A DIFFERENT LIGHT

Copyright 2011

Excelsior Publications

No part of this book may be reproduced in any form, or by any means, without the permission of the publisher.

International Standard Book Number:

978-0-9844760-0-8

Printed in the United States

First Edition

Library of Congress Control Number:

2010924187

Don,
No sailing, but I hope you enjoy the powerboat scene.

Michael

A DIFFERENT LIGHT

By

Michael J. Bourke

To the woman

I'm waiting to meet

He crawled a few inches forward and then slumped down again, just a dusty lump in the middle of a long stretch of dusty road. A short distance away, hidden behind a rock, two women watched him as he moved again but made no progress.

He couldn't hear them as they argued, and again he attempted to move forward but gained no ground. For a long moment there was no movement at all, until one of the women stood up from behind the rock and slowly approached him.

She walked through the dry grass and onto the road, stopping a few feet from the man's head. When he didn't react, she stepped closer, knelt down and touched his neck. Still he didn't move.

The woman coaxed her companion to come forward, and together they made a litter with two sticks and their backpacks. As they were rolling the man onto it, his eyes opened to a narrow slit; and he saw a pretty face and a flash of brown hair highlighted by the sun behind. The vision hurt his eyes, and he closed them again.

Pulling together at the head of the litter, the two women dragged him into town, down the main street, over line after diagonal yellow line marking parking places where there were no cars. A single traffic light, unlit, swayed in the evening breeze. Dust and a scrap of paper were all that greeted them from the line of single- and double-story buildings on either side of the street.

Occasionally a face would appear in a window, then a figure in a doorway. In groups of two and three, a handful of people watched the two women. But none of the watchers spoke, not a word; and none moved to help the two women with their burden.

The man was conscious, though delirious; and he was able to walk from the litter into their house with a woman on either side of him, guiding him. The other people in the town watched until after the trio had disappeared from sight; and then still without speaking and in the same groups of two and three, returned to the houses from which they had emerged.

The two women lived on the second floor, and they struggled to get the man up to their living room, where they laid him on a couch against the wall.

The first woman knelt next to him, tending to him, loosening his clothes, splashing water onto his face and into his mouth.

Once, weakly, he brushed his hand against her face, and

she held still and let him do it, but then he groaned and eased back into the darkness of unconsciousness.

Outside, the setting sun also was easing the town into darkness. The woman lit a candle and watched the man as he slept.

He was about thirty years old, handsome, with a lean and muscular build. His dark hair, uncut for months, curled about his ears; and his beard showed it had been several days since he'd been clean-shaven.

For that day and most of the next he slept, half-waking when the woman spooned water or broth into his mouth, not waking at all when she undressed and washed his body with a wet cloth.

All the while he slept, she stayed close to him, responding every time he made a sound or a movement. She watched him as if he were a faintly flickering fire, one she desperately needed to keep herself warm. She habitually searched for on-going reassurance that the light still burned inside him.

When he awoke late on the afternoon of the second day, after having slept through most of her ministrations, it was her gentlest touch that roused him, when she pulled the sheet up around his shoulders.

He opened his eyes and saw her beautiful face, framed by flowing brown hair, just as he'd seen it in his dreams many times since yesterday. Her smile was so delicate that he wasn't sure it was there at all, but her eyes betrayed her happiness at seeing him awake.

"Hi," she said softly.

He blinked, surprised that this vision before him also was capable of speaking.

"You've been asleep a long time," she added. "I was wondering if you were going to return to *our* world."

While she spoke he watched only her lips, and now he touched them with his finger tips. Then his hand fell back to his side.

"You're beautiful," were the first words that he said to her.

She smiled and diverted attention by straightening the sheet, savoring the compliment while giving him neither coy denial nor any endorsement.

Then she asked, "How are you feeling? Can I get you anything?"

He thought for a moment, then said, "I'm hungry."

"Good, good," she answered, eagerly. "Of course you must be hungry. I'll get something. How about a roast beef sandwich?"

"That sounds wonderful."

She jumped up and ran for the kitchen, then stopped abruptly in the doorway and turned back toward him.

"It's not real bread," she said, her voice subdued. "It's homemade, and we haven't gotten the knack of it yet. It's kind of heavy and crumbly. And the meat's from a can."

"Sounds fine," he answered.

She went into the kitchen; and, while she was gone, he looked around the room.

The flat was small, and the room he was in was narrow. At the outside wall, a double window overlooked the street. From where he was lying, he could see down the short hall to the two bedrooms and the bathroom which was next to the kitchen.

The furniture, a couch and two chairs, was old, clean, and comfortable. In the corner was a television set, its blank screen reflecting the simple furnishings of the room.

The woman returned with the food, handed it to him, and sat down.

"I brought you a can of pop, too," she said. "It's not cold but it still tastes good."

He accepted the food and ate slowly, deliberately. Though their eyes occasionally met, neither one spoke at first.

Before the silence became too awkward, she said, "I don't know your name."

"Jim, my name's Jim," he answered. "What's yours?"

"Missy."

"I'm happy to meet you," Jim said.

"Me, too."

Their first run of conversation was over, and nothing more was flowing. Jim filled the time by taking another bite of his sandwich, and chewing slowly.

Looking at the sandwich and not at her, he said, "I was wondering if anyone else was alive."

Missy leaned forward. "I know what you mean. We couldn't believe it, when we saw you."

Now he looked at her. "We? You mean there are others?"

"Bess and I found you. She's my best friend. You don't remember seeing her? We worked so hard to get you up here. But that means…oh, my…" Missy paused as she realized the full import of what Jim had just said. "That means, you've been alone, all alone, all this time?"

He didn't answer, but the silence answered for him.

Missy allowed the moment to ebb before saying, "That must have been awfully hard, all these months, not knowing."

Jim redirected the conversation by asking, "Are there others, more than two?"

"Oh yes, quite a few," Missy answered. "There's Kate and Susan and Allyson. There's Ernie and Bob. There's Pamela. And there's Harry and Frank and Anitra. Let's see. That means, with you, we're up to a dozen now."

"Where are they?"

"Oh, different places, you know, around town," Missy said. "We really don't see each other too often. We just…we just don't. Except for Bess, of course. We knew each other before…well, before."

"I'd love to meet Bess," Jim said, "to thank her."

"She's out getting water," Missy replied. "We have to bring it in from the river. It's a lot of work, hauling it up a flight of stairs, but we're used to it. When we first moved in, the water heater still worked. It was heaven—hot baths! But after a few days the water turned cold, and after a few more days it stopped coming altogether."

Jim had finished eating, and Missy took the plate from him.

She continued, "I suppose it's foolish of us to keep living here. If we moved to the ground floor, we wouldn't have to haul our wood and water up that long flight of stairs. But this place seems like home to us now. It's what we've got to hold on to."

She stood up and took a step toward the kitchen.

"And besides," she said, "the view from the kitchen window of the sun setting behind the mountains is breathtaking."

"You don't need any better reason than that," Jim answered, "A place that feels like home, with a good vantage for the setting sun."

Missy took the plate into the kitchen, set it in the sink, and paused to look through the window framed with sheer curtains. The sun was just beginning to contemplate its journey behind the mountains.

Without turning around, she called out over her shoulder, "Would you like me to help you come in here so you can look at this view?"

Jim sat up on the couch and picked up the sheet that was covering him.

"Uhmmm, I would," he said, "But I don't seem to have any clothes on."

He put the sheet back down.

Missy walked into the room, laughing and also blushing.

"Your clothes were a mess," she said. "I threw them

out."

He looked at her with lips pursed and head tilted to one side. Still smiling, Missy held out her hands as if to protect herself from his gaze.

"There's a little department store right across the street," she said. "I'll go get you something. They should have a good selection, because no one else in town is your size."

"Thank you," Jim said, with a gentle smile. "But don't you want to know my size?"

"No," she answered. "After shopping for four brothers, I could do it with my eyes closed. Shirt, pants—want anything else? It's all on sale, 100 % off."

"Underwear?" he asked.

"Right," she said, touching her finger to her temple as she walked out the door.

A few minutes later the door opened, and Jim called out, "Back so soon?"

He looked over his shoulder; and there in the hallway, holding a bucket, was a woman he had not seen before. She had short, light brown, curly hair and a very pretty face. She was wearing slacks and a blouse, and the material around the buttons of her blouse puckered to contain her well-rounded breasts. She held the bucket in both hands in front of her; and, after quickly meeting Jim's gaze, she kept her eyes to the floor.

"Oh, you're awake," she said softly.

"You must be Bess," he responded. "Hi."

"Hi, she said with a brief smile. Then, not thinking of

anything else to say, she said "Excuse me," and backed away through the door into the kitchen.

Bess didn't reappear. Missy returned 15 minutes later, carrying several packages, which she placed on Jim's lap.

"Here," Missy said, "guaranteed to fit."

Before Jim could acknowledge, Bess made a noise in the kitchen; and Missy said, "Oh, Bess's here. Did you two meet?"

"We said 'Hi,' " Jim answered.

"Well, I'll go talk to Bess," Missy said. "I'll give you some privacy so you can get dressed."

Missy went into the kitchen. Jim heard her and Bess talking softly while he was putting on his clothes.

Sitting up made him dizzy, so he took his time dressing. Missy glanced into the living room once and saw him standing, with his back to her, fastening his pants. She nodded to herself when she noticed that the jeans she selected did fit well.

By the time Missy went back into the living room, Jim was sitting down on the couch again and buttoning his shirt. She noticed he was moving slowly.

"You feeling okay?" she asked.

"Yeah, I'm okay," he said. "I'm still just a little…tired. I think I'll have to pass on that sunset until tomorrow night."

"That's okay," Missy said, rearranging his pillow and helping him lie down again on the couch. "You just lie back and relax. You can't expect to get well all at once. You've made a lot of progress today."

Out of habit, she pulled her easy chair up to her usual

position of vigilance before she realized that now, things were different. Now, for the first time since he had come into her life, he was *aware* of her sitting there, watching over him.

In response to his questioning glance, she said, "Mind if I just sit here beside you for a while?"

The gentle tone of her request moved him, and it took him a while to answer, "You're the first person I've seen in over half a year. I'd love to have you stay here longer."

They remained together in silence. Bess stepped out of the kitchen, said a soft "Good night" in their general direction and, without pausing, walked down the hall to her bedroom. Jim and Missy both called "Good night" after her. They heard her bedroom door close behind her.

"Is something wrong?" Jim asked.

"No," Missy said. "Well, at least nothing we can do anything about. Bess is a little bit afraid of you."

"But I hardly said anything to her, nothing more than 'Hi.' "

"I know. It's nothing you did. It's just…it's just that you're here."

Jim tried to make eye contact with Missy, but she was avoiding looking directly at him, so he said, "I don't understand."

"I don't either, exactly. Our routine here doesn't change very much, hasn't for months. We get up. We get what we need to get through the day. When it gets dark, we go back to bed. You've interrupted that."

"I don't know what to say. I'm sorry."

Missy looked at him now and said, "No, don't be sorry. It's not your fault. We just haven't been thinking about it, not for all this time. The only things Bess and I talk about are things we did before...the change. You're forcing us to think about it, again."

"I don't want to hurt you. But there's so much I don't know, don't understand. I need to know more. I need to know what you know. I need to know what happened."

"Of course. Of course," Missy was nodding, quickly, with her eyes to the floor, "but we don't really know what happened. I've never talked about it, not even with Bess. We just lived through it; we just lived; and after a while it was over; and there weren't any more surprises."

"Please...please tell me."

Missy took a deep breath, and began, "We were on a boat. Bess and I were on vacation, and we'd just flown in to meet this guy that Bess knew pretty well. I guess it was kind of a double date, since I was fixed up with his buddy. He was the one who owned the boat. I had just met the guy, but he seemed as if he was nice..."

Her voice trailed off, and it was a moment before she continued.

"We'd left Monday night and motored for a few hours to get to a place where there was this sunken ship. We dropped anchor to spend the night. The only radio we had was the marine radio, and we didn't turn that on. We didn't know anything was happening. We spent the night laughing and drinking and playing cards. Bess was so happy.

"The next day we went scuba diving. I wasn't very good at it. I'd only gone a couple of times before. But we were teasing the guys, saying that we were better divers and that we were going to find a fortune in sunken treasure, and not give any of it to them. So that's why we went in the water first while they stayed with the boat. We didn't stay under for more than about 10 minutes."

"When we tried to get back in the boat, we kidded the guys about being poor sports, not helping us in. Then we saw that neither one of them was moving."

Tears welled up in her eyes. Jim put his hand on her knee to comfort her, and she put her hand on top of his and squeezed it.

"I'm sorry," he said. "I'm sorry this is so hard. I'm sorry it's so hard on you."

"It's okay," she answered, and one tear glistened down her cheek. "I can't believe I haven't talked about this before. Bess and I never talk about it; and there's no one else, really."

"What happened after you found them?"

Missy reached for the pillow and clutched it to her chest before continuing.

"I guess we went a little crazy then," she said. "We didn't know what had happened. We thought it was pirates, or fumes, or food poisoning. But they looked so peaceful, like they had just fallen asleep. Only we couldn't wake them up. I felt *guilty* trying.

"I was working with the radio, seeing if I could call someone for help. Poor Bess! She wanted to give her boyfriend CPR, and she didn't know how. She kept shouting at me, asking me what to do; and I didn't know either. Eventually we realized that it was hopeless. I just held Bess in my arms, and we both cried.

"When we couldn't cry anymore, I tried to use the radio again. For a while I thought I wasn't doing it right, because I couldn't hear anything. But then the weather report came in, as clear as anything. But all the other channels were dead quiet. It was so spooky.

"Eventually we figured out how to start the engines and raise the anchor. I didn't even know where we were. I just kept going, hoping that we would hit land, afraid that we were going straight out into the ocean. Finally we found the shore and followed it till we came to the marina.

"We called out for someone to help us, and no one came. That was the worst part. All I wanted was to be able to turn everything over to someone who would take care of us. There was no one. No one knew we were in trouble. No one was going to make it better. It was as if, in the whole world, no one cared. That was the worst moment of my life. I felt so helpless. If it wasn't for Bess, I don't think I could have stood it."

Jim asked, "You didn't see anyone?"

"No, nothing, no one," she answered. "It was as if everyone had just evaporated. All the cars were gone too, even our car. Every minute I kept expecting to see someone, some person, somewhere; but there was no one.

"The phones hadn't stopped working yet, so we tried to call, every number we could think of. We even made some up. We got a few recordings but no one live. Even the long distance calls we tried just kept ringing forever. No one was answering the phones anywhere.

"We kept phoning. We took turns. We should have figured it out, but we didn't want to. It just couldn't be

13

happening. We kept thinking we were going to get help. We kept hoping it was all just a crazy mix-up, and everything was going to be okay. But it wasn't."

Emotionally spent, Missy stopped talking. Jim, unable to comfort her with his arms, let the silence and the minutes do it for him. The sun had set, and the twilight was fading.

Missy got up, lit a candle, and sat back down, more composed.

She continued, "We spent that night at the marina, raided their kitchen for food. That was such a long night.

"The next morning, nothing had changed. We were still alone. We went back to the boat. I remember envying the guys. They looked so at peace. I felt they were already in heaven, and we were left in hell.

"We spent the rest of that day sitting on the shore, not talking much. Bess wasn't even crying anymore. That seems like it was a million years ago.

"Sometime that evening, we heard a car drive by, racing along the road next to the marina. It happened so fast, by the time we got up to look, the only thing we saw was a cloud of dust it had left behind.

"But that car brought us to our senses. Maybe there *was* something we could do. So we grabbed a few things and started walking in the same direction the car had gone. We walked all night, and it was dawn before we found the car, smashed up against a tree, with no one in it. That was just outside this town.

"Harry was the one driving the car. He was drunk; that was why he smashed it up. This is his town. There's a big supermarket here, and I guess Harry used to be the manager or something. There's plenty of food. Harry gave us some food, and we moved in to this place. We've been here ever since."

"How did Harry survive?" Jim asked.

"We never asked him," Missy answered. "And he never asked us either."

The candle flickered and sputtered, then burned brightly again, casting dancing shadows on the walls around them.

"Are you tired?" Missy asked. "I've been doing all the talking for a long time. Would you like to get some sleep?"

"I am tired," Jim answered, "but I don't feel like sleeping."

Missy waited, savoring the respite from her narrative. When it didn't seem like Jim was going to speak, she said, "I've told you my story. You're the only person in the world I've told my story to. I'd like to hear about what happened to you."

Jim wasn't quick to begin. Speaking softly at first, so softly that Missy had to strain to hear, he said, "I'm the only person in the world you've told your story to. I haven't told my story to anyone, because there wasn't anyone."

Missy said nothing, and Jim continued, "I was in a cave, and my two buddies were still outside. We were amateur spelunkers. It was a great cave, right next to a lake. Parts of it were under the lake. There were underground waterfalls and some fabulous rock formations—a great cave.

"We never even got started. I was inside, and my friends were lowering supplies down to me. We were going to spend the whole day inside.

"I did a little exploring, waiting for them to join me.

They never did. I shouted up to ask what was taking so long, and there was no answer. Eventually, I had to pull myself out of that hole.

"One of my friends was gone, and so was the truck. My other friend was on the ground, *so very still.* I figured at the time that it must have been a heart attack. It looked like he had just gone to sleep. I got the notion in my head that all I had to do was go over and wake him up. But I knew it wasn't true, and I felt that it would be wrong, even rude, for me to try, like talking in church, or something.

"So I waited. I was sure that my other buddy was coming back with help, but I waited all day, and he didn't show up. When it started to get dark, I figured I'd better try to get help myself. But we were pretty far off the beaten path, and I hadn't been doing the driving, so I hadn't been paying that much attention. I got lost, and the night overtook me, and I had to just stop, right were I was, in the middle of nowhere, and wait for daylight. That night was so dark. Every time I looked at my watch, I expected a few hours had gone by, and it was only a few minutes.

"When the sun finally rose, I had no idea where I was. I couldn't find any signs of civilization, and I couldn't find my way back to the cave. I stumbled around all that day until I finally found a road, and I followed it until I came to a little store and gas station.

"I called out for someone, but no one was there. Just like you, I tried using the phone, but no one answered. I remember, I called the operator, and I counted the rings. I'd gotten to over a hundred before I hung up.

"I found myself something to eat. That was when I saw the paper, the early edition from the day before. The headline read, 'Communication Blackout Covers Asia.' I read the article, and it was pretty clear to me that whoever wrote it didn't have a very good idea of what was going on—just some poor newspaperman rushing to meet a deadline. All the article said for sure was that all communication with that side of the world had ceased, and there had never before been a blackout that lasted more than just a few seconds, and nothing that total.

"That was my first clue that this was a lot bigger than just me and my friends in trouble. Everything was different. Why hadn't I even seen a single car on that road? Why was it so quiet? Not only the people, but there were no birds, no animals.

"I loaded up some food, and I started walking. I had to find out what was going on! But I never did get very far. I couldn't carry that much food. I'd go two or maybe three days in one direction, and then I had to turn around. Every time, it got harder for me to go out. That store was my safe place. Everywhere else seemed full of risk. I started skipping days, first just one at a time, and then more. When the weather turned cold, I stopped going out at all. What was the point?

"I spent the winter in that store, eating most of the food, reading every word of that newspaper—sports scores, advice columns, comics, front page article about an unknown phenomenon striking the Asian continent. I wondered about the outcome of 'tomorrow's' ball games, ones that hadn't been played. I tried to improve on the answers in the advice column, as if the people had written directly to me, asking for my help. I guess that sounds pretty 'off the wall'."

Missy smiled her subtle smile, but said nothing.

"Anyway," Jim continued, "spring came, and I was almost out of food. I knew I had to do something. I packed up everything I could carry and decided that, no matter what, this time I wasn't going to turn back. This was it.

"I'd been out of food a couple days when you found me. I don't think I could have crawled very much farther."

Jim shifted his weight to look directly at Missy. "And then I found myself looking at the most beautiful face I had ever seen."

"You were delirious," Missy smiled.

"I'm not delirious now."

They looked at each other and felt the rush of communicating without words. The candle flame flickered and danced, adding to the softness of the night that surrounded them, robbing outlines of their definition and blending objects together, and still the two held each other's gaze.

"Nothing's changed," he said. "You're beautiful."

At that moment, the candle popped loudly. Missy turned to see the flame die. She looked back at Jim. Moonlight coming in through the kitchen window provided just enough light for Jim to know she was looking his way.

"I'm afraid I can't spare another candle," she said. "They're scarce."

"That's okay," he answered. "I like the moonlight."

They remained silent for a while. Though she couldn't see him in the shadows, she could hear his breathing and an occasional rustling of the sheets.

"I'm glad you're here," she addressed the shadows. "Maybe things aren't hopeless."

"I gave up thinking things were going to get any better a

long time ago," he answered. "I'm glad I was wrong."

The night progressed. Missy could tell by Jim's steady breathing that he was asleep. She soon fell asleep too.

She slept peacefully for an hour or so; and when she awoke, she decided that Jim was well enough that she could spend the night in her own bed. Before leaving the room, she knelt down beside the couch, pulled the sheet over Jim's shoulders and straightened the pillow behind him.

He awoke to her touch while she was bending over him; and, with his dreams still flavoring this reality, raised his head and kissed her chest.

She did not move at all while his lips lingered there, and then she leaned forward the slightest possible amount, just enough to communicate to him that she didn't object to what he was doing.

He moved his hands from under the covers and undid one, two buttons on her blouse. As he moved the material away, he kissed her several times along the slope and the curve of her breast until his lips touched her nipple. He kissed her there. She braced her arm against the back of the couch. He kissed her again and drew her nipple into his mouth and let her feel his teeth. Then he kissed her again and allowed his lips to just barely touch her body. They both held still, in the gentlest contact, and the slightest motion by either one of them registered at his mouth and at her breast.

A soft sigh escaped her lips. Then, abruptly, she stood up, bent over, kissed him hard on the mouth, and walked to her bedroom, shutting the door behind her.

He closed his eyes; and, in his mind, she was still there, straightening his pillow and granting him the pleasure of her beautiful body.

* * *

The next morning, Missy woke early, put on a long, flowing, red bathrobe, and walked past the living room on her way to the kitchen. She was surprised to see Jim sitting up, with the sheet already folded on the couch next to him.

She asked if he was okay, and he told her that everything was fine—he'd just had all the sleep he needed for quite some time.

They went into the kitchen together. A door from the kitchen led to a back porch where Missy went to light a wood fire in a large barbecue grill. She prepared a breakfast of canned potatoes which she fried, toast made from homemade bread, also jam, juice and tea. He helped her set the table.

"Is Bess going to join us?" he asked.

"I know she's up," Missy said. "I heard her just a few minutes ago."

She called out to Bess that breakfast was ready; and soon Bess appeared, wearing satin pajamas and a satin robe and with her hair neatly brushed.

"Why Bess," Missy said. "You look so nice this morning."

"You look lovely," Jim said.

Bess smiled and looked down and whispered "Thank you" and helped finish preparing breakfast.

The talk at the breakfast table was meager at first, with Missy and Jim carrying most of the burden. Bess's reticence slowly dissolved; and, by the time they were well into the meal, a pleasant conversation developed. Missy again apologized for the quality of the bread, which Jim said tasted delicious. Bess gave Missy credit for being the better cook, and they good-naturedly argued the point.

They ate well and took their time finishing the last of the tea and toast. By then, the sun was shining brightly through the living room window and promising to chase away the morning chill.

"Well," Missy declared, "We have a whole beautiful day ahead of us. How are we going to spend it?"

"My days don't change very much," Bess moaned. "If we want to take baths tomorrow morning, I have to start hauling the water now."

"I'd be glad to help out," Jim said. "I'm feeling much stronger today."

"No, no, that's okay," Bess declined, while not meeting Jim's gaze. "I kind of count on doing it."

"As a matter of fact," Missy said, "I've got a lot of kitchen work to do. You have no idea how hard it is to bake bread on a barbecue."

Jim laughed. "I'll bet there are a lot of difficult things you've somehow learned how to manage to get done."

"We get by," Missy answered. "Getting water and wood occupy most of our time. We use the wood for cooking because we don't have any heat in here. A couple of the houses have fireplaces, but ours doesn't. I didn't get too cold last winter—nothing a few extra layers of clothing didn't take care of.

"We save our bath water to wash our clothes in, and then

we save our laundry water to flush the toilet. I've always been afraid someday the sewer would fill up and overflow, but so far that hasn't happened.

"We go to bed when it gets dark, and when the sun comes up we start all over again.

"If we need anything, there's a lot of little stores in town that are still pretty well stocked—clothes, hardware, stuff like that. We just go around and take what we need."

"What about food?" Jim asked.

"Harry controls the food," Missy said.

"Why?"

Before answering, Missy looked at Bess, who just shrugged.

"It's always been that way," Missy said. "Harry's the one who belongs here. It's like, this is his town; and he's just letting the rest of us stay.

"Anyway, he passes out food everyday between ten and eleven o'clock. He makes us earn it sometimes, by working in the market. We'll have to go see him today, now that we have another mouth to feed."

"And how about you?" Bess asked of Jim. "How are you going to spend your day?"

He said, "I'm going to find myself a place to live."

The conversation fell silent.

After a moment, Missy spoke. "You're moving out? You don't want to stay here…with us?"

Jim cleared his throat before answering.

"That's the best offer I've had in...well, that's the best offer I've ever had. But it's an offer I'm going to decline, at least for now.

"I did a lot of thinking last night and this morning. The last thing I want is to be alone. But I need to feel that things are getting back to normal. I need to have a place of my own. I need to set up a life for myself."

Missy placed a few of the dishes in the sink.

"Where will you move?" she asked quietly.

"Not far, I hope," he said.

"The place next door, over the hardware store, is nice. The entrance is all the way on the other side of the building, so you have to go on the street to get there from here. But we share a common wall."

"I like that," Jim replied.

They finished the last of the meal, and Jim and Missy offered to help with the dishes, but Bess wouldn't let them, since it was already past ten o'clock and "Harry won't wait."

Missy changed quickly into slacks and a blouse, and she and Jim went down the stairs on their way to the street. Jim took Missy's arm when they reached the bottom of the stairs and turned her to him.

"I want to make sure you understand, Missy," he said.

It was the first time he had spoken her name, and the sound of it made her smile.

"I'm not moving out because I want to move away from you," he said. "In fact, I was hoping for just the opposite. I was hoping I might be able to...court you."

She tugged on his shirt front while she answered him. "That sounds funny. You mean an old-fashioned courtship? Does that mean you're going to bring me flowers and candy?"

"Well, flowers, anyway."

She turned her head down. "I forgot," she whispered. "No candy."

"But," he responded, ducking down in an attempt to look into her eyes, "I was hoping that we could have a date tonight, maybe to see that sunset. Are you willing to go out with me?"

She looked up at him.

"Yes," was all she said.

He put his arm around her waist, and they walked out into the sunshine and turned left toward the supermarket.

"Right across the street is where Pamela lives," Missy said. "She's the only one who lives all alone."

"Why's that?"

"I don't know. People, who knew each other before, live together. But after, people just sorta drifted in, found this place. Bess and I don't talk to them much, because it would mean talking about it. Maybe they feel the same way."

Jim stroked her waist gently. "What about you and me? We talked about it."

"You're special." She turned to look at him, and he kept just his finger tips touching her side. "You're good for me. You showing up shattered my routine, Bess's too. I think I needed to talk about it, but I didn't know how to get started."

He brushed a strand of hair away from her face, and let his hand linger against her cheek. They turned and continued walking, arm-in-arm.

They came to the corner where the lone traffic light was—a three-way intersection. To the south, the main street ran straight to the horizon; and to the north it ran for a half mile, past a power plant and a bridge over the river, before curving out of sight. No road went east into the valley. The road west stretched away into the mountains.

"Over there," Missy said, pointing across the street to a gas station, "is where Ernie and Bob live. They're both retired, gray-haired, sweet-looking guys. They spend all day, every day, working on junk cars and arguing with each other and working some more, but they never get anything running. There are no working cars here.

"And this," Missy said, stopping, "is where our food is."

They were in front of a large supermarket. Most of the street side of the building was a long row of plate-glass windows, and the customer entrance and exit were at the far corner. At the near corner, however, the wall was brick with only one door and a waist-high window that looked into a small room, barren except for a few folding chairs and a counter along the wall away from the window. Standing at the counter, with her back to them, was a tall, attractive woman, late thirties, with long, black hair.

"That's Pamela," Missy said.

Jim opened the door, and he and Missy went inside. Pamela held herself perfectly straight and did not react to the sound of the door behind her. Only when Missy walked up to the counter and stood next to her did Pamela turn stiffly and acknowledge Missy's presence with a nod.

"Hi," Missy said in return.

They stood in silence. Jim walked up and stood next to Missy. Almost imperceptibly, Pamela turned so that she could just see him out of the corner of her eye.

At that moment, a dark-haired man with a sharp nose and wispy, graying sideburns entered the room from a door behind the counter. He carried a box full of canned goods and placed it in front of Pamela.

"Here," he said.

"Thank you," Pamela responded.

As she turned toward Missy and Jim before walking out, she took an extra second to look Jim over quickly, up and down.

Pamela left, and the man behind the counter turned to Missy, said nothing, just waited for her to speak.

"Harry," she said, "This is Jim. He's going to need some food, and we could use a little more, too."

"You're late," Harry answered.

"It's not eleven yet," Missy shrugged.

To Jim, Harry said, "So you're the new one. You don't look too bad off."

"I've had some good, loving care," Jim answered, looking at Missy.

Harry grunted and turned back to Missy, saying, "I need someone to count cans today."

"Gee, Harry," she answered, "I was going to help Jim get settled today and…well, okay, I guess I can do it."

"In back," Harry's voice was emotionless. "Anitra and Frank are there already."

"Can Jim get some food?" Missy asked.

Harry waited a long time before answering. Missy shifted her weight once, sliding her foot, a small sound to fill the void.

"Yeah," Harry answered finally. "What do you want?"

"Soup, vegetables… maybe some meat?" Jim said.

"Meat's scarce," Harry answered, as he turned to go into the back.

Jim waited until Harry was out of earshot. "This seems so strange. Why is everyone so…unfriendly? I can't say I've actually met anyone yet."

Missy hesitated before answering. "It didn't used to seem strange. It does now, now that I'm looking at it through your eyes. It's just the way things are, the way they have been. Pamela's nice enough, but she keeps pretty much to herself. I guess that's the same thing Bess and I are doing. And Harry…well, Harry is Harry."

Harry returned with a box of food, about half full; and placed it on the counter.

"Frank's waiting," he said to Missy.

Missy faced Jim, put her hands on his arms, and rubbed them up and down, playfully.

"I'm sorry I won't be able to help you get settled," she said. "See you later?"

"Before sunset," he answered.

27

She walked around the counter and into the market. Jim was left standing in front of Harry.

Jim asked, "Is there anything you want me to do for this food?"

"I'll let you know," Harry said.

Jim waited; but, when he realized that Harry wasn't going to say anything more, he said, "Well thanks," and slid the box off the counter; but halfway out he stopped and asked, "By the way, have you got any candy?"

"Candy? No."

"Any sugar?"

"No."

"Maple syrup?"

Harry harrumphed, but he went back into the market and returned with a jar of syrup, which he dropped into Jim's box.

"Thanks," Jim said, and walked out.

Harry didn't answer.

The sun had fulfilled its promise, and the chill was gone from the air as Jim walked down the center of the street. He went farther north, past where he and Missy had walked, to get more of a view of the town, which consisted of a half-dozen blocks. He stood in the street between the gas station and the supermarket and looked north. There were no signs of life in the houses and shops.

He turned around and walked back down the street, past the traffic light, past Missy and Bess's, to the hardware store next door.

The windows still had banners in them advertising sales and new products. A sign in the corner of the window announced that the upper flat was available to rent.

"I think I'll take it," he said to himself.

The front door was locked. Jim walked around to the side of the building where he found a door that had been pried open. He entered the small back room of the hardware store which also contained stairs leading to the upper flat.

Jim set his box of food on a counter and walked through the store. Most of the shelves and bins were well-stocked, but there were a few exceptions: empty boxes which used to contain flashlight batteries and an empty shelf where propane canisters had been displayed.

He went upstairs and found what was, except for dust, a neat apartment. The place was almost a mirror image of Missy and Bess's, except that there was a front balcony instead of a back porch. He set about exploring the cabinets and cleaning up.

The afternoon passed. Missy worked at the supermarket until after four o'clock. Bess spent most of the day hauling water.

Jim found a red wagon and went around town picking up clothes, bed linens, and a barbecue, which he set up on the balcony.

Throughout the afternoon, he and the red wagon made several trips up and down the street. He got a load of books from the library, an exercise treadmill from the sport shop. Once he came upon Bess and loaded her buckets of water into his wagon and transported them to her flat for her.

Jim visited the gas station, where he introduced himself

to Ernie and Bob, each of whom shook his hand warmly but immediately returned to tinkering with the junk cars scattered about the place. They paid him no heed while he loaded a half-dozen car batteries and a few other automotive parts into his wagon. He wished them good luck, they each looked up from under the hood of a car and waved, and he continued on his way.

By late afternoon, Missy was home, deciding what to wear and putting on make-up that had been in her purse, untouched, for months. Bess sat on the bed, listening to Missy talk and offering helpful advice.

At his place, Jim had put on a dress shirt and slacks, a sport coat and tie. He spent most of his time over his barbecue, boiling maple syrup and dripping the thickened mixture onto wax paper, where it formed pathetic-looking, teardrop-shaped lumps. He had hoped it would be chewy, but the end product had become more crackly.

He also went to the field in back and picked a small bunch of tiny flowers with delicate petals.

Armed with his presents, an hour before sunset Jim walked down the stairs on his side of the building, over the sidewalk in front, and into the stairwell on Missy's side of the building. She heard him coming up the stairs. At the top of the stairs, he adjusted his tie and patted down his hair before knocking.

Missy opened the door, and Jim stood before her in his off-white silk jacket, red striped tie, dress shirt and pants and spit-shined black shoes that reflected the light. He carried the flowers in one hand and the make-shift candy, gift boxed and gold wrapped, in the other.

Missy wore a red, fuzzy, v-neck sweater that outlined the shape of each breast, a gold pendant that hung between, black slacks and low-heels. Her shoulder length hair was loose, flowing.

"I've come a-courtin'," Jim said at the same moment that Missy said, "Hi Jim, c'mon in."

He stepped through the doorway.

"You look great," he said.

"So do you."

They continued looking at each other. From behind Jim, Bess cleared her throat.

"Hi Bess," Jim said, turning to look at her but quickly returning his gaze to Missy.

"Do you want to sit down?" Missy asked, gesturing toward the living room with her open hand.

Realizing he still had the candy and flowers, he held them out to her and said, "These are for you."

She took them with a smile, and he sat down in the chair.

"The flowers are beautiful," she said as she sat down on the couch across from him. "Bess, would you…"

"I'll get a vase," Bess volunteered, taking the flowers with her into the kitchen.

"And what is this?" Missy asked, starting to unwrap the gold foil.

She opened the box and saw the misshapen amber lumps.

"Why…why, they're wonderful," Missy stammered.

She looked up at Jim, hoping for more information, but all he did was smile at her. Bess returned with the flowers in a vase and placed them on the table between Missy and Jim.

"Look Bess," Missy said, showing her the box. "Look what Jim brought."

Bess looked, and then looked again, and the confusion registered on her face. She looked from Missy to Jim without getting a clue.

"They're very nice," she said, cautiously.

He kept them dangling for a while longer before he said, "It's candy."

"It's candy!" Missy and Bess said in unison.

"It's very nice candy," Bess added.

Missy's hands, holding the candy box, collapsed to her lap; and she looked fondly at Jim.

"You brought me candy," she said, "candy and flowers."

"I took a shot," Jim answered, shrugging his shoulders. "Try one," he went on, "but be careful, unless you tell me we have a dentist here in town."

Missy took a piece and held out the box to Bess, who selected one carefully.

"They're good," Missy said, not quite concealing her surprise.

"I boiled up some maple syrup," Jim confessed.

"They *are* good," Bess agreed; and then, turning to Missy, she whispered, "He can cook."

Bess sat down on the couch next to Missy and asked, "So, where are you two kids going on your date tonight?"

"Well," Jim answered, "since it's our first date, and I want to make a good impression, I'm taking her to the biggest show in town."

He paused for effect before continuing, "We're going to watch the sunset. I've got a blanket to sit on. I've got some crackers and a bottle of wine. And, if we want, we've got the maple blobs. "

Both women laughed.

"You've got wine?" Missy asked. "How did you manage that? Harry usually keeps all the alcohol for himself."

"Harry's not the only source," Jim replied. "I did a lot of exploring today, and I found plenty of places with some interesting stuff."

"Stuff?" Missy asked. "You found stuff?"

Jim shrugged, "Maybe useful stuff. It all depends on how you put it together."

"And in all your exploring," Missy asked, "Did you find the best place to watch the sunset?"

"I did," he exclaimed, "And would you believe it? It's right here in your own backyard."

"Isn't that convenient," Missy minced.

"Isn't that," Jim answered. "I figured that hill out there would be a good place. I've already got the blanket set up and the wine...well...the wine is at room temperature."

"Just the way I like it," was Missy's gracious response.

"Would you care to join us Bess?" Jim asked.

"No," Bess demurred. "No thanks. I'm going to go...shopping."

"You can come with us if you want to Bess," Missy said.

"No, it's okay," Bess answered. "I really do want to do some shopping. Maybe I'll go looking for some interesting 'stuff' of my own."

Jim accepted her declination with, "Well, okay," and then, to Missy, said "Shall we go? I think the show's going to start soon."

They went out, and Bess closed the door behind them. She stayed in.

The hill in back was a few hundred feet from the buildings. It was about 12 feet high, with grass and sand near the top and thicker vegetation at the base. Jim had placed the blanket on the far slope so that they could lean against the hill and have the full panorama before them.

They climbed the hill and settled down on the other side, near the top. The sand under the blanket yielded to their weight so that, when they lied down, it shaped to their bodies, like a hug from Mother Earth.

Jim had set the bottle of wine in the sand, with three glasses next to it. He started pouring the wine.

Missy looked at the third glass and said, "I see you were sincere about inviting Bess. It's starting to look like you're a nice guy."

"Not that nice. It didn't escape my attention that I had a chance to spend the evening with two lovely women."

"Are you disappointed that you only got me?"

He had moved his face close to hers and held up a glass of wine so that he looked over the top of it to see her eyes, before saying, "The only thing better than having a date with two women is being able to concentrate all your attention on one extraordinarily beautiful woman."

He offered her the wine.

"Thank you," she said, as she accepted both the wine and the compliment.

She watched the horizon, and he took the opportunity to watch her, the way her hair teased her cheeks in the breeze, the way just the corners of her mouth curved up when she was pleased, the way she breathed.

"I always loved watching sunsets," she sighed, "partly because I felt I was sharing them with all the other people in the world, all at the same time. It doesn't feel the same anymore. It feels so lonely, now."

"We can't be sure," he answered. "If a dozen of us are still alive, there may be others, there probably *are* others, somewhere. They may be too busy to be watching this sunset, though."

"I wish I could talk to them," she said, "even if we could never meet. Just to tell someone that we're still alive, that we're still looking at sunsets, and that…and that we love them."

The sun continued its slow descent as more and more, the distant mountain peak blocked it from view. They sat in silence, watching it. The March breeze didn't hold the heat; and, as it blew, it chilled them. He put his arm around her shoulders. She put her arm around his waist.

"I'm so glad I'm here with you," he said.

She squeezed his waist in reply.

He continued, "I don't think I've thanked you yet for what you did for me. When I was crawling down that road, I know I was getting pretty close to running on empty. I didn't want to die, but I was starting to think how nice it would be to just go to sleep, and it would all be over. I wouldn't be here now if it wasn't for you. You saved my life."

She wasn't looking at him, but instead watching patterns in the sand she was making with her feet.

"You saved me too," she said, "and you don't even know it."

"How?"

"When I saw you in the road there, struggling so hard to move just one more foot, I found myself..." she took a deep breath, "...I found myself starting to cheer for you. I wanted you to make it. You just had to make it!

"And in the time I spent taking care of you, hoping that you were going to live, I found myself wanting to live, too. I didn't even know I had lost that until you gave it back to me."

The jagged mountain had nearly divided the sun into two narrow segments. Jim refilled the wine glasses and put his arm around Missy again.

"Tell me one thing," she asked. "Why did you keep trying so hard? There was nothing good in front of you, just more of the same dusty road. Why did you keep going when it didn't seem like it was doing you any good?"

"You're going to think it's strange."

"Tell me."

He swirled the wine in his glass before answering.

"Boredom," he said. "Boredom gave me the reason to keep going. When I got to the point of thinking, 'Why do anything, why try?' the answer was 'I might as well.' Something was better than nothing. I knew it was going to end, sooner or later. That's the only guarantee. Until then, I figured I might as well have something, do something.

"So when I was lying in the road in a heap, unable to move, I'd say to myself, 'This is boring' and I'd move. Even the ache in my muscles and the dust in my mouth were better than the boredom of nothing. I guess that sounds pretty crazy. I guess I was crazy."

"Maybe not," she responded.

"But now," he said, "I've really got something."

He kissed her cheek, and she rested her head on his shoulder. The sun now was gone from view, but the daylight lingered. The pair nestled down farther and held each other closer.

"How do you think Bess is doing?" he asked.

"She's better," Missy said. "She has her good days and her bad days. You notice she's warmed up to you quite a bit, though she was terrified of you at first."

"She was?"

"It's because we don't know what happened or where all the people went. Bess thinks maybe there was an invasion, or a plague. She didn't want me to bring you to town at first. She thought you might be infected with a terrible disease or that maybe you were an alien."

"An alien? You mean, from another country, or from another planet?"

"She was too afraid to say."

The twilight was fading. The few wispy clouds that had drifted by in the darkening sky were joined by more. There was no moon, and there were no lights. Soon, it would be very dark.

Abruptly, Missy rolled over so that she was on top of Jim, and her face was very close to his.

"You're not an alien, are you?" she asked.

"No," he answered, surprised. "I'm a man, born on this planet 32 years ago, and I've been here ever since. And, until lately, I've had a pretty uneventful life."

"Good.".

Slowly, excruciatingly slowly, she brought her lips forward and pressed them against his mouth. He hugged her; with one arm at the small of her back and the other below her shoulders. He hugged her tightly so that he could feel as much of her body against his as possible.

Her hands were on either side of his head, and she tousled his hair and kissed him again. She paused to look into his eyes, just visible in the ever-increasing darkness.

"You're pretty good at this," she said.

"Don't stop...want more practice," he uttered, the shortness of his breath the product of the pounding of his heart.

She kissed him again, several light, easy kisses; and she slid her lips back and forth against his.

"You know," she said, drawing away from him, "There's something about a man who wears a tie…" She began pulling on his tie, loosening it. "…something that says that he's got things under control, that he likes himself and he's not afraid to show it…" She undid the knot and began sliding the tie out from around his neck. "…something that says he's confident, proud of his accomplishments…" She took his tie off, threw it to the side, and started unbuttoning his shirt.

"Yes," she said. "A tie makes a man look special."

"But I don't have a tie on, anymore."

"Too bad."

She continued unbuttoning his shirt and started kissing his chest, also biting his chest hairs and pulling on them with her lips. He stroked her hair and caressed her head and gave her free rein to do whatever she wanted. She started kissing his stomach.

In the distance, they heard Bess's voice calling out, crying for Missy. Several times Bess called out Missy's name, and also once Jim's, and once she cried out in pain. Missy answered right away, but at first Bess didn't hear.

Missy and Jim stood up and climbed back to the top of the hill. They were barely able to discern Bess below them, stooped over and holding her leg.

"Missy, oh Missy," Bess cried.

"Bess, what's wrong?" Missy shouted. "What's happened?"

"It's dark; it's so dark," Bess sobbed. "You never stay out after dark. I thought…I thought you had disappeared, like everyone else."

Missy climbed down to Bess, and Jim followed.

"No, Bess, no, we're right here, we're here," Missy soothed. "We didn't realize how dark it was. Everything's okay."

Missy hugged Bess and straightened her hair.

"Are you okay?" Missy asked.

"I...I hurt my leg in the dark. I tripped over something," Bess cried. "Oh, Missy, I was so frightened. I thought you had gone away forever. I thought everyone had gone away. I thought I was all alone, the only one left. And it was so dark. I couldn't see anything. I couldn't see the hill; and then, when I came looking for you, I couldn't see the house, or anything. Don't leave me."

Missy and Bess hugged again while Jim stood alongside.

"Everything's okay now, Bess," Missy comforted. "You're all right now. We won't leave you."

"We'd better get back to the house," Jim said. "I'll lead the way. You take care of Bess."

Jim turned in the general direction where he thought the buildings were and couldn't see a thing.

"Where the hell is the house?" he muttered.

They made their way slowly through the darkness, Jim leading the way, Missy and Bess walking arm-in-arm behind. Once Jim fell down, cursed, and Missy reached out to him as he got back up. She hooked her free hand into his belt in back to keep the three of them closer together.

They groped their way until Jim found the back of the

buildings. He was almost on top of it before he saw it. They felt their way along the wall till they came to the back door leading to the stairwell. The women went up the stairs first, and Jim followed.

"I don't have any candles," Missy said. "I was supposed to ask Harry for some, and I forgot."

"I'm okay now," Bess said. "I didn't mean to ruin your date. I'm all right as long as I know that you're okay."

"You didn't ruin our date," Jim answered. "We shouldn't have stayed out that long. We weren't paying attention to how dark it was getting."

The three of them stood in the living room in the dark, only being sure of each other's presence by the sound of their breathing or the rustle of their clothes when they moved.

"Well," Bess broke the silence, "I should leave you two alone, so you can finish your date. I'm sorry I was such a baby."

"No Bess, you're fine," Jim responded. "I think I should go. I don't want to wear out my welcome on the first date. We've had a full day."

"Are you sure, Jim?" Missy asked. "I could put on some water for tea. We could see by the firelight."

"No thanks, Miss," Jim answered. "I have some things I want to do anyway. And the two of you could use some time together to relax, get things back to the way they were. You sure you're okay, Bess? Is your leg all right?"

"I'm fine, now," Bess replied.

Jim reached out in the darkness, found Bess's arm, pulled closer to her and gave her a comforting hug.

41

"Sleep tight," he said.

"Good night, Jim," Bess responded.

Then he reached out for Missy's arm, hugged her, and gave her a kiss on the neck.

"Good night, beauty," he whispered. "Thanks for a lovely evening."

"See you tomorrow?" she asked.

"Yes," he answered. "Good night."

Jim felt his way to the door and started down the stairs. Missy called out after him.

"Be careful, Jim," she said. "It's dark out there."

Jim laughed.

"I know," he answered. "I'll talk to you in the morning."

Missy closed the door behind him.

"So, how was your date?" Bess asked. "Did I ruin it?"

"Not at all," Missy replied. "It was just perfect. C'mon, I'll tell you all about it."

Outside, Jim had found his way through the darkness and had gone up the stairs to his flat. He mounted the treadmill in his kitchen that he had hooked up to a car generator connected to the bank of batteries on his porch. In the living room, he had a microphone stand to which he had attached an automobile tail light.

Jim walked on the treadmill in the dark for a while, then

42

worked his way to the living room and threw a switch he had in line with the tail light.

The bulb glowed brightly, so brightly that he held up his hands to shield his eyes, and he had to avoid looking directly at it. It chased all the darkness away, save for the shadow that Jim cast as he walked around it.

Jim took a shade from one of the lamps in the room and bent it so that it fit, loosely, atop the glowing bulb, mellowing the light. Then he sat down to do some reading before going to bed.

Across the street, Pamela, staring out the window from her private darkness, saw the light spilling into the street. Since it was the only light in a totally dark world, she felt drawn to it, hypnotized by it. She stood at her window and watched it, wondered about it, for as long as it was still glowing. Even after it went out, she was still standing there, watching, waiting. Only when she was sure that it would not reappear did she feel her way through the darkness to her bed and lied down.

At first, she did not even bother to close her eyes.

※ ※ ※

The next morning dawned bright and cheerful. Missy had gone with Bess to her room the night before to console her and also to talk about the date with Jim, and wound up falling asleep there. The morning sun streaming through Bess's window woke them both up at about the same time.

Bess took her bath first, while Missy began some of the preparations for breakfast. Because the sun was shining so brightly, Bess, anticipating a warm day, dressed in shorts, along with a sleeveless white top. She wrapped her hair in a towel.

As Missy prepared for her bath, she and Bess discussed how they would spend their day. The wood supply was adequate, so they could work together hauling tomorrow's supply of water. In the afternoon they would pay a surprise visit on Jim.

Missy took her bath and had just stepped from the tub. She had a towel wrapped around her, another one in her hands to dry her wet, disheveled hair. Drops of water still glistened on her face and on her bare legs.

Then, the phone rang.

Both women froze where they stood—Bess in the hall on the way to her bedroom and Missy standing in the doorway of the bathroom. They looked at each other, surprised and uncertain. A drop of water trickled down Missy's face, and a self-willed lock of wet hair flopped over in front of her eye. Missy brushed it back and looked from Bess to the telephone and back again. Missy motioned with her head toward the phone in a suggestion that Bess should answer it, and Bess warded off the idea by holding up her hands and taking a step backward.

Slowly, and with measured steps, Missy walked, barefoot, over the living room carpet until she stood before the table on which the phone was sitting.

She looked over to Bess for reassurance. Bess motioned her toward the telephone, but didn't herself dare to step any closer. Missy faced the phone again, which remained silent before her.

Slowly Missy reached out, took a deep breath, and, with just thumb and forefinger, picked the handset up from the cradle and held it out away from her. She turned so that she could face Bess. With her other hand she pushed the hair away, and carefully she put the handset up to her ear and listened. She shook her head towards Bess to indicate that she heard nothing.

Missy drew another deep breath and said, her voice shaking, "Hello?"

Jim's voice answered, "I hope I didn't call at a bad time."

"Jim!" Missy shouted as loud as she could. "It's Jim!" she said to Bess.

Bess ran up to the phone.

"Jim, what are you doing to us?" Missy cried. "We didn't know what to expect. It's been so long since I heard a phone ring!"

"So it's true what they say," Jim teased, "that the prettiest women never get any phone calls. But why did it take you so long to answer? I heard it ring through the wall, but it took you forever to pick up. Did I get you out of the shower?"

"Yes you did, you bad boy!" Missy giggled.

"So now you're all wet and glistening and…"

"Hold it right there, fella," Missy interrupted, laughing. "The first time I've used a phone in months, and it's an obscene call!"

"Okay, okay," Jim retreated. "I'll pick a better subject. How's Bess feeling this morning?"

"She's right here," Missy answered. "Talk to her."

Bess took the phone.

"Hi, Jim," she said. "How did you make the phone work?"

"Frankly, I don't know," he answered. "I just kept poking wires till something happened. How are you? How's your leg?"

"I'm fine. It was just a scratch. I always feel better when the sun is shining. Are you coming over for breakfast?"

"Nope. I've already had breakfast. But I was hoping after breakfast you two could come over here. I have a business proposition for you."

"He wants us to go over there after breakfast," Bess said to Missy. "He has a proposition for us."

"Sounds intriguing," Missy answered.

Just then there was a knock at the door.

"Jim, hold on." Bess said. "There's someone at the door, and Missy's not dressed."

"That's okay. I'll hang up," Jim said. "I'll talk to you when you come over."

"Okay," Bess replied. "We'll be there. Bye."

"Bye, Jim," Missy called out before Bess hung up.

Missy ran to her bedroom while Bess went to open the door. In the landing was a man, about 30, stoop-shouldered, heavy set, wearing dress pants a size too small and a white, short-sleeved shirt, stretched open between each of the buttons. The pocket of his shirt was filled with pens.

"Hi, Frank," Bess said.

Frank spoke slowly, as if he was checking every word, rolling each one on his tongue, tasting it, before he would let it out of his mouth.

"Harry...Harry wants everybody to come to the store around noon today," he said.

"Okay," Bess replied.

Frank stood, waiting, thinking, before saying, "That's all."

He turned to leave, then stopped and turned back.

"Uh, do you...do you know where that new guy lives?" he asked.

"Next door, above the hardware store," Bess answered, "But we can tell him for you."

"Uh, okay," Frank replied.

He turned partway, turned back, and then turned away fully and walked down the stairs. Bess watched him leave.

Missy and Bess had a quick breakfast and went over to Jim's. He showed them his treadmill, charger, side porch full of batteries, and the 12 volt floor lamp.

"Welcome to Jim's Power and Telephone Company," he said. "I can run a line through the wall, and you can have light anytime you want. As my first customers, I can get you hooked up for a special, introductory price."

"How much?" Missy asked.

"A smile," Jim answered.

Missy smiled. She couldn't help it.

"I see you believe in paying your bills in advance," Jim teased. "Excellent."

Missy and Bess told Jim about the meeting at noon. Then the three spent the rest of the morning running wire and rigging lights so that each woman had a light in her bedroom as well as one in the kitchen and the living room.

They ate lunch at Jim's, just snacking and talking. Each woman took a turn on the treadmill, charging the batteries and having fun. The activity energized not only the batteries but also the people, and their conversation remained lively even while they were walking down the street to the store for the meeting.

They stopped at the same little room in the corner of the building that contained the supermarket.

"Do you do this often?" Jim asked, just before they walked in.

"Never," Missy answered. "This is a first."

They opened the door, doubling the amount of sunlight in the room. The liveliness of their conversation collided with the quiet inside. Jim closed the door, and the subdued light and somber mood enveloped them.

Inside the room, the folding chairs were set up facing the counter, as if for a meeting, but there were only seven chairs. Ernie and Bob were seated by the window. Three women Jim had not seen before sat closest to the counter. No one was talking.

"I feel like I'm in church," Jim whispered to Missy, intentionally letting his lips brush against the exquisite curve of her ear.

She nodded at him, but said nothing. He ushered Missy and Bess to the two remaining chairs and stood behind them.

Except for the occasional cough or scrape, the room was

silent. Three people walked in from the storeroom and stood behind the counter.

Jim bent his head toward Missy, and she whispered in his ear.

"You know who Harry is," Missy said. "The other guy is Harry's brother, Frank. And the woman with them is Anitra. I thought she was Frank's girlfriend, but I've never been sure. Sometimes Harry acts like she's his girlfriend too."

Jim raised his eyebrows. Missy shrugged.

Anitra was a tall woman, taller than either Harry or Frank. She had flowing black hair that reached nearly to her waist. She was dressed in hip-hugger slacks and a cut-off top. She wore one or two gold rings on every finger, a gold necklace, and a thin gold chain around her bare midriff, carefully positioned so that it's single, tiny gold charm dangled in front of her navel.

Harry stood in the center of the trio, an amalgam of tall, lean Anitra and short, overweight Frank. When he shifted his weight in Anitra's direction, she darted to give him more room.

"The other three women," Missy whispered, "are Kate, Susan, and Allyson. Kate's the brunette. They live at the end of town, on the other side of the market from us."

Jim nodded. Harry cleared his throat. Missy stopped whispering to Jim; and, after a moment, Harry started speaking.

"People are going to have to earn their food," Harry said. "We here have too much to do, with all the work, running this market, to get our own wood and water. You don't know what it's like."

No one said anything.

The door to the street opened, and Pamela walked in. She stood in the open doorway, not knowing which way to go.

"You're late," Harry proclaimed.

"I don't have a clock," Pamela responded, wilting. "I have no way of finding out what time it is."

Harry waved her off. Awkwardly, Pamela sat down on the window sill.

"What I need," Harry continued, "is a pile of wood, in front of the market, so we don't have to go all the way up in the hills to get it. And we're going to put some garbage pails in front of the market for water. I need them kept full."

Still no one said anything. Jim rubbed the back of Missy's neck with one hand, and she moved her head in syncopation with his massage.

"You," Harry barked, pointing at Jim. "You want wood or water?"

"Doesn't matter," Jim shrugged. "Water, I guess."

"You've got wood," Harry replied. Then he pointed to Pamela. "You've got water." And he pointed to Missy. "You've got inventory to finish. Meeting's over."

Harry walked out the same way he came in. Frank and Anitra stood, uncomfortably, in front of the group.

"You can all leave now," Frank muttered, so quietly only the three women closest to the counter heard him.

They stood up, and the others did likewise. Frank moved to walk out, hesitated once, then went through the door. Anitra followed him.

Everyone else filed out the front door, wordlessly, and went straightaway back to their own places. Only Jim, Missy, and Bess lingered out front.

Jim was shaking his head. "That was so strange. I couldn't call it a meeting. More of a sermon. That guy sure doesn't waste any words."

"But why is he picking on us?" Missy asked. "The inventory is foolish! There's no reason to count it over and over. I don't know what he wants from me."

"I think I know what he wants from you," Bess said.

"Oh, Bess," Missy groaned. "Please tell me you're kidding."

Bess answered, "All I can say is, you better change out of those tight jeans before you go to do inventory."

Jim sighed, "I guess I don't get a vote."

"Go chop your wood," Missy teased. "I'll worry about how I dress the next time. And you, Bess, how are you going to spend your day?"

"Water," Bess answered, gloomily.

Missy went back inside the store to help with the inventory, and Jim and Bess walked to the corner.

"Catch you later, Bess," Jim said.

"Aren't you coming back home first?"

"Nah, I want to look around in back."

"How come?

"If I can make a phone call next door, there's no reason I can't make one to the next block."

"Can I watch?"

"Sure."

Bess and Jim examined the phone lines in back of the store, and then traced them where they ran to the pole, across the street, through their back yard, and to a junction box. In all, several dozen wires were involved.

"How do you know what you're doing?" Bess asked.

"I don't," Jim answered, "But that's no reason not to take a shot at it. This used to work. The only question is if we can make it work again."

But after an hour of trying without success, Jim and Bess agreed it was time they got their chores done. They would leave the phone for another time.

Bess went off to the river to begin hauling water for the next day; and Jim, hatchet and ax in hand, took off on the road heading south of town, for wood.

A quarter mile out of town, Jim left the main road and followed a smaller road that curved gently west up into the hills. Another half mile later, all uphill, he came upon an old and rusty station wagon that had been abandoned by the side of the road.

Jim inspected the car thoroughly. There was no gas in the tank, no life in the battery, and the tires were soft. Jim found a hand pump in the back, stripped off his shirt, and pumped up the tires till they were extra hard. He knocked out the lock on the steering column. Then he began foraging in the woods for dead branches, which were plentiful. In less than two hours he had the station wagon full, packed right up to the roof with wood. He stopped to rest; and, from his vantage up on the hill, in the distance he saw a lone figure walking south of town toward him. He went to meet her.

Bess had tired of hauling water and had come out to see how Jim was doing. He met her near the fork in the road, and together they walked back to the station wagon.

"Does it run?" was the first thing Bess asked when she saw the car, loaded so full, sitting flat on its springs.

"Nope," Jim answered, "But that's why I was so happy to see such an attractive, healthy woman walking this way with those lovely, well-muscled legs."

"Okay, Mister Smarty Pants. You want me to push, don't you?" Bess asked.

"Yup," Jim replied.

They pushed, and they pushed, but the car did not budge. Jim's muscles bulged, and the sweat dripped off his face and down his chest. He pushed straight on; he put his back to it. Nothing worked.

They rested, and Bess leaned against the car. Jim got a long branch and propped it under the car.

Again they struggled, shoulder to shoulder, pushing with all their strength on the branch. They moved the car up, but they did not move it along. His sweat mixed with hers. He reached to the top of his form and held on, muscles tight and straining, for as long as he could.

And then, the car moved.

Slowly it moved forward while they pushed. Jim quickly positioned the branch again, and they pushed again, and the car kept on moving, slowly but undeniably. Gravel under the wheels crunched sharply.

They dropped the branch and threw themselves against the back of the car. Jim groaned as he put his full weight into it.

The car kept moving, easing downhill, massive and unstoppable now.

"Get ready to jump in!" Jim shouted.

"I hope my door is unlocked!" Bess called back.

"It better be!"

They were trotting behind the car, just touching it.

"Now!" Jim shouted.

They both got into the car, banging shins and elbows as they did. The speed increased—ten, twenty, thirty, forty, forty-five miles an hour.

"Wheeee!" Bess cried out as the car rounded a bend with the tires squealing.

"I wonder if the brakes work?" Jim asked.

"Now you wonder?" Bess shouted as the car rounded another curve with dust flying and gravel spitting. She grabbed his bicep and held on.

"Doesn't matter," he shouted. "This is no time for caution. We need the momentum!"

Two more screeching turns, and the car careened onto the main road, where Jim almost lost control. From there it was a straight shot into town, and the car started gradually slowing down.

"What brakes?" Jim shouted. "We don't need no sissy brakes!"

"Wow, that was great!" Bess said, letting go of Jim's arm. "I wasn't scared at all."

Jim smiled at her.

"Me either," he said.

The car continued to slow down; and, when they entered town, they found themselves rocking in their seats, urging it forward. It kept on moving, until it was right in front of the gas station, across from the market. Jim applied the brakes.

"Whatya know," Jim said. "They work."

"Brakes?" Bess shot back. "We don't need no sissy brakes!"

Jim laughed. They got out of the car and stood on the sidewalk, looking at their accomplishment—a rusty white station wagon, sitting alone in a deserted street, loaded so heavily with wood that it looked in danger any minute of collapsing under the weight.

"That ought to last Harry for a while," Bess said.

"I think so," Jim replied. "The hard part's going to be pushing the empty car back up the hill when we have to refill it."

"You're on your own on that one," Bess laughed.

Together they walked back toward their homes.

"Well, that was fun," Bess said. "Now what?"

"Now," Jim answered, "I think I could use a shower. Maybe I'll try just grabbing a towel and washing off in the river."

"I don't think you want to do that," Bess cautioned. "That water is coming right out of the mountains, and it's still ice cold. You'll catch pneumonia. Even when we use the water we leave sitting overnight, it's an adventure taking a bath in the morning."

They were in front of Bess's now.

"If you want to come up," she said, "I'll treat you to some fresh, room-temperature, bath water. I'll even warm a couple kettles full on the barbecue. That's what we usually do."

Jim protested, "I don't want to take *your* bath water away. You worked so hard for it. And I know how much you dislike having to get it every day."

"Actually," she answered, "I kinda like the exercise. I just hate the boredom. But I had so much fun today, even hauling water doesn't seem quite so bad anymore. C'mon."

She was standing two steps up on the stairs and tugging on his arm, her eyes wide and openly pleading.

"Pleeeease," she entreated.

"Okay, okay," Jim consented, laughing. "Just let me go to my place and get a change of clothes first."

"Oh, right," Bess giggled. "That <u>would</u> be a good idea."

Bess bounded up the stairs while Jim went next door. She lit the barbecue and put several pans of water on to heat. He joined her at the kitchen table while they were waiting for the water.

"Are you sure this is okay?" he asked. "I don't want to

deprive you two of one of the very few luxuries we have around here."

"I'll get more water," Bess answered. "It won't kill Missy to take her morning bath in the evening for a change. Besides, she should be home soon, and I want to surprise her with you. We can have dinner together."

"You want to surprise her with me? What does that mean?"

"You know. It was my fault you didn't get to finish your date yesterday. She really *likes* you. And I was being such a baby. But now maybe you can take up where you left off."

Jim sighed, "I really like her too. But you're not going to be afraid tonight?"

"I've got a light I can turn on now."

The fire in the barbecue crackled, and the smoke drifted lazily away from the porch and toward the distant mountains.

"This is a luxury," Jim almost whispered, "Just being able to sit still, without having to struggle every minute to survive, just being able to relax, and think, maybe even daydream."

"I know," Bess agreed. "Hauling wood and hauling water. Except for eating and sleeping, that's all I do, all day, every day."

Jim was tracing the design on the tablecloth with his finger, but his mind was elsewhere.

"Do you think about before," he asked, "how we took it all for granted—heat at the flick of a switch, water at the twist of a knob, music? I miss music."

Bess moaned, "Ohhh, music. I'd forgotten about music. I miss it too."

"Spare time is what we need most. If it takes all our strength and all our time, just to survive, we've got nothing left to figure out how to make surviving easier."

"You picked up some spare time today, Jim. I know Harry expected you to be busy for days, hauling wood for him."

Jim's smile was bittersweet.

"Yeah," he agreed, "and that was fun. But in the long run, it's not going to count for much. Next week, there won't be an abandoned car at the top of the hill."

"You're not going to push it back up?" she teased.

He knew she was kidding. He let the moment linger, before he continued. "Worst thing is, despite all our effort, we're not really making it. We're counting on work people did in the past. Sooner or later that supermarket will be empty, and we'll either have to move to another town with a supermarket, or figure out a way to get the food here. But eventually the cans are going to rust, and by then we'd damn well better know how to grow our own food, or we'll die."

Silence enfolded them. The somber mood reached a place in Bess's mind.

"There's something I've been worried about," she said. "Something we've just been lucky about so far."

"What?"

"There's no doctor. If someone gets sick, even just a little, it could be serious."

"Whoa," Jim groaned. "I hadn't thought about that. There's so much, so much we counted on, so much that we're missing."

"There's a doctor's office across the street. I went in there once for aspirin."

"Any books?"

"Hundreds."

"Maybe you should read them."

"Me?"

"I know I won't be any good at medicine, but I can haul *your* water for you. The best way I can spend my spare time is by giving it to you."

"Jim, that's so sweet. But I don't know that I'd be any good at medicine either. There's so much to know."

"You'll probably be terrific."

Bess beamed. "You're sweet. Now I know why Missy likes you so much."

It was Jim's turn to smile.

By now, wisps of steam had started to rise from the smaller containers on the grill.

"The water's about ready," Bess said. "So if you want to get started…"

"You want me to help with the water?"

"Sure."

They each carried some of the water to the bathroom, where there was already several inches of cool water in the tub. They poured the hot water in. Jim took his shirt off while Bess got the rest of the water.

She knelt by the tub and mixed the water with her hand.

"It's just barely tepid," she said. "I'll put more on, but you can get started. Would you like bubble bath?"

"I'm not the bubble bath type."

"Sure you are!"

She mixed in the soap till the water was frothy.

"Enjoy," she said. "I'll let you know when the rest of the water is hot."

Bess closed the door behind her, and Jim undressed and got into the tub. He sank down until the bubbles were just under his chin, closed his eyes, and let the water relax him.

When the rest of the water was hot, Bess knocked on the door.

"Do you want me to leave it by the door, or are you decent?" she asked.

"I'm decent as long as my bubbles hold out."

Bess brought the water in and carefully poured it into the tub, near Jim's feet. When she was finished, she leaned against the sink.

"You look very contented," she said.

"Ohhhh, this is a treat," he replied, swirling the water. "You could go into the Turkish bath business. I'd pay for this."

"Should I put it on the list of what's important to us—food, medicine, bubble baths?"

Jim said nothing, just sighed contentedly as he made waves in the water.

"Speaking of food," Bess said, "since the fire is already going, and Missy is late, I might as well start cooking. What would you like?"

"I'm easy to please," Jim answered. "What does Missy like?"

"Corn and potatoes are her favorites."

"Mine too."

"I knew that."

Back from the market, Missy bounded up the stairs. The door to the bathroom was mostly closed, and the pair inside did not hear her come in. She, however, heard them.

"There's something else I want to say, Jim," Bess said. "You were wonderful today. You made me feel so good. If I've ever felt as good as I feel right now, I don't remember it."

"You were wonderful too, Bess," he replied. "You're a very special woman, and you have something great to offer."

He reached out his hand to her. She offered her hand to him. He took it and squeezed it.

"And I loved swappin' sweat with you," he said.

"Maybe we can do it again?"

"Sure," he answered.

He let her hand go. Bess backed closer to the door.

"Put some clothes on," she said. "I'll start dinner."

Missy stood in the middle of the living room, not moving, listening to the conversation, uncertain about what she should do. She took a step toward the kitchen and stopped. Then she went back through the outside doorway and again stopped. She turned around and looked at the bathroom door and the narrow opening through which she saw Bess moving.

Missy went back out to the landing and blocked out the scene by closing the door. She backed down the first several steps, holding the handrail. Then, in a daze, she turned around and walked down the rest of the way. She stopped at the bottom and sat down on the very last step, hunched over.

For a long time she sat there, not moving, staring at the wall in front of her. Then the tears started to roll down her cheeks, and she began to sob. Once started, she sobbed so hard that it hurt her chest, and she hugged her knees, and she rocked, and she wanted to stop sobbing, but she couldn't, and she couldn't catch her breath either.

The violence of her crying diminished slowly, and Missy sat there, rocking and hugging her knees, as outside the darkness started to creep in and take over the town for yet another night.

Around town, the people were preparing for the approaching darkness, settling in to await the time when the darkness again released them from its hold.

Across the street, Pamela was busying herself about her apartment; but she was also frequently looking out her window, to see if the light would appear again tonight. Up the block, Ernie was closing the door of the gas station behind him and heading diagonally across the street to Missy and Bess's place.

Missy roused herself and dried her tears with her hands as well as she could. Her face was red and the area around her eyes, swollen. As quietly as she could she tiptoed up the stairs and listened at the doorway. She heard Jim and Bess in the kitchen.

Missy walked in quickly and headed straight for the bathroom.

"Hi, hi," she said to both Jim and Bess without looking at them, as she walked past the kitchen doorway. "Don't look at me. I'm a mess from work."

Jim and Bess both said "Hi" as Missy closed the door to the bathroom behind her.

"I've started dinner," Bess called to Missy through the door. "It's your favorite."

"Okay," Missy called back, her voice wavering. "I'll be out in a minute. I'm not too hungry. I ate a little at the market."

Missy braced her hands against each side of the sink, looked at her face in the mirror, and gave a deep, pained sigh. She splashed cold water from the basin onto her face and toweled off. Then she applied make-up, using both hands because she was still shaking.

There was a knock at the outside door. Bess was on the back porch, stirring food on the barbecue, but at the sound of the knock she poked her head into the kitchen.

"You have a visitor," Jim said.

"No one ever visits here," Bess replied. "Would you…"

Jim nodded. "I'll get it."

Jim opened the door, and Ernie was standing there, holding his hat in front of him, and moving it around by the brim, from hand to hand.

"Why, you're Ernie, right?" Jim said. "C'mon in."

"No, no, I don't want to bother you folks," Ernie replied. "I'll just stand out here in the hall. Well then, okay, maybe I'll step inside just for a minute, but I don't want to bother you."

"C'mon in, Ernie," Bess said, wiping her hands on a dish towel as she entered the room.

Ernie came in, and Jim closed the door.

"I don't want to disturb your dinner none," Ernie said. "I gotta git right back cuz Bob is settin' out a spread for us right now."

"What can we do for you, Ernie?" Jim asked.

"I just want to thank you for bringing that car in to us. It means a lot, you having faith in us like that. And it's mighty nice to have some fresh work to do. Me'n Bob was going around in circles, there. But now we got a real project to work on, and we're gonna do our best for ya, t'see if we can get 'er runnin' agin'."

Jim gave a knowing glance to Bess before saying, "If anyone can fix it, you can Ernie."

"Only thing though, only thing," Ernie said. "It might be tough. Looks like we're gonna need a new piston or two, and we ain't got the size. Used ta be you could get something turned, but not anymore. Its tough getting' parts."

"Well, do your best for me, Ernie," Jim said. "Maybe we can figure something out."

"I'll get started on it right away," Ernie said. "There'll be a whole lotta work to do, a whole lotta work. Gotta rebuild the carb. She's an old one, y'know. Gotta check the differential. A whole lotta work."

"You can do it, Ernie," Jim said.

Ernie put his hand on the doorknob to let himself out.

"We'll get started on it first thing in the morning," Ernie said. "It's getting dark now, but we'll do it first thing in the morning. I'll do the carburetor first. Yeah, the carburetor. First thing in the morning. Yeah. First thing."

Ernie opened the door and backed out.

"Thanks for coming over, Ernie," Jim said. "I'll stop by the garage soon and see how it's coming along."

"Thank you for bringing the car in," Ernie repeated. "And thank you, ma'am," he said to Bess. "I hope I didn't disturb you none."

"Not at all, Ernie," Bess answered. "I'm glad you came over."

"Thanks again, folks," Ernie said, and walked down the stairs.

Bess closed the door.

"I think we made someone very happy," she said. "I've never heard Ernie say so much before."

"I think we made someone happy," Jim agreed.

They walked back into the kitchen. It was darker now, and so Jim turned on the light.

65

"Jim," Bess asked, while opening a can of fruit juice, "Do you ever wonder, sometimes, about why there are no cars left anywhere?"

"Yeah, I wonder," Jim answered. "It doesn't make any sense. No cars and no people."

"And no animals," Missy added, stepping into the kitchen.

"Hi, Miss," Jim greeted her, standing up to kiss her cheek.

Awkwardly, she responded, though she wound up missing his cheek and kissing his collar.

"Not even any bugs," Bess continued. "I wonder if we'll ever know what happened."

Jim shook his head and sat back down at the table. "They still aren't sure what killed off the dinosaurs, but that doesn't mean it wasn't obvious, if only someone had been around to see. Maybe this will become obvious to us soon."

"I hope so," Bess sighed.

"Maybe it's something we'd be better off not knowing," Missy added. "Maybe it's too horrible."

They fell silent for a moment.

"What I'm most afraid of," Bess said, "Is that it's not over. That whatever it is, it's still out there, waiting for us."

Again, silence, gloomy silence, which Jim broke by saying, "We don't know what the shape of our enemy is, or from what quarter to expect him."

"Let's talk about something else," Bess said. "Dinner's

ready."

Bess served up a meal of canned vegetables and fruit juice.

"How were things at the market?" she asked. "How was Harry? Did he make a pass?"

"No," Missy answered. "He never even talks to me. But I catch him looking at me sometimes, when he thinks I'm not watching. It's creepy."

"It's the blue jeans, Missy," Bess said. "You've got to start wearing baggier clothes when you're around Harry."

"Maybe I will, tomorrow, when I have to go back."

"You have to go back again?" Bess asked.

"Harry promised this would be the last time," Missy answered. "It doesn't make any sense, though. I'm not doing anything that needs doing."

"If I'm right," Bess said, "Harry's going to see to it you *never* finish your job."

Missy groaned, "I promise, I'll wear the ugliest clothes I can find, tomorrow."

"You haven't asked us about our day," Bess said. "We had quite an adventure. You should have seen…"

Bess was interrupted by another, very tentative, knock on the door.

"You ladies seem to be very popular tonight," Jim said.

Missy offered to answer the door.

"Maybe it's Ernie," Bess said. "He's come back to thank us some more."

"You have a wicked tongue, Bess," Jim responded.

Bess pretended to pout.

"But I love that about you," Jim added, and Bess smiled.

Missy opened the door. Standing there was Pamela, dressed in a black sweater and black slacks. She stood at an angle, not quite facing the door, and with all her weight on one foot. In her hand she held a small, wind-up alarm clock.

"Pamela," Missy said. "I'm surprised. Please come in."

Both Jim and Bess stood up from the kitchen table and went into the living room to greet the newcomer. Pamela ventured only one step into the room, and gestured weakly with the hand that held the alarm clock.

"I found a clock today at the novelty store," she said, not making eye contact with anyone, "but I didn't know what time to set it to, and I couldn't think of any way to find out. I guess everyone else knows what time it is, because they were all on time today. Could you please tell me what time to set my clock?"

Missy reached out, took Pamela's arm, and brought her farther into the room.

"Come into the kitchen," Missy said. "Would you like some juice? Of course we'll help you set your clock."

Though the first step was reluctant, Pamela allowed herself to be led into the kitchen.

"You have light," Pamela said. "I saw it last night too."

"Jim rigged it up," Missy explained. "It was part of a car. He's very good at figuring out how to make things work."

Missy looked at him, but turned away quickly before he met her glance.

She directed Pamela to sit at the table and poured her a glass of juice. They all sat down, following which there was an awkward pause.

Missy reached across the table, touched Pamela's arm, and broke the silence by saying, "I'm so glad you came over. It must be so very hard for you, living all alone."

Pamela shrugged, and took a sip of her juice.

Softly, and with difficulty, she answered, "I do what I have to."

"I don't know how you manage," Bess said. "Missy and I have to work pretty much non-stop, all day long, just to get what we need; and *we* share the work."

"I don't have any choice," she answered, very quietly. "I don't know anyone."

"I…" Missy began, but choked up before she could continue. "I'm so sorry."

They talked for about an hour, on topics that were of most pressing concern to their daily existence—what foods they were eating, how they were heating food and staying warm on cold nights, how they got their water and wood, where they stored it. Once started, the conversation flowed, not like that of strangers forced together by tragedy, but like old friends catching up.

Jim told Pamela to help herself to the wood in the station

wagon in the street, but he didn't mention the adventure he and Bess had getting it there. Bess remarked about how strange it was that there were no working cars anywhere around.

"I had a car," Pamela said. "I drove here in it. I was looking for help. It was before I knew how bad things were."

"Where were you," Bess asked, "when it happened?"

Pamela's eyes filled with tears, but she didn't cry. She grimaced once, twice, before she started her story.

"I was home, with my husband. We have a summer home, up in the mountains. We always spent Sundays in bed together, you know, eating a slow breakfast, doing crosswords, turning the heater down on the water bed, snuggling for warmth, being close. We wouldn't listen to the radio or TV; it was our escape from the outside world."

She stopped talking and was staring hard at her glass on the table. No one broke the silence, and after a while she continued.

"But that day we had a fight," she said, and her voice broke. "I was mad at him, and so I left him, and I went to the downstairs bedroom. I could hear him above me. He was pacing around, but then he stopped, and he didn't come down to see me. I took some pills and fell asleep. When I went back upstairs, he wasn't moving. He was just lying there in bed, so…very…still."

Pamela stopped talking. Missy moved her chair closer and put her arm around Pamela.

Pamela sobbed once, and continued.

"Anyway, when I couldn't get anyone on the phone, I got in the car and drove for help. When I got to town, it was empty— completely empty—except Harry was standing in the middle of the intersection, under the stoplight, swaying back and forth, holding a bottle in his hand. I asked him for help, but all he did was force his way into the driver's seat. He insisted on driving, and I let him before I realized how drunk he was. I couldn't get him out again. He almost hit a building at the end of the street; and, when he stopped to back up, I jumped out. He drove off and left me.

"I ran all over town looking for someone to help. There was no one, anywhere. I couldn't believe it. No one was going to help me. I was in front of a flat, so I crawled upstairs and knelt by the front window. I don't know how long I was there. It seemed like hours. I saw Harry drive back into town with Frank and Anitra. By then, I didn't care anymore. He left them and drove off in the other direction.

"I stayed in front of that window all night. I don't think I slept any. The next morning, I saw Harry, on foot, staggering back into town. A few hours later, I saw you two walk in. There was no sign of my car, and I never found out what happened to it. I didn't care. It didn't matter anymore."

Pamela stopped talking. She straightened up in her chair, and wiped her eyes with her fingertips.

"When did the rest of the people come into town?" Jim asked.

The three women exchanged glances, waiting for someone else to answer. When no one else did, Missy brought herself to speak.

"It seems funny now, hearing myself say it," she began, shaking her head, "but I don't remember. I don't think I was paying attention. All I could think about was what I had seen, and I was so afraid of what had happened. It's like a dream, a nightmare. I guess Kate, Allyson and Sue came some time after us, and, later, Ernie and Bob. It might have been the other way around, though. I don't like thinking about it. I want to forget."

"I'm pretty sure Ernie and Bob were last," Pamela confirmed, with a shrug. "I'm like you. I wasn't paying attention, either. For that whole first month, when I wasn't getting supplies, all I did was look out the window. I didn't care about what I saw, but it was either look out the window, or stare at the floor, so I looked out the window."

Pamela started to cry again.

"It's getting better," Missy soothed. "We can make it better."

"I feel better," Bess said. "It makes me feel better doing things to improve how we live. I feel better because I helped get the wood today. And I feel much better because I have a light I can turn on now."

Their eyes drifted to the ugly bulb, taped to the top of its pole, the unattractive, twisted wire spiraling around the pole and out to the porch.

"Yes, the light," Pamela sighed. Her tears made the harshness of the bare bulb even more intense, and she closed her eyes briefly, and a tear trickled down her cheek. "I wouldn't be here if I hadn't seen the light. I needed the light."

"There's no reason we can't rig up a light for you, too," Jim responded. "As a matter of fact, we should be able to wire up at least one light for you right now."

"I'd like that," Pamela agreed, nodding briskly. "That would mean a lot to me. You're all welcome to come over and see where I live. You've never been there. No one has."

Missy tried to decline.

"You three go," she said. "I'd better stay here. I have a lot of things I need to do."

Pamela reached out to her and touched her arm.

"Please come," she said.

Reluctantly, Missy agreed.

Missy got a candle that she'd just picked up that day at the market, and the four of them went out into the street. Missy and Pamela waited in the alley next to Jim's place while he and Bess went upstairs and got a battery, wires, and bulbs. Then everyone went across the street to Pamela's.

Most of the buildings on the east side of the street, Pamela's side, were single story. Pamela's was an exception. She led the way up the stairs, followed by Missy with the candle.

Jim quickly wired the battery up in the living room, so that they could see. The room was spotlessly clean, and every shelf, every possible space, was decorated with countless vases, figurines, and pottery that Pamela had collected from around town.

Embarrassed, she explained, simply, "It's how I keep busy."

Pamela treated them to a bottle of wine she'd found in the apartment and had no occasion to open until now.

"I'll come back tomorrow and do a good job," Jim said. "We'll have to get the battery outside, and we'll have to set up a way you can recharge it."

"We run on a treadmill at Jim's place to keep the

batteries charged," Bess gushed. "I'm going to talk Jim into hiring me full time. I'll get to stay in shape, and I've always wanted to work for the phone company."

"Phone?" Pamela asked.

"Jim made the phone work between his place and ours," Bess answered. "So now he can call over to our place and whisper sweet nothings anytime he wants."

Missy fidgeted, but no one noticed.

"It's been so long since I've heard a telephone ring," Pamela said, "I don't think I remember what one sounds like."

"We're working on hooking everyone up," Jim replied, "but figuring out the switching is tough. We may just have all the phones ring at the same time. It's hard enough just tracing the right wires. But Bess and I are working on it. We had a lot of fun together today."

"We had a <u>lot</u> of fun together today," Bess agreed.

Missy stood up abruptly.

"I should leave," she said, brusquely, looking at no one. "I don't like staying away this late."

"Hang on," Jim replied, standing up. "I'll walk you back."

"No, no, you stay," Missy responded. "I'll manage on my own."

Without waiting for an answer, Missy walked out and started feeling her way down the stairs in the darkness. Jim turned to Bess and Pamela.

"I should go with her," he said. "Are you two okay

here?"

"Go on, Jim," Bess answered. "We're fine. You and Missy could use a little privacy. Maybe Pamela and I will have a pajama party here tonight."

"I'd like that," Pamela responded.

"Go on, Jim," Bess urged.

Jim walked out and started working his way down the stairs.

Missy had reached the middle of the street and stood there in the dark, bewildered and upset. By the time Jim had navigated the stairs and reached the street, she had turned around and was running back. Crying, she ran right into Jim's arms.

"I don't want to be alone," she cried. "I don't care whatever else happens. I don't care what you did! I just don't want to be alone!"

While she was crying so hard, he just hugged her and smoothed her hair, and he kept on hugging her as they slowly swayed back and forth in the middle of the street. He brushed her hair back from her forehead and kissed her there, tenderly, several times.

"You're not alone," he whispered. "I'm here. We've both survived this far; and we're going to continue to survive, together, you and me."

She cried quietly with her head on his shoulder. He let her cry. The two of them stood, holding each other, two together in the middle of that deserted street, in the middle of that little town, in the middle of all that open country.

When she was no longer crying, they stood there, feeling

each other breathe.

"Do you want to go for a walk?" he asked.

"In the dark?" she sniffed.

"It's not that dark tonight," he answered. "Not like last night. There aren't any clouds at all. Look at all the stars."

They separated to arm's length, still holding each other's shoulders, and each of them looked up to the sky. The blackness of space was perforated by countless sparkling white and blue lights. Missy was awe-struck.

"I never noticed. I've never seen so many stars before," she sighed.

"There's no more light pollution," he answered. "Nothing to turn the night sky murky. We're seeing the stars the same way our ancestors did, thousands of years ago. Want to walk?"

"Yes."

"You're not afraid?"

"No, I'm not afraid."

She eased gently out of his arms, and they walked up the center of the street, towards the river. The night was cool, but there was little breeze. They walked along in silence. The only sound was their footsteps, echoing back to them from the empty doorways.

They continued past the market, past the gas station, beyond the edge of town, until they approached the river. Passing the power plant on the left side, they stood on the bridge over the river, leaned on the railing, and looked eastward to the grand expanse of the valley and the grander expanse of space.

A pale glow appeared on the horizon.

"We're going to be able to see the moon tonight," he said. "Should be almost full."

They watched in silence as the glow increased. The top of the moon appeared, sharply defined, red—a small, round segment with a flat bottom. He spoke without taking his eyes off the moon.

"This is the first time I've heard you cry," he whispered. "I didn't like it. I didn't expect it. I didn't know what to do."

She also kept watching the moon as she spoke.

"I'm a woman," she shrugged. "Sometimes we cry. There's nothing to do. Just let it happen."

The moon continued easing away from the horizon, becoming less red as it became more round. A few renegade clouds ventured in front, making the moon look as if it had been sliced in two pieces.

The man and woman stood on the bridge, watching. They were not touching each other, they were not speaking, but the moon was joining them together. The line from her eyes to the moon, the very sharp angle, and the line back to his eyes brought them together, uniting over a distance of a half-million miles two people who stood only inches apart.

"It's beautiful," she sighed.

"Yes."

A breeze blew across the bridge, gentle, but enough to make her shiver. He sensed it.

"Are you cold?" he asked. "Do you want to go back?"

"No," she answered. "I don't want to leave this."

He put his arm around her. She felt the cold of her own thin blouse as it pressed against her, and then she felt the warmth of his hand.

"Tell me why you were crying," he asked.

It took a while for her to answer. "The world is such a big place, and we are so small, and so few. I feel like I don't belong. I was envious of the closeness you and Bess shared today."

"You and I can be close, too."

"No, Jim," she replied. "It can't be. This little town may be the start of a whole new civilization. We have to be faithful."

The word took him by surprise, and he turned to look at her.

"Beauty," he whispered, "I have been faithful to you. I started being faithful to you years ago, long before we met. I knew you were out there somewhere. I've been waiting for you all of my life."

"Really?" she asked, turning now to look back at him.

"Really," he answered, simply.

She kept looking at him, searching his face, wanting to believe, waiting for him to say or do more. He only smiled at her gently, saying nothing, waiting for his innocence to flow from him, reach her soul, and illuminate it. It was irresistible. She let go of her defenses, put her arms around his waist, and hugged him.

"I believe you."

The bottom of the moon cleared the horizon, and the huge orb, now yellow, floated in the air, casting its most golden light over the valley, across the river, and upon the woman and the man who were embracing. Across the entire Earth, from pole to pole, over five oceans and seven continents, even though they did not know it at the time, *they* were the <u>only</u> two people in each other's arms that night. For that moment, the whole planet belonged to them.

The embrace lasted while the moon rose higher in the sky, and the golden color turned to bluish white. He took her by the hand and led her away from the bridge and toward the power plant. He put his arm around her shoulder, and she put her arm around his waist. They walked together up the sloping ground to the front door of the building.

There he squeezed her shoulder and bent over to kiss her neck. She leaned her head toward him to cradle his head between her cheek and shoulder.

"Shall we go in?" he whispered.

"Here?" she said. "I've never been in here."

"Neither have I."

He tried the door. It was locked. He picked up a brick from the flower bed in front of the building, moved her safely away, and threw it at the door, shattering the glass panel. A burglar alarm whooped once loudly, once quietly, and then stopped, its backup battery having thrown all of its precious few remaining electrons into a futile effort.

He reached inside and unlocked the door. As he opened

it, the broken glass scratched noisily against the sidewalk. They stepped over the glass and went inside.

The power plant was the tallest building in the area. Its first floor was built into the side of a hill, so that in the back, there were only small windows high up in the wall. But the second floor was of double height, an 18-foot-high ceiling, and the entire front wall, facing east, consisted entirely of glass panels, panels that were alternately smooth or deeply beveled.

Missy and Jim passed the lobby and found their way up the dark stairs to the second floor. There the moonlight shining through the 18-foot-high wall of glass provided enough light so that they could see everything.

The room they were in was a large lobby that serviced offices that lined the other three walls. There were a few couches and chairs, a couple of end tables and floor lamps, a receptionist's desk near the windows, and a broad expanse of highly-polished hardwood floor that shined in the moonlight.

Holding hands, they walked into the room silently, reverently. As they walked past the different panes of glass, the image of the moon jumped and danced for them.

They stood in the center of the room, hand-in-hand, absorbing the crystalline image. Missy slipped her hand out of Jim's, walked up to the glass wall, and delicately ran her fingers along one of the beveled edges. He watched her do it, her beautiful body outlined by the shining glass. Moonbeams reflecting from the window flirted with her hair. When she had finished, she turned to him, smiled, and held out both her arms. He went to her, and they hugged again.

"C'mon," he said. "Let's explore."

"What for?"

"We're going to build a nest."

Childlike, they went from office to office, poking and prying, looking in drawers and cupboards and behind doors. They found blankets, a flashlight that worked, crackers too stale to eat, a still-sealed bag of potato chips, paper cups, and a bottle of 20-year-old scotch with only an inch gone.

They piled their booty in the middle of the lobby floor. He moved the receptionist's desk out of the way, shoved a couch into place, facing the window, to serve as a back rest, and threw the cushions on the floor. They placed cushions and pillows from all the chairs and couches on the floor and fit them together.

When they finished their work, they were both on their knees, on the cushions; and they met in the middle and hugged and kissed; and he caressed the back of her head.

They fell over sideways onto the cushions and blankets, and he bumped his head on the scotch bottle.

"Are you all right?" Missy asked, with a mixture of laughter and concern.

Jim emerged from the pile of pillows, holding the bottle and rubbing the side of his head.

"I'm fine," he answered. "Shall we drink this before I destroy it?"

They nestled down and pulled the blankets up close. He poured scotch into two paper cups and gave her one. They hooked each other's elbows, and looked into each other's eyes before taking their first sip. She promptly made a face in response to the strong taste of the scotch.

"No water, no ice," he sighed. "I'm going to have to

start treating you better."

"You're treating me just fine," she answered, brushing her hair back and taking another sip, displaying for him her willingness to drink the liquor, unflinching, just the way he expected her to. "When I think about what a difference it's made, since you came here…"

"Not that much," he replied. "So far all I've done is make one phone call and light up a couple of car tail lights. I wish I was doing more."

"In me," she whispered. "You made a difference in me. I was dead, and I didn't know it. I'm alive again, now."

He looked at her, couldn't stop looking at her, at the gentle beauty of her face, shining in the moonlight, looking back, *at him,* unflinching, accepting him the way she accepted the scotch, because she willed it.

"I can relax then," he answered. "No man can hope for a greater accomplishment than that."

"But I don't want you to stop."

He put his arm around her and placed his mouth against hers. He kissed her fully on the lips and then kissed her delicately around her lips and on her chin and down her neck. She laid her head back on the couch and fondled his hair while he kissed her.

With each button of her blouse that he undid, he continued kissing her, between her breasts and down to her stomach, leaving no part of her beautiful body unkissed; then, up again, kiss by kiss, until he was once again at her mouth.

He hovered over her, whisper-kissing her mouth, and she started unbuttoning his shirt. When she finished, she pulled his shirt out from his pants, put her arms around him under his shirt, and pulled him towards her. The couch she was leaning on slowly slid back across the shiny wood floor, until he was lying completely on top of her. They experienced the full contact of their naked chests, and they kissed each other as hard as they could.

He kissed her ears, neck, and cheeks and then very hard he kissed her open mouth and kept his lips against hers as gradually the kiss became less forceful, slowly and steadily becoming gentler until once again his lips were just touching hers. He kissed her several more times, gently, and stood up. Standing fully in front of her, he finished undressing, taking his time while she watched.

When he finished, she stood up, facing him; and, matching his achingly slow and deliberate moves, she slid out of the rest of her clothes. More than seeing, he experienced her beautiful nakedness as if he were floating, seeing her close and from afar at the same time. They stood face to face, and then they reached out to each other, at first only their finger tips touching, until they slowly came together and experienced the shock of naked body hugging naked body.

Gently, she separated from him and lied down in the middle of the cushions, reaching out to him to restore their communion. He took her hand and lied down, first next to her and then fully on top of her.

The moon watched over them while they completed their closeness.

✹ ✹ ✹

The moon continued its patient, diagonal journey along the checkerboard of glass, its image passing through pane after pane as it headed to its next destination in the southwest. The two lovers now were resting in each other's arms, comfortable and warm in the center of the cushions. He kissed her glistening shoulder, and she sighed and kissed his chest. Together they fell asleep.

Inexorably, the moon kept moving, past one glass panel after another. Jim awoke when he sensed that they were in the moon's shadow, and he had to sit up to see the moon shining through the very last window pane on the right. Soon it would be blocked from view by the brick wall. He awakened Missy by kissing her breasts; and, sleepy and contented, she put her arms around his neck. He straightened up and brought her with him. They walked as close as possible to the windows to share the last of the moonlight. Dreamily she sought the warmth and comfort of his body, and she held on to him while he led her in a slow waltz in the silence, swaying back and forth, turning slowly, turning back, their naked bodies now as one, now separate and sliding along each other, now united again. They continued their dance for as long as the moonlight lasted; and then, in the increasing darkness, he led her back to the cushions and laid her down. She curled up in the center of the cushions, and he wrapped his body around her, his chest against her back, his arm caressing her naked stomach. He kissed her neck and joined her in sleep.

They slept as one for the rest of the night, without changing position, comfortable in the harmony of their union. When the next morning's sunlight began to filter into their love nest, she groaned and tried to pull the covers over her head. He awoke long enough to help her pull, thereby capturing under the covers and prolonging the last darkness of their first night together.

Only when the sun was well started on its journey across the sky, tracing its individual path along the same panes of glass the moon had graced the night before, did the two yield to the fact that the new day had begun.

He awoke slowly. She awoke quickly. She straightened and stretched her lean body, looked toward him to see that his eyes were still closed, and then she pounced on him, pinning his arms with her hands and his thighs with her shins.

He jerked awake, then relaxed when he saw that it was her. He closed his eyes again, surrendered himself to her, and relished the last few moments of his sleepiness.

"Good morning," she chirped. "You're so grumpy in the morning!"

He grunted at her. She dangled her auburn hair in his face, brushing wisps of it across his eyes and his lips. He smiled; then he captured a lock of her hair in his mouth. Slowly she pulled her head back, drawing her hair from his lips.

She kissed his forehead, then slid her legs out so that she was lying on top of him with her arms around his head, touching as much of his naked body as possible with her own.

He touched her cheek with his hand and kissed her mouth. She kissed him slowly, lightly, everywhere on his face; then cuddled up with her head under his chin. He stroked her shoulders.

"We're going to have to get back," she sighed. "I have to work at the store. And Bess might be worried."

"Just one more moment," he pleaded. "Bess is with Pamela. She'll be fine. And Harry can wait."

She drew her answer out elegantly, "Ohhhhkaaaaaay."

She slid her body down along his and then back up so that she was nestled securely under his chin. He placed his hands on the small of her back and pressed her closer to him. She wiggled her way even closer and then relaxed. The only sound was their breathing.

"There are two things that I want," he whispered. "I want to work hard today at something, anything, so that I can feel proud of myself. And I want to be with you again tonight."

"We can work together at the store," she offered. "Then we'll *still* be together tonight."

"No, I doubt if Harry wants *me* at the store," he answered. I'd be better off staying here. I want to study this place. It doesn't look as forbidding inside as I thought it would."

"Okay," she breathed. "But I'm not looking forward to seeing Harry today."

She hugged him hard, pushed away from him, kissed him once, and stood up.

While she made her morning reparations, he spent the time exploring the offices, now in sunlight. When she finished, she found him back on the cushions, lying on his stomach and propped up on his elbows, reading technical manuals. She knelt beside him and smoothed her hand over his shoulder blades.

"Water still works here, a little," she said.

"Must be dribbling out of the water tower," he answered without looking up from his reading. Then he stopped what he was doing, looked at her, and kissed her hand.

She kissed him between his shoulder blades and then rested her chin on his shoulder, looking with him at the papers before them.

"What are you reading?" she asked.

"Engineering reports on this place," he answered. "Very interesting. They were experimenting with a second source of electricity. Not only did they have the water turning turbines, but they were trying to use these piezo electric plates that generate electricity when they get stretched and twisted in the current."

"Do you understand all this stuff?"

"Not all of it, but a little. They weren't sure there was enough water current here to produce a reasonable amount of electricity; but it might be enough for us, if you promise not to use your electric hair dryer too often."

She grabbed at him, and he rolled over to receive her. She wrestled in his grasp, squirmed to get away, and then stopped struggling and kissed him.

"My hero," she said, looking into his eyes.

"My lady," he answered.

The warmth generated by the contact of their naked bodies increased, and she softened to it, but then she pushed away.

"I've got to go," she declared. "I don't want Bess to worry."

He reached out to her as she was backing away and just managed to hold her fingers against his finger tips.

She kissed his fingers, drew one of his finger tips into her mouth, then slid it out and kissed it again. Then she stood up.

"I've got to go," she said.

She put on her clothes. He buttoned her blouse for her.

"I like to redo what I've undone," he explained.

She stood, head down, hands at her side, like a little girl, while he finished buttoning her blouse.

When he finished, he asked, "Do we have a date tonight?"

"Yes," she answered.

He kissed her forehead, then her lips, and she kissed him back and hugged him hard. She kissed his lips and his chin and then put her hand up to his lips to stop him as he tried to kiss her again.

"Don't bother to see me out," she teased. "You're not dressed for it."

He smiled.

"This evening?" he asked.

"Yes. You can cook dinner for Bess and me. Then we'll give her a quarter and send her to the movies."

"It's a date."

She backed away from him and didn't take her eyes off him until she turned to go down the stairs. He heard the scrape as the outside door crunched more of the broken glass. He stood in the wall of windows and waved to her, and she waved back to him. Then she turned and ran down the street into town.

He returned to the cushions and pulled on his pants before sitting down and surrounding himself with the technical papers.

Missy kept running until she reached the first buildings; and then, winded, she changed her pace to a brisk walk. When she reached the block where she lived, Bess was just coming out of Pamela's flat; and the two women met in the middle of the street and put their arms around each other's waists and walked toward their own place.

"How was your night?" Missy asked.

"Fine," Bess answered. "Pam and I talked most of the night about everything. How was your night?"

Missy only smiled, and Bess jostled, and Missy laughed, and Bess squeezed her.

"I'm happy for you," Bess laughed. "Are you going to tell me about it?"

Still laughing, Missy said, "No," and then changed it to, "Maybe, some."

The two women walked into their building and up the stairs.

Bess sat on the bed, cross-legged, while Missy was changing her clothes. Missy told her about standing on the bridge with Jim watching the moon rise and being mesmerized by it, spending the night at the power plant. She told her how magical the second floor lobby was, with the moonlight streaming through the wall of windows and bouncing off the shiny wood floor. She told her she remembered dancing, naked, with Jim and wasn't sure whether or not it had been a dream. She told her how wonderful Jim was.

"I noticed you were fond of him," Bess teased. "I think he's pretty nice too."

Missy finished dressing, in a baggy blue jogging suit and

white tennis shoes.

"This is what a woman in love wears?" Bess asked.

"This is for Harry."

"Smart girl."

Missy and Bess split a can of peaches for breakfast. Bess said that while Missy worked at the store, she would tidy up around the flat. She also promised to haul enough water so that they could clean up before dinner.

Back at the power plant, Jim spent the morning exploring the first floor and studying all of the machinery there. He returned to the cushions on the second floor where he had piled all the information he'd found about the operation of the place. While reading, he ate some of the potato chips and took one sip of the scotch, made a face, and pushed the bottle and the cup away from him. He finished the potato chips and crumpled the bag and tossed it toward the waste can, missed, got up and placed the bag in the waste can without ever stopping reading.

He kept at it until past noon, when he cast about for more food and found none. He stretched and limbered his stiff legs, then went downstairs to the river to splash some water on his face and bare chest. He reached the river bank and became lost in thought while he watched the gush of water from the melting snow in the distant mountains, churning vigorously around and over the diversion to the power plant.

"Hi," he heard a tiny voice say.

Jim turned and saw Kate standing just a few feet away, under the bridge, with a bucket in her hand. She was wearing trim-fitting slacks and a blouse that was knotted under her chest so that her midriff was bare. Her dark hair was mostly concealed by a scarf, and she was barefoot.

"Hi," he answered. "I didn't see you standing there."

Kate brushed from her face a wisp of hair that had escaped from the scarf and, teetering under the weight of the large bucket, walked up the embankment a few steps closer to Jim.

"You looked so deep in thought, I didn't want to disturb you," she explained.

"Power plant," he responded, looking back toward the gushing water. "It's amazing that a place that seems so forbidding is actually so simple. Water, turned into electricity."

"You've been inside?"

"Yeah. It's an interesting place, lots of dials." He said. "You want to see?"

She hesitated, looked down at the ground where she had placed her bucket, then back up at Jim.

"Yes, I would," she said.

"Good, come on."

He turned and began walking toward the plant. She started after him. He stopped abruptly, turned back; and Kate, a bit startled, pulled up short. He held out his hand to her.

"My name's Jim," he said.

She smiled and shook his hand.

"My name's Kate."

He showed her the first floor of the power plant, told her

91

about what he had been reading, explained how he thought it was supposed to work. She listened and offered suggestions.

"You sound as if you know a little about this," he said.

"I'm an architect," she said, then added, in a lower tone, "Well, I <u>used</u> to be an architect. I know a little bit about electricity. Nothing like this though. You sound like you know what you're doing."

"Not really. I just try to figure things out, then take a deep breath and go for it. I figure not being sure is no reason not to try. But it *is* a little scarier dealing with something that can turn me into ashes if I make a mistake."

"If there's anything I can do to help…"

"Turn everything off."

"What?"

"Turn everything off," he repeated. "Pull all the circuit breakers in town and turn off all the switches. My best guess is that if the electricity's going to come back on, it's got to be done slowly."

"Do you really think the electricity's going to come back on?" she asked, eyes widening.

He shrugged. "I'm going to be very careful not to fry myself. If anything good comes out of what I do, so much the better."

She looked at him without saying anything. He looked back at her for a moment; but then, when she didn't speak, he turned his gaze downward.

She smiled and said, "I'll go turn everything off. I'll get

Sue and Allyson to help me. At least it'll be a different way to spend the day, that's for sure."

She walked to the outside door and opened it, then turned to him before leaving.

"Good luck," she said.

"Thank you," he answered.

She left, and he returned his attention to the manuals and the control panels.

While Jim continued studying, and Kate enlisted Sue and Allyson to help turn off everything electrical, Missy was working at the supermarket.

The only windows at the market's main area were in the front of the building, so that even during the brightest part of the day most of the area was dimly lit, in a day-long twilight. The store was kept spotlessly clean; and the chrome and enamel of the once-refrigerated sections, long since emptied of their putrid cargo and washed out, occasionally glistened in the pale light.

Harry was keeping Missy busy rearranging stock on shelves and counting and recounting the amount of food remaining. She worked alone; Frank and Anitra spent most of their time in the stockroom in back. Harry occupied himself with his own matters, but he often walked past or along where Missy was working and looked at her.

The sweat suit she wore was baggy and limp, yet its inherent lack of definition was still not enough to conceal the pronounced curves of Missy's firm, trim body. She wore the sleeves pushed back above her elbows. Her arms were bare. Her ankles were bare. Occasionally, when she bent over, a section or two of her vertebrae was exposed; and, once in a while, when she reached to a high shelf, there was a flash of her toned, tanned stomach, contrasted against the dark blue material.

Harry's visits past where Missy was working became more and more frequent.

Sometime after noon she joined Frank and Anitra in the back room and ate a lunch of dry cereal and a can of fruit juice. Harry hovered nearby, but did not venture close enough to join them in their casual conversation about the store and the work they were doing.

Lunch was brief; the conversation listless. Soon Missy excused herself and stood up to go back to work.

"I'll be done in a couple of hours," she said to Harry. "This is the last of it, right?"

"I'll let you know when it's time for you to know," he replied.

Missy returned to work, straightening shelves and counting merchandise.

Concentrating on her work, she was startled by a figure standing in the dimly-lit aisle, a shadow outlined by the light from the windows at the far end of the store. Missy gasped and put her hand to her chest.

"I'm sorry," Kate said, coming forward and holding out her hand to touch Missy's shoulder. "There wasn't any way to knock."

"That's okay," Missy exhaled, her hand still to her chest. "It's kinda spooky in here. You surprised me. Are you here to pick up some food?"

"No," Kate answered, "though I'd never say no to a little

extra food. But I'm here to pull the circuit breakers. Jim asked me to do it."

"Jim? You saw Jim?" Missy's voice sparkled. "When did you see him?"

"About an hour ago. He's down by the power plant, trying to turn the electricity back on. It'll be a miracle if he does it, though."

"Why?"

"He doesn't know what he's doing. He's just winging it."

"He's pretty good at that," Missy sighed.

Missy led Kate to the back room, where Frank and Anitra were still sitting and talking.

They said hello to each other, and Kate told them why she was there. Hovering nearby, Harry walked over as soon as he heard Kate speak.

"I don't want you messing with the electricity around here," Harry grumbled. "There's no telling what kind of trouble you could cause."

"There is no electricity around here," Kate responded. "So there's nothing to worry about, is there?"

Harry grunted. "You're asking for trouble when you start doing things you don't know anything about. People should just stick with what they know. That's what I say."

"I designed houses for a living," Kate shot back. "I think I can handle this."

"I don't want you doing anything that can damage this

store," Harry snorted. "This store is more important than anything else. This store is everything."

Kate walked over to the far wall where several electrical conduits came in. There were three large junction boxes, two with levers and one without. Harry followed her.

"You'd better know what you're doing," he warned.

She went to the two boxes with levers and simply threw them into the off position. At first she couldn't open the third box, but she found a rusty butter knife on the shelf and pried the box open. Inside were two large fuse holders; and with a hard tug on each, she pulled them out and laid them on the shelf.

"The bigger they are, the easier they are," Kate beamed.

"There better not be any trouble because of this," Harry growled. "It'll be all your fault if there is."

Walking back to the table where the other three had been watching her, her back to Harry, Kate merely shrugged her shoulders. But then she turned around to face him.

"As long as I'm here, can I get some food?" she asked.

"This isn't the right time. Come back tomorrow when you're supposed to," Harry grumbled.

Kate grimaced, but she didn't say anything more. Missy walked with her part of the way out.

"How was Jim when you saw him?" Missy asked.

"Like an absent-minded professor," Kate answered, "Focused on one thing only. He certainly can be intense."

Missy's sigh was prolonged, "Yes, yes he can."

Kate said good-bye and left, and Missy returned to her counting and sorting.

It was late afternoon before Missy finished all the work that Harry had set out for her. She sought him out at a desk in the back where he was doing paper work and told him that she was done. It took him a while to look up from the work he was doing.

"I'm going to leave now," she said.

"Wait a while," Harry replied. "There's something I want to do before you leave."

Missy stood there in front of him, fidgeted, twisted on her heels.

Harry left her standing there several moments before he looked up and said, "Wait for me in the little room in the front."

"Where we had the meeting?"

"Yeah."

Missy walked out of the back room. Her hips swayed gently—delicate and lady-like—and Harry watched her closely, staring even after she was out of sight.

She had reached the front room before he reached under the desk, took out a cardboard box, and placed it on top. Inside were canned goods—baby peas, sardines, canned lunch meat, spaghetti, pudding. Harry studied the contents of the box before taking several of the items out and leaving them on the desk. He then stood up and took the box with the rest of the food toward the front.

Missy was waiting in the small front room, on the outside of the counter.

"C'mon Harry," she said, under her breath, "I want to get home."

Harry walked into the room.

"I'm all set," Missy said, "I'll be leaving now."

"Hold on," Harry replied. "I have something for you. This is the good stuff. I don't let everybody have this. There's not much of it left."

He held out the box to her, and she took it, but he didn't let go. Her eyes were on the box and its contents, but he watched her; and as long as he held on to the box, she was forced to face him.

"This is all special food," he insisted. "Some of *them* wouldn't appreciate it."

"That's very nice of you, Harry," Missy responded. "Bess and I will enjoy it."

Still Harry held on to the box.

"You'll be back same time tomorrow?" he asked. "There's a lot of work to do, and there's nothing more important than this place."

Missy let go of the box.

"Honestly, Harry," Missy bristled, "The work here is not that important. We're just counting food; we're not making any more of it. The work we do here doesn't matter very much."

"You'd be surprised," Harry countered, a tinge of hurt in his voice. "This is the most important thing there is, controlling the food. It's the only thing that matters. Do you want it or not?"

He held out the box to her again. She hesitated, then started to reach for it again. At the same time, he pulled the box away.

"Maybe I'll just keep it and give it to you when you show up for work tomorrow," he said, "just to be sure."

"I'm going to be busy tomorrow," she snapped. "I'm going to help Jim. Kate got to help him today, but I'm going to help him tomorrow."

Harry shook his head.

"Jim's a fool," he sneered. "What he's doing isn't important. The food is the only important thing. *I* have the food, and *you* still have to eat."

"You're not being fair, Harry," she pleaded. "We all have our own work to do. Why are you picking on me all the time?"

Harry set the box down on the counter. He looked at Missy, first at her face, but he was unable to continue looking her in the eye, so he looked down at her breasts, which even Missy's baggy outfit couldn't conceal too well, and when he began to feel nervous about staring, he let his gaze rest safely on the box in front of him.

"There is something, something more," he said, without looking up.

He sidled his body closer to the end of the counter, closer to Missy's body. He raised his eyes first, so that his glance could linger again at her breasts, and then he raised his head to meet her gaze. He took a deep breath, to start to speak; but, before the first word came out, the wall phone rang.

Harry jumped like a frightened cat and dug his nails into

the counter. He looked at the phone on the wall as if it were about to attack him. It rang again, and Harry jumped again.

"I'll get it," Missy said cheerfully.

Eyes wide with fright, Harry looked at her as if she had just started speaking Martian. His mouth agape, he watched her walk over to the phone, pick it up, and say hello.

"Hot dog!" Bess squealed at the other end. "I did it! Where are you?"

"I'm at the market," Missy answered. "In the little meeting room."

"Hold on," Bess said, "while I mark the wire."

Missy turned to Harry, who still hadn't managed to close his mouth.

"It's Bess," she said, with cheerful matter-of-fact-ness.

She turned her back on him to attend to her call. Harry finally was able to close his mouth, but he continued to stare at her in disbelief.

"I can't believe this worked," Bess said. "I've been playing with it for hours. There are *so many* wires."

"Congratulations," Missy beamed. "There's no end to your talent."

"Are you coming home soon?" Bess asked. "It's almost dinner time."

"Right away," Missy answered. "Have you heard from Jim?"

"No," Bess replied. "I thought by now he would be with

you. Have you seen him?"

"Not lately," Missy said. "He was going to fix dinner for us tonight. I think maybe I'd better start it for him."

"I'll help," Bess offered, "But hurry home. We have to celebrate my finding the right wire."

"I'll be right there," Missy replied, and hung up. Then to Harry she said, "Gotta' go. Thanks for letting me use the phone."

Missy hied herself from the room, not giving Harry a chance to respond, but her speed was unnecessary, since no utterance from him was forthcoming. Still clinging to the counter, he watched her departing figure in disbelief. It was several moments after she was out of sight before he sat down, alone, in the small room; and it was close to sunset before he stood up and went back into the store.

Missy ran the distance from the market to her place and bounded up the stairs. Bess was on the floor of the living room, surrounded by wires she'd strung in from a back window.

Missy surveyed the messy scene, and Bess smiled up at her sheepishly.

"I suppose there's an easier way to do this," Bess said. "But I haven't figured that out yet. I'm just trying to do my own little bit of good."

"Good? You're a life-saver. You got me out of the market just in time. Harry was getting creepy."

"It must be nice having two boyfriends."

"Don't even joke about it. I wish Jim would come home."

"Kate was here to pull out our fuses. She said Jim was still at the power plant."

Missy sighed, "He'll be along. I guess I'd better start dinner."

"Want help?"

"No, no thanks, Miss Alexandra Graham Bell. You stay with your telephones."

By the time Missy had dinner ready, Bess had cleaned up most of the mess. She had assembled a small electric panel near the phone with switches labeled "Jim," "market," and "Kate." Missy came into the room to look at her project.

"That might be all I'm going to get," Bess said. "Everyone else lives on the other side of the street, and their wires might not run through our backyard."

"Kate? You're wired up to Kate?" Missy asked. "Can we call her?"

"Sure. She was here when I found her wire. We both talked to Susan by phone this afternoon."

Missy held the phone to her ear, and Bess threw the switch next to Kate's name once, then again.

Missy heard the sound of someone picking up the phone at the other end, followed by giggling, then someone saying "Hush!" and finally Allyson's voice saying, meekly, "Hello?"

"Hi Allyson," Missy chirped. "We're just checking out the phone."

Allyson laughed.

"I didn't believe it was possible," she said. "We have a

phone again."

Missy talked to Allyson and then to Kate. She asked her if she had seen Jim.

"About an hour ago, about five o'clock," Kate said. "I went back to the power plant, and he was still there, sitting on the floor, reading and eating from a box of old crackers. He was incredibly focused. I told him that we had pulled all the fuses, and he answered me; then twenty seconds later he seemed surprised to see me standing there."

"But was he okay?" Missy asked.

"He was fine," Kate answered. "Do you want me to walk up the road and tell him anything?"

"No, no," Missy said. "As long as he's okay. I don't want to disturb him."

The two women said good bye and hung up.

"Don't worry," Bess said to Missy. "He'll come when he's ready."

"I know," Missy agreed. "I'm sure he's okay. But I guess we can't wait dinner for him. We'd better start eating without him."

The two women sat down at the table. They took turns recounting how they had spent their day. Bess told about hauling water in the morning and working on the phone in the afternoon. Missy told about Harry offering the choice food.

"The strange thing is," Missy said, "I believe he thinks he's being nice. But I hate it when he makes me stand there like a beggar, with my arms out. It's like he's the only one who has any right to eat, and the rest of us have to wait for him to throw us a crumb."

"We *are* a little low on food," Bess mentioned. "Maybe I'd better be the one to go get more tomorrow."

"Yeah, maybe so."

The women continued their meal. As the amount of food on their plates dwindled, so did their conversation. Missy's rate of eating also slowed, so that she sat for a long while rearranging the last few bits of food on her plate. When it began to get dark, Bess got up and turned on the battery-operated light. The women finished their meal and drank their tea in silence.

They cleaned up the kitchen together, talking infrequently and only about the task at hand.

When they finished, they went into the living room. Bess sat in the chair and read; Missy sat on the end of the couch nearest the window and looked out, resting her head on her hand with her knuckles against her lips. It grew darker outside, while Missy remained lost in thought. After a while she looked toward Bess.

"What're you reading?" Missy asked.

Bess closed the book with her finger holding her place and looked at Missy before answering.

"Doctor books," she said, softly. "I'm starting with pharmacology, then basic anatomy and physiology."

"My goodness, girl," Missy proclaimed. "Why on earth are you doing that?"

"It was Jim's idea. He thinks I could be a doctor. We need one. Sooner or later someone is bound to get sick."

"Ah, yes, Jim," Missy sighed. "It's a good idea. We really *do* need a doctor. Let me know when you get to stomachaches. My poor belly hurts a lot right now."

Bess perked up.

"I already know something that'll help," she declared. "You can be my first patient!"

Bess made a concoction of water, baking soda, and sugar. She swirled a teaspoonful of vinegar into the glass before Missy's eyes, and told her to drink it fast, while it was still foaming. Missy made a face but swallowed it in several gulps.

"That's not bad," Missy admitted. "Did you learn that from your books?"

"No, that's from my gram, her old home remedy. We used to make them when we were kids, even when we weren't sick. Do you feel better?"

"Yes, a little. I'll be all right."

Bess returned to her reading, and Missy went back to staring out into the darkness. A light came on at Pamela's place across the street, and Missy saw Pamela walk past her window. Except for that, everything else outside was in blackness.

"It's so dark out tonight," Missy said.

"It's not like last night," Bess responded. "Did you see the moon? It was so bright and round! It cast so much light you could see everything."

"Yes," Missy answered softly. "We saw the moon last night."

"I guess the moon won't be out till later. It won't be

105

quite full, tonight."

Missy returned to her reverie. Bess, tired of reading, closed her book and joined Missy in looking out the window. Time passed. Pamela turned out her light across the street.

Bess broke the silence. "I'm sure he just got involved in what he was doing and lost track of the time."

Missy stood up.

"I'm going to go look for him," she declared, pacing to the end of the window and back.

Bess stood up too and walked closer to Missy.

"Are you sure?" she asked. "It's pitch black out there."

"I've waited too long already," Missy answered. "He's working with electricity. He doesn't really know what he's doing. He could be lying hurt somewhere, unable to help himself. I've got to go. I've got to find him."

Missy was moving frenetically, but in no particular direction. Bess grabbed her arm.

"Take it easy. Go steady," Bess soothed. "Do you want me to come with you?"

"No, you stay here, in case he comes home. You can send him out to look for me. I wish I had a flashlight."

"We've got a candle, a stub, that Pam gave me last night. You can take that."

Bess got the candle while Missy put on a jacket. Bess handed the candle to Missy at the doorway.

"Maybe you shouldn't go," Bess cautioned. "There's

something evil out there—something that makes people die or disappear without any warning."

Missy's eyes grew wider; and she took a deep breath, in, and out.

"I've got to go," she said. "I've got to know if Jim is all right."

Bess lit the candle for her. "I'll watch you from the window for as long as I can."

"I'm going to try to walk right down the middle of the street," Missy replied, "and just keep going till I get to the power plant."

"Be careful."

They looked at each other, and then they hugged each other, Missy using one arm so that she could hold the candle away from them both.

They separated.

"I'm going," Missy said.

"Go," Bess answered.

Missy went out the door, and Bess went to the window to watch her.

Missy had trouble going downstairs, trying to protect her candle from her own wind of motion and hold on to the hand rail at the same time. She made it to the bottom door and walked out onto the street, still protecting her candle. Taking small steps, Missy worked her way out to the center of the street and then turned toward the power plant.

From her window, Bess saw the faint light as it moved

away from the sidewalk, but she could scarcely make out Missy's form.

Although the candle cast enough light that Missy was able to see the ground just in front of her, the bright flame before her eyes blinded her so that the darkness beyond seemed even blacker.

She knew that she had reached the intersection because she heard rather than saw the stop light swaying over her head.

She was past the intersection and had started on her way along the second block, in front of the market, when she heard something, a scrape, off to the left, on the market side.

She looked in that direction and strained to see through the darkness. She held her candle out to where she had heard the sound, but that blinded her and she couldn't see anything beyond the flame.

She put the candle lower and to her side and waited for her eyes to adjust. Again she heard the slightest scraping sound coming from in front of the store. Her heart started to pound against her chest.

Missy took cautious steps to walk closer to the sound. Ahead she saw a pale glow, like a cluster of fireflies, moving about the lamp post.

She stopped when she was ten feet away and held her candle a little more forward.

Ahead of her, a shadowy figure was hunched over, manipulating something inside the junction box of the lamp post. The figure held a flashlight with batteries so nearly dead that the bulb just barely emitted a soft, orange light.

"Jim?" she asked softly, with a tremor in her voice.

There was no reaction from the dark figure, still hunched over and fussing with the junction box. Missy took one step closer, then one sideways, circling the lamp post, trying to see better without getting any closer. Her voice was shaking.

"P-please, Jim," she cried, louder.

The figure spun about.

"Missy?" it asked.

It was Jim! Missy ran up to him, dropped her candle and hugged him. He was surprised, confused, and it took him a moment before he hugged her back.

"Missy?" he asked again. "Missy! It is you! What are you <u>doing</u> out here?"

"I was so scared. I was afraid I'd lost you too. I was afraid you'd disappeared like everyone else."

"I'm sorry, love, I'm so sorry," he murmured. "I'm fine. Are you all right?"

"Now," she sniffed. "Now."

He held her at arm's length and handed the flashlight to her.

"It's almost gone," she said, holding up the barely-glowing light.

"It served me well, for as long as it could," he replied.

He backed one step away from her, and she could see by the faint light that he was smiling.

"What are you doing?" she asked.

Still smiling, he leaned against the lamp post with his hands behind his back.

"Jim, you're acting so strange," she said.

"Trust me, my beauty. Have faith in me. All is well."

He stood there fidgeting behind his back, and then, with a final bump, he stood up straight. There was a low hum, a crackle, and then a flash, followed by darkness, and then a steadily increasing glow until they were bathed in the light from the street lamp above them. Quickly, and in falling-away succession in both directions, every street lamp on the main street lit up, both sides of the street—brightness, radiant brightness, existed where moments before there had been total darkness. In one bold stroke the darkness was pushed away, away from the store fronts and out of the doorways, away from this couple standing on the sidewalk. Darkness was pushed away, forced away, as much as twenty feet up, and hundreds of feet in each direction along the street. Their circle of light, their umbrella of illumination, which only moments before reached no farther than their finger tips, was now expanded to a distance of several blocks.

Awe-struck, Missy gazed around, turning slowly, with her arms outstretched and her palms up, like a little girl in a rain shower, bathing in the unexpected light. Jim, smiling broadly, watched her. He reached out to her, and she ran into his outstretched arms.

"I love you," he whispered.

She pulled back, surprised, and then she kissed him, as hard as she could.

They embraced while the lights in the town began warming up and burning off six month's accumulation of dust.

Then, arm-in-arm, they walked to the center of the street and began strolling back toward Missy's flat, regally like a king and queen parading for their invisible subjects. At the intersection, the traffic light was now working—amber, red, then green—and they waited for the green light before proceeding, then laughed together as they passed underneath.

Bess, who had been watching from the window, came running downstairs as soon as the lights came on, and now she joined the couple in the middle of the street. The three held hands and danced in a circle, first one way and then the other, laughing and shouting. They moved their dance to encircle the nearest street lamp, its metal detail mellowed by countless layers of paint, chipped in places to reveal varying colors.

Disorganized, they danced around the post, reversing directions unexpectedly so that they were bumping into each other and breaking the circle open.

Attracted by the light and the sound, Pamela had come downstairs and watched them for a moment from her doorway before walking over to join them.

They opened the circle to include her and again rounded the lamp post until their unbridled enthusiasm fragmented the circle; and they danced on, as couples, trading partners in an unprogramed square dance. The dance ended when the performers were too winded to both dance and laugh and opted for laughter.

Their rest lasted only a moment.

"C'mon," Missy said, grabbing Jim's hand and then Pamela's and urging Bess forward.

They ran diagonally, through the intersection and across the street, until they were in front of the gas station. Ernie and

Bob were inside, leaning against one of the big, glass-paneled doors, and gazing out at the miracle of light.

Missy waved at them and shouted for them to come out; and, slowly at first, they pulled open the door and joined the people on the sidewalk.

Missy was about to lead her troupe away.

"Wait a minute," Jim said and ran into the gas station.

A half-minute later, the large sign in front of the station creaked and started rotating atop its pole. By the time Jim was back outside, the fluorescent tubes inside the sign flickered and then shone brightly.

The group around the sign cheered and moved into the street to better take in the view of the sign, turning and shining.

Next Anitra and Frank walked out of the front door of the market and stood, diffidently, on the curb. Missy ran to them, engulfed their shyness with her enthusiasm, and started pulling them closer to the group in the street.

Though he was partly obscured by the reflection of the gas station sign on the grocery store window, Missy saw Harry inside the store, looking at them. She waved at him to come outside; but Harry, surprised to discover he was visible, pulled farther back into the darkness of the store.

With a shrug, Missy turned her back on Harry and steered Frank and Anitra toward the group in the center of the street. Bess was dancing an impromptu reel with Ernie while the others stood around clapping. Bess traded partners, began dancing with Bob, and Pamela danced with Ernie.

Then Bess traded partners again and started to dance with Frank, who danced several steps, clumsily, before returning to the side, where he continued clapping his hands and grinning broadly.

Jim and Missy weaved their way between Pamela and Ernie, and the four of them danced in a circle.

The street lights dimmed. The dancing continued, but Jim pulled Missy aside.

"I've got to go to the power plant. I've got some dials to spin," he said.

"We'll all go!" Missy shouted.

Jim led the way up the street, and Missy brought up the rear, like a school teacher directing her class on the playground at recess.

Halfway up the block, Kate, Allyson and Susan, unavoidably attracted by the lights and sounds, were standing on the sidewalk; and they were immediately deluged by the wave of festivity. Missy and Bess weaved among the three newcomers, Jim and Kate held hands and spun around, and the enlarged group continued merrily toward the power plant.

Back at the store, Harry had the side of his face pressed against the window, watching the group for as long as possible. When they reached the edge of town, the numerous streetlights gave way to only a few lamps on tall wooden poles; and all Harry could see were surreal silhouettes. He backed away from the window, away from the light, and sought his refuge in the darkest reaches of the store.

The group paraded up to the front door of the power plant and went inside, trampling on the broken glass as they went. They spread out on the ground floor of the building and watched while Jim, accompanied by Kate, studied gauges and made adjustments.

"This is going to have to be monitored," Jim said. "Till we find out how much flexibility we have."

"I'll do it," Kate volunteered.

"It's likely to be a pretty boring job," Jim cautioned.

"I don't mind. It'll feel good to be able to do something useful. I'll get Allyson and Susan to help me. We'll take shifts."

"You've got the job," Jim replied, and he gave her waist a squeeze.

The celebration of light continued throughout the building. On the second floor, Ernie asked why all the cushions were spread on the floor. Missy smiled shyly at Jim, and he winked at her, but neither one answered.

Bess and Allyson ran from room to room, turning on every light they could, until the building was ablaze in light.

"Hey, take it easy," Jim cautioned in jest. "Someone's going to have to pay the electric bill this month."

"Not me," Bess teased.

With every increase in power usage, Jim called downstairs to Kate, who reported that they hadn't even caused a ripple on the gauges.

Gradually the celebration mellowed. Everyone began the walk back into town except Kate, who stayed to watch the console. Susan agreed to relieve her the next morning.

During the walk back to town, the moon was hanging low in the sky, adding its mellow light to the light of the street lamps. Jim and Missy walked with their arms around each other's waists.

As the parade had been joined, so in reverse did it disband. The people walked down the center of the street, and Susan and Allyson went to their house, with a "Good night!" and a promise to meet again in the morning.

In the next block, Ernie and Bob departed to the left, and Frank and Anitra to the right. At the intersection, Jim tried again to wait for the green light, but this time Missy good-naturedly forced him to go through on the red. He protested that they were going to get a ticket, but she would have none of it. Pamela said good night, and Jim promised to come over the next day to start up her electricity.

Jim climbed the stairs with Bess and Missy. Still jovial, the three of them collapsed in a heap on the living room floor in front of the sofa. They settled down, talked about the events of the day, and Missy scolded Jim for eating nothing more than stale crackers all day. Missy got a quick meal ready for him and by the time she returned, Bess was sleeping with her head on a pillow on Jim's lap. Missy handed Jim a plate and sat beside him with her arm around him while he ate.

By the time he consumed half the food on the plate, sleep became a stronger need than food. He set the plate down and leaned back against the couch with his hand on Missy's knee and closed his eyes. She leaned her head on his shoulder.

"A good day," he said.

"A good day," she repeated.

They were silent for a while.

""Shouldn't someone turn off the street lights?" she whispered.

"Automatic," he mumbled.

They both fell asleep.

* * *

The waking process the next morning was gradual and relaxed, each one in turn coming to a higher level of wakefulness, responding to the presence of the others, and drifting back to share a twilight sleep, none of them ready to admit that it was time to wake up fully.

Eventually, Missy and Jim moved at the same time, and neither one could deny that the other was awake.

"Hi," Jim said softly.

In response, Missy brushed her hair back from her eyes and kissed his forehead.

Gently, Jim shook Bess's shoulder.

"I'm awake," Bess mumbled, but she didn't open her eyes.

The sun was shining brightly through clusters of white, sharply defined clouds; and, looking out the window, Jim remarked, "It's going to be a nice day."

"It's a beautiful day," Missy answered, but she was looking at Jim when she said it. He turned to meet her gaze, and they shared a smile.

Missy roused herself and went toward the kitchen.

"Coffee for everyone," she announced as she left the room.

Bess and Jim got up and, still groggy, followed Missy into the kitchen. Slowly they completed their journey to wakefulness, as they drank their coffee and finished the last of Missy's homemade bread.

Daubing the crumbs on her plate, Bess broke the silence by saying, "Last night seems like a dream. The lights, and all the people. I felt like I was at an amusement park. I still can't believe it was real."

"Bright lights on a dark night," Jim replied, "that always seems dreamlike to me."

"Do you realize," Missy added, "that was the first time everyone here has gotten together? The first time we acted as a group? It's like we just came back to life, after being asleep way too long."

"Maybe we are coming back," Bess agreed. "Maybe we are."

They made their plans for the day. Missy and Jim determined that, whatever else they did, they would spend the day together. Bess was going to clean up the flat, pick up groceries from the store, and spend the afternoon trying to locate the wires from more telephones. Missy and Jim were going to visit around town to make sure there were no problems with the restored electricity, also visit the power plant to check things there, and spend the afternoon replacing Missy's gas water heater with an electric one. Hot baths were promised to everyone that evening, the thought of which made the ladies moan with delight.

While Bess stayed at the flat, Missy and Jim set out on their errands. They visited Pamela, turned on her electricity, and got rid of the car battery. They decided not to visit Harry.

"I'm just not up to seeing him today," Missy said. "Bess can tell us later if he's having any trouble."

They visited Ernie and Bob, who hadn't gotten used to the fact that the power was back on. Jim helped them set up shop lights and hook up the compressor. When Jim and Missy left, Ernie and Bob were working enthusiastically, still faithfully trying to breathe some life back into the rusty, white station wagon, all the while arguing about the best way to proceed.

The next stop was Kate's place. Before they even knocked on the door, Missy and Jim saw through the window that Kate and Allyson were sitting side by side on the couch. Allyson was crying, and Kate was staring blankly at the wall.

Jim knocked; and, after a brief delay, Kate answered the door.

"What's the matter, Kate? What's wrong?" Jim asked.

Kate stood for a moment without saying anything.

"You'd better come in," she said at last.

"Is it Susan?" Missy asked. "Did something happen to Susan?"

Kate answered as if coming out of a trance.

"What?…oh, no. Susan's fine," she said. "She's down at the power station. She's all right."

"What is it then?" Jim asked.

"I think you should sit down," Kate answered. "There's

something you have to see."

Kate returned to her seat next to Allyson, who was still crying softly. Jim and Missy sat along the wall perpendicular to them. When Kate didn't speak, Jim prompted her.

"What is it?" he asked, again.

"This morning," Kate said, "After I got home. I slept for a few hours, but it was too nice a day to sleep."

She paused.

"Go on," Jim coaxed.

"We realized that, for the first time, we could watch television," Kate explained. "There's a whole bookcase full of video tapes in this house. We each chose a movie; and we got ready to start watching…but we found out there was already a tape in the player."

Kate now started crying too. Missy put her hand on top of Jim's. They waited until Kate was willing to continue.

"I'll play it for you," Kate said.

She picked up a remote control and pressed a button. The video player in the corner whirred into rewind, emitting a gradually shifting scale of sound as the tape moved from one spool to the other, and then clicked into forward.

The screen was gray and filled with static. Green numerals displayed the time of recording: 11:50 a.m.; and then the static changed to the image of a newscaster in mid sentence.

"…that communication to and from the stricken area simply stopped. There were several reports of numerous casualties, but attempts to confirm those reports have so far been unsuccessful, since the stations making the reports themselves have fallen silent.

"The phenomenon, whatever it is, appears to be traveling west. Since early this morning, New York time, communications with European countries began terminating. We have been unable to reach our correspondents in Paris and London since about 7:00 this morning, local time."

While he spoke, the newscaster's eyes nervously darted away from the camera and back again. News personnel frequently passed back and forth behind him, exchanging scraps of paper and whispers.

"The President is, at this moment, unavailable for comment: but a White House spokesman, speaking for the President, has urged that everyone remain calm and has promised that everything possible will be done as quickly as possible to determine the nature of the disturbance."

The pace of the activity going on behind the newscaster increased. A piece of paper appeared from off camera and was handed to him.

"We have a report now that there has been some trouble along the east coast, in Montreal and in Maine."

The newscaster paused and held his hand against the earphone in his right ear, and he stared hard into space as he concentrated on what he was hearing.

"It seems that communications have also been lost to the New England seacoast. No one is answering the phone at our affiliate in Portland…or anywhere else in Maine, for that matter. The nature of the disturbance still is unknown, but once again we wish to say that everyone is urged to stay calm.

"We have reports, also unconfirmed, I'm afraid, that people are attempting to flee from the approach of this...phenomenon...by traveling west; but we have no knowledge as to how many people are involved or whether there is any reason to justify such actions."

The newscaster paused to listen to his earphone. Beads of sweat were breaking out on his forehead and his upper lip. The background sounds became more pronounced, a conglomeration of people's voices, occasionally punctuated by a high-pitched cry.

"I'm informed that even phone calls to places just a short distance east of our location are going unanswered, though areas west appear to be unaffected."

The newscaster twisted in his chair as he glanced hastily over his shoulder and then returned his attention to the camera.

"We're hearing some sound in our area now, sounds of people moving, people in the streets. We'll try to see if we can discover the nature of the disturbance."

Several people were seen in the background, running along the wall and leaving the room. Soon there was no one else on camera except the newscaster. His image moved erratically as the broadcasting camera bounced once, and then again. The newscaster stood up haltingly and then sat back down.

"I'm trying...I'm sorry...It's very difficult...I hope that..."

His eyes darted around the room.

"I'm sorry...I can't...I'm sorry...I'm so sorry..."

The newscaster stood up, clumsily throwing down his microphone and earphone, and ran off camera. The camera remained steadily focused on the empty chair for several moments, and then it swung away abruptly and focused on a nondescript spot on the wall. A few more sounds were heard, muffled sounds, something banging, and then all was silent.

For several long minutes that same motionless image stayed on the screen—the corner of a desk, a mostly blank wall with a few notes tacked to a small bulletin board, an open door leading to another door.

Moments later the scene switched to that of another newsman, with hair not quite combed and tie crooked, just sitting down at a desk and attaching a microphone to his coat.

"We're not quite sure what happened at our New York…"

The screen returned to static. Kate allowed the static to remain on the screen for a while before she reached for the remote control and shut the recorder off.

No one in the room spoke. Allyson was no longer crying, but she sat with a tissue pressed against her lips. Kate got up and walked part way out of the room and then returned to her seat without having accomplished anything. Missy and Jim sat quietly. Without looking at her, Jim reached for Missy's hand; and she took his hand and squeezed it.

Kate broke the silence. Without looking up, she said, "That's all the machine was programed to record. We played the tape to the end. There's nothing more on it."

"They didn't know," Missy moaned, shaking her head. "They didn't know what was happening. I always expected they must've known what was happening to them. We're the ones who don't know. But they didn't know any more than we do."

No one responded to what Missy had said. Each sat quietly with his or her own thoughts.

Almost at once, they all reacted to the sound of footsteps on the porch, and Susan burst in, her blonde hair flying.

"Quick!" she shouted. "You've got to listen to this!"

She was carrying a small, multi-band radio with the cord trailing behind her. She plugged the radio in and knelt on the floor in the living room to adjust the dials.

"I was bored," she said, "And I turned on the radio, just pretending there was music, and I heard something!"

They listened while she spun the knobs back and forth. The only sound was an occasional crack of static.

"It's there," she declared. "I didn't imagine it. I really heard something."

She spun the dial rapidly, and they heard one blip of sound among the static. She turned the dial back slowly.

From the radio, they heard a male voice:

"C-Q, C-Q, C-Q. Please answer me, anyone."

The voice paused and the static returned. After a while the voice came on again.

"I'm running out of time. This is the end of my transmission for today. I'll broadcast again tomorrow at noon and six o'clock. Someone answer me please."

There was a sigh, and another static-filled pause, then, "This is David, from the Delray farm. Out."

The static returned, unbroken.

From her position kneeling on the floor, Susan looked up, searching the faces of the other people in the room, seeking a response to what she'd discovered.

"Wow," Jim exhaled, "there's another survivor."

"He sounds desperate," Kate said.

"He sounds lonely," Missy added.

"Can we answer him?" Susan asked.

She was still on her knees; and, her eyes wide and moist, she looked at everybody in the room, until her gaze settled on Jim. But he shook his head.

"I saw that radio at the plant," he said. "It's a short wave receiver. But I didn't see a transmitter, there or anywhere else in town. We should probably organize a search to see if we can find one. But if not, all we can do is monitor that frequency. If he tells us where he is, maybe we can figure out a way to get to him."

"Do you think he's far away?" Susan asked, her eyes pleading.

"He could be on the other side of the planet. With no one competing for the airwaves, no interference, radio ranges get a lot farther."

"We've got to find him," Susan moaned, weeping. "I think he's all alone. He sounds so…desolate. So sad."

They made plans. Kate took the responsibility for telling everyone else in town about the video tape and the short wave broadcast. She suggested everyone meet back at her house that evening, to discuss the latest developments.

Jim and Missy went with Susan and Allyson back to the power plant and spent time there, improving their understanding of the workings and cautiously adjusting the settings. They also decided that the person monitoring the electric output would also monitor the short wave.

When Jim and Missy left, Allyson was monitoring the console; and she had paper and pencil ready to write down anything she heard over the radio. Susan's shift was over, but she volunteered to stay with Allyson, just in case there was another broadcast.

Before heading back to town, Missy and Jim went to the water tower that was a few hundred feet behind the power plant. Jim broke into a utility shed that was attached to the tower. He reset a circuit breaker that was inside the shed, and an electric motor came to life, driving a pump that began sucking water from the river.

A little nervously, Missy called out to him from outside the shed, "Do you know what you're doing this time, or are you just winging it again?"

"Winging it," he answered, grinning, as he emerged from the shed, wiping his hands on a cloth. "But as long as no one grabs hold of a live wire, we don't have anything to lose, even if it doesn't work the way we think. And this one should be pretty easy. It's the weight of the water that provides the pressure. As long as we keep the tower full, we should have running water."

"But it's taking it right from the river," Missy grimaced. "Shouldn't it be purified?"

"It's the same water you've been bringing in by the bucketful," he answered. "And for sure no one's put any contaminants in it for almost six months now."

"It just seems different when we have to do it ourselves," Missy sighed. "I like thinking that someone is out there, taking responsibility, making sure it's good enough."

"Maybe you'd better boil it before you drink it," Jim allowed; and then he tapped his finger against her chin and added, "And you have to use your own fluoride."

"I will," she promised, smiling and revealing her beautiful teeth.

They began their walk back to town. The sun shone brightly, and a few fluffy clouds drifted serenely by. Missy walked with her hand in Jim's back pocket, and he had his arm around her with his hand on her stomach.

"Do you think we'll hear him again, that guy on the radio?" Missy asked.

"He sounded like he's been calling for some time. He'll come on again. I just hope he tells us how to find him."

"That still may not do us much good," Missy cautioned. "How far can we walk in a day? How much food can we carry?"

Jim nodded, "Nothing's easy anymore."

Missy continued, "We'll have to find another supermarket. It'll be like climbing Mt Everest, moving from base camp to base camp. It could take a long time."

"I'll need a spare set of wheels for my little red wagon," Jim joked, and Missy laughed.

They walked through town and returned to Missy's flat, where Bess was putting away groceries.

"Look at this!" Bess complained as they walked in.

"Look at how little food Harry gave me. It's not enough for more than a day, and he made me beg for even this much! He said something about how you were supposed to show up for work today."

"I wish he'd pick on someone else for a change," Missy groaned. "I'm not the only person in town who can count."

"Bess thinks Harry's interest in you has nothing to do with your counting," Jim teased. "You *could* take it as a compliment."

"We'll see how flattered I feel after he lets me starve to death," Missy replied, glumly.

"At least we have plenty for today," Bess said. "We should all go talk to Harry tomorrow. That is, unless he shows up at Kate's tonight."

"You think he will?" Jim asked.

"Kate invited him, while I was there," Bess answered. "But I don't think he'll show. He and Kate had quite an argument about the electricity. He refused to let her turn it on, said it wasn't safe."

"Sounds like Harry," Missy agreed. "Did you go with Kate, to see the newscast?"

"Yes," Bess answered softly. "It was very sad." She shook her head slowly. "All the noise in the background, all the people, they all sounded so frightened."

Bess's eyes got moist, and Missy put her hand on Bess's shoulder. Bess touched Missy's hand and then she wiped away a single tear.

"Kate said to tell you," Bess changed the subject, "that

she's making tonight's meeting a movie party also—a double feature, with popcorn. And isn't it wonderful there might be someone else alive out there?"

"Maybe our little town's population is going to grow again," Missy agreed. "There hasn't been a growth spurt since I recruited Jim."

She grinned at Jim mischievously, and he grabbed her around her waist, and she squealed.

The playful conversation set the pattern for the rest of the afternoon, as they set about replacing the water heater in the closet in the kitchen—sawing out the old one, capping the gas line, carrying the gas heater down the stairs and carrying a new electric heater from the store across the street back up the stairs, fitting it into place. The three of them worked together.

Jim was just finishing, soldering the last pipes; and Bess and Missy sat down to rest.

"So," Missy asked, "Do you know what you're doing, or is this another one of those 'try something and see what happens' deals?"

"Actually," Jim replied, "for a change, I have done this once before. Still, you never know what you don't know until it leaps up and bites you."

"Is that why you haven't even tested to see if there's any water pressure yet?"

"Why spoil the surprise?" Jim answered. "And, if there's no water, we can still use the heater. We'll just still have to bring the water up by hand."

He finished soldering, put his hand on the intake valve, and called out, "Ready?"

"Ready!" both women answered together.

He turned the valve, and there was an immediate rush of air, followed by silence, and then a distant banging sound, more silence, more banging, a prolonged whoosh, and the dull gurgle of water dribbling into the tank.

Everyone cheered.

Playfully they argued about who would take the first hot bath, with everyone claiming the right. When Missy and Bess couldn't decide between themselves, they offered the honor to Jim, who declined, saying he still intended to first make good on his promise to fix dinner, albeit using their kitchen.

"My place is the opposite of yours," he said. "I've got an electric water heater and a gas stove. Plus, I don't have any food," he confessed.

While waiting for the water to heat up, they worked together, cleaning up the mess from the installation. Then Bess went to take the first shower while Missy and Jim started dinner, an inventive concoction of spaghetti, powdered milk and Parmesan cheese that Jim called, "Pasta, a` la James." It was the first time they were able to use the electric stove instead of the barbecue on the porch.

Bess showered noisily, exaggerating the sounds of her enjoyment so they could be heard in the kitchen. Missy affected a motherly tone and admonished Bess to not use up all the hot water.

Missy showered next, and then Bess took over in the kitchen while Jim showered. Clean and fresh, they sat down to a filling meal of spaghetti, with sweet pickles on the side, water, and fruit cocktail for dessert.

They cleaned up the kitchen, with hot water for washing the dishes; and they set out for Kate's.

Jim walked between the two women with an arm around each one's waist; and the three traveled in unison, laughing and jostling when one of them got out of step.

Darkness was just setting in, and the street light had just come on.

The trio walked past the market, still dark inside, past panel after panel of glass showcasing one check-out line after another, cash registers all unlit and silent, conveyers all unmoving.

At the next to the last panel, they saw Anitra standing and staring out, her dark eyes wide and shining in the subdued light.

With their free hands, Bess and Missy both signaled Anitra to come out, but she shook her head no, pointed obliquely around her body back towards the shadows of the store and lowered her eyes to the ground.

The three kept walking.

When they arrived at Kate's, Ernie and Bob were already sitting on wooden chairs near the window, and Pamela was sitting on the couch. Bess sat next to Pamela, and Missy and Jim sat in the love seat along the far wall. More than one person talked about being surprised by the return of the water, when it came dripping or gushing through faucets long left open.

True to her word, Kate served popcorn; and Allyson served pop, ice-cold from the now-working refrigerator.

Nervously, Kate stood in front of the TV and addressed the group.

"I guess this is everyone," she began. "Susan's at the power station, and I don't think Harry's group is coming.

"I know I called this a meeting, because I thought we should get together and discuss the new developments. But now that you're all here, there's not really that much to say. Everyone here has already seen the newscast tape. It seemed so important this morning, but I guess we really don't know very much more than we did before."

Missy cleared her throat, and Kate looked her way.

"We do know a little more," Missy offered. "We know it didn't happen all at once, worldwide; and we know it happened around noon in New York."

"I remember that day, but it seems like a hundred years ago," Kate sighed. "Noon, on Monday. Our last happy day…"

Kate's voice drifted off; and the sorrow she felt, the sorrow they all shared, supplanted any further conversation. But Jim prodded her.

"Tell us, Kate," he urged. "Tell us what happened. Tell us how you found out."

She looked at him, but took the time she needed to recover from the wave of emotions her memories had evoked. The silence in the room became the gentle urging for her to speak.

"We were at my cabin," she began, "about 30 miles north of here. I designed the place myself—nothing showy, but elegant, efficient. It was our week-end to christen the cabin, 'girl's week-end away,' no phones, no TV, away from all the noise and the crowds." Kate laughed a single, mirthless laugh. "Noise and crowds sound good to me now. Why were we spared? What happened? Why were some people uneventfully eating lunch while other people were disappearing, dying?"

"We weren't eating lunch yet," Allyson interrupted. "Don't you remember? We were waiting for Karen to get back from the store. We were in the hot tub, drinking mimosas. We were being so silly." Allyson added, softly, "Poor Karen— she never came back."

Allyson hung her head. Kate walked over to her, and the two women embraced.

"Was Susan with you?" Jim asked.

Kate straightened a strand of Allyson's hair and smiled encouragement to her before turning and answering.

"Yes," Kate nodded. "Susan too. The three of us. It seems so frivolous now. Karen took so long getting back, we figured she'd met some guy and forgotten about us. By evening we were worried, and we called to report her missing, but no one answered the phone. I remember we took turns listening to it ring, thinking someone would surely answer; and we'd give them hell for keeping us waiting so long; but it just kept ringing, forever.

"By the next morning, we were more frightened than anything else. Nothing was working the way it was supposed to. I guess deep down we already sensed that something serious was wrong. We just didn't know what. But somehow we knew that if anything was going to change, we'd have to be the ones to change it.

"Karen had our only car, so I left Susan and Allyson behind and started walking into town. At first I expected to hitch a ride, but mile after mile went by, and I didn't see anyone. It took me all day to reach town, and when I did only Harry and

Frank and Anitra were here. They told me everyone else was gone, and there was no one who could help me. I couldn't believe it. But I spent the night in town, and the next day I walked back to the cabin. It didn't take long for our food to run out, so we all walked back here. There was nowhere else to go. We've been here ever since. There was nowhere else."

Allyson said nothing, but she nodded her head. The somber mood settled over the group like a blanket.

"We was in the desert," Ernie volunteered, and the unexpected sound of his voice jarred the company. "At the old school house. They was talking 'bout using the place agin'; and our job was to try and see if the old boiler had any life left in it.

"Ceptin' we had inch-'n-a-quarter pipe, and we needed inch-'n-a-half. Somebody brought the wrong pipe."

Ernie looked at Bob.

"And somebody forgot the pipe cutter," Bob defended himself. The two men exchanged accusatorial glances.

"Anyway," Ernie continued, "We wuz workin' on the boiler, and we never did know nuttin' was wrong, 'cept when I think back, I recollect maybe things did get mighty quiet, all of a sudden like. Felt kinda creepy."

Ernie shuddered at the memory.

"How did you get back to town?" Jim asked.

"We drove," Ernie answered proudly. "Had my '63 Super Sport. " 'Cept we burned out the engine 'bout a mile or two from town."

"Someone forgot to replace the oil in it," Bob said.

"Someone forgot to remind me," Ernie countered.

Bob and Ernie continued their argument, so Kate started the movie, which was <u>Silverstreak,</u> and Ernie and Bob settled down to watch it with the others. Halfway through the movie, Allyson left to relieve Susan at the power station.

Susan arrived during the final minutes of the movie. She was wearing pale blue jeans, her blonde hair was tied in a pony tail, and she carried a note pad. She waited just inside the doorway until the movie was over, and she shifted her weight from one foot to the other.

After the movie ended, and the conversation it had generated began to subside, Susan spoke.

"He called again," Susan said, softly. "On the radio."

The conversation stopped, and all eyes turned to her. She looked at the note pad before speaking again.

"It was quite a bit the same as before," she said. "His name is David, and he's calling from his own radio on his farm. He's got a gas-powered generator, and he puts a half cup of gas into it each time he broadcasts, to get electricity for his radio. He said he's getting very low on gas. He promised to broadcast every day at noon and eight p.m., until his gas runs out.

"That's about it, except he kept begging someone to answer him, and no one did."

"But did he say where he was?" Jim asked.

"Just that he was at the 'Delray' farm," Susan answered. "He doesn't sound like he's even thinking about someone coming to find him. All he's thinking about is getting an answer on his radio. He wants someone to know that he's alive. I heard him wondering out loud if maybe he's the only one left alive, on the whole planet. It sounded like he was crying."

Susan's announcement was followed by a discussion of who the newcomer was and how he could be reached. There were more talkers than there were listeners.

Amidst the chatter about how much territory anyone could expect to cover by walking, Bob said softly, "We could take the car."

No one heard him, and the conversation continued. A few minutes passed before once again, and a little louder, Bob said, "We could use the car."

This time Bess heard him and asked, "Car? What car, Bob?"

The flow of conversation ebbed, and, as Bob became the focus of attention, he squirmed, then sat up straight in his chair and pulled on his collar.

"The station wagon," he said. "It's all finished, except we need one piston ground to size."

Ernie joined in.

"Ya' ain't going no where without that piston," he declared. "It's hard steel, and it's gotta be ground perfect."

"I'll grind it for you," Jim offered. "There's a whole bunch of machines in the shop at the other end of town."

"It's gotta be done right," Ernie cautioned. "What we got is a piston from another motor—hard, hard stuff. Gotta take off mebbe 30 or 40 thousandths, but it's gotta be on the money. Kin you do that?"

Jim nodded, "We'll get together on it in the morning."

"Well, that's it then," Kate declared. "We have a plan. All we can do is monitor the broadcasts and hope that he tells us how to find him."

Kate and Susan provided refills of popcorn and drinks, and Kate started the second movie, A Man and a Woman.

As the movie started, Missy whispered to Jim, "Is tomorrow going to be another one of your 'figure something out and plunge ahead' deals?"

"Not this time," he answered softly. "Machining is how I made my living, before."

Missy kissed him on the cheek.

The group settled in to watch the movie.

When it was over, Jim and Missy left; and Bess stayed to talk. Later, when Bess went home, she heard from Missy's bedroom the sound of Jim and Missy whispering and giggling. Bess tiptoed into her own bedroom and silently slipped into bed.

The next morning, Bess was awakened by the sounds of them together in the bathroom. With feigned innocence, Bess knocked on the door and asked what they were doing in there, and Missy called back that they were saving on water.

When Jim and Missy finally emerged from the bathroom, the three breakfasted on tea, since it was all they had, and then went to the store to talk to Harry.

The main part of the supermarket was locked, but the little meeting room in the corner was open. Susan was already there, and Frank was behind the counter.

Susan was wearing shorts, and her blonde hair was loose and flowing. She greeted them enthusiastically.

"Good morning," she beamed. "Isn't it a beautiful morning? I woke up, and I felt like going down to the town diner for some bacon and eggs. But since that's impossible, I came here instead."

"We don't have eggs," Frank said, apologetically. "We've got canned bacon, though."

"Really?" Susan chirped. "I was just kidding. Tasting bacon again would be heaven"

"They've got several cans," Missy confirmed. "I've counted them often enough."

"Can I have one?" Susan asked, shyly.

Frank fidgeted.

"Lemme' check," he said and walked into the back.

"This is great," Susan declared. "I can cook bacon at home and take some down to Kate at the power plant."

"I thought you three were working in shifts," Jim said. "But you seem to be there most of the time."

"There are four of us now, because Pamela wanted to help out too," Susan answered. "But I don't mind staying there. I want to be around when the broadcasts come in."

Frank returned and placed one can of bacon on the counter. Anitra stood behind him, leaning in the doorway with her arms folded.

"Here," Frank said. "Harry says that's all you can have. It's not 10 o'clock yet."

Susan took the can sheepishly and, with a wincing smile, said to Jim, Bess, and Missy, "See you guys later?"

"I'll stop by in time for the next broadcast," Missy promised. "Let's hope this time he tells us more about where he's located. 'Delray Farms' is not much of a clue."

Abruptly Anitra stood up straight and unfolded her arms. She took a halting step forward and hesitated. But with a quick glance at everyone in the room, she retreated again into the back.

Susan said her good-byes and walked out. Jim asked to see Harry, and Frank went into the back. After considerable time he came back and told them Harry was coming. Many more minutes elapsed before Harry appeared.

"Yes?" Harry said, flatly.

"How's the food supply?" Jim asked.

"I don't like to reveal that," Harry answered.

Bess stepped in front of Jim.

"The lives of all of us depend on this food, Harry," Bess scolded. "You're not special. You have no special rights."

Harry backed away from the counter and Bess's ferocity.

"What I'm d-doing is for the best for everyone," he stammered. "The food supply has got to be controlled."

"You're making yourself out to be some kind of boss, and you're not," Bess snapped back.

From behind, Jim put his arm around Bess's stomach and drew her back. Missy helped by pulling on Bess's arm.

Still holding onto Bess, who was squirming, Jim said, "We'd like some food."

"You're too early," Harry declared.

"We'd like to have breakfast," Jim answered in a clipped voice.

"Come back tomorrow," Harry replied.

"But we have nothing to eat for today," Missy protested.

"You should have thought of that when you didn't show up for work yesterday," Harry snarled.

"I work here more than anyone else in town," Missy shot back. "And it's such a waste of time. We just keep counting the same things over and over."

"You didn't show up," Harry blustered, "And we had to do your share of the work."

"Give us some food," Missy demanded.

"Tomorrow," Harry answered.

"You bastard!" Bess blurted out, still squirming to get out of Jim's grasp.

"Come on," Jim said. "Let's leave. We don't need him today. There are still plenty of pantries in town we haven't tapped into yet. And when the car is running, we won't need him at all, ever again."

Again Bess shouted at Harry, "You lousy bastard!"

Jim put his other arm around Bess and picked her up off her feet and turned with her toward the door. Missy opened the door for him, and he carried her out of the shop.

"You don't understand how important my work is," Harry called out after them. "My work matters."

Once outside, Jim eased his hold on Bess's midsection,

and she wrestled out of his grasp.

"He makes me so mad," she shouted. "He tries to act important, and he's not."

"It's no good meeting him head on," Jim soothed. "We'll have to figure out an end run around him. Come on; let's look for food. I bet there are a lot of kitchens that are still stocked."

They went toward the south end of town; and, by visiting several houses, collected a full box of canned goods. They also broke into the machine shop, and Jim removed calipers and micrometers.

After a quick meal, Bess went to the power plant; and Missy went with Jim to the garage. He talked with Ernie and Bob and measured the bore of the cylinder and the diameter of the piston.

Then Jim and Missy went back to the machine shop, and Missy watched while Jim ground the piston down to size.

With every pass the grinding wheel made, the spinning piston got shinier, first on one side, and then over a larger and larger area, until the whole circumference was glistening.

"It's pretty," Missy said.

"That's one of the fringe benefits of the job," Jim answered, "making dull things shine."

"Too bad it won't stay that way."

"Yeah, too bad."

Jim measured the diameter and adjusted the grinder to make another pass.

"Jim?" Missy broke the silence.

"Yeah?"

"What are we going to do about Harry?"

Jim worked a few dials on the grinder before answering.

"It won't do any good to confront him," he said. "We'll just have to figure out another way to get our supplies. Then we can avoid Harry altogether."

"He has no right making us beg for every scrap of food, begging like a dog for a bone," she complained. "No one should ever go hungry as long as there's food anywhere."

"No one should ever go hungry."

"I'll bet Harry's more afraid of us than we are of him," she said.

Jim said nothing.

When the piston was finished, they took it to Ernie and Bob, who enthusiastically received it and immediately set to work installing it in the engine. Then Missy and Jim went to the power plant.

Someone had swept up the broken glass on the sidewalk, and the door opened smoothly. Kate and Bess were inside, talking; and Susan was adjusting the knobs on the radio.

"Anything yet?" Missy asked.

"No," Kate answered, "But it's still a few minutes before noon. There's still time."

They talked, in hushed tones, pausing between each sentence in anticipation of a sound coming from the radio.

Twelve o'clock came, and still there was no sound. Susan adjusted the radio more frequently.

Anitra walked into the room, and the surprised silence that greeted her hung in the air like a question.

"I wanted to hear," Anitra said simply.

The seconds ticked by. With each passing minute the conversation became more somber.

The radio remained silent.

But at ten minutes past noon, the radio came to life.

"C-Q, C-Q, C-Q, this is KQA-6650 calling any station, any station. Answer me please."

There was silence, followed by "Any station, answer me please."

Another silence.

"I'm broadcasting on a frequency of 148.85 megacycles, and I'm trying to reach anyone. Anyone. Come in please."

Silence.

"Is anyone out there? Can anyone hear me?"

The silences became longer.

"Is anyone else still alive?"

Silence.

"I...I don't know what date it is. I should have kept track; I should have marked it off, but I thought I'd remember, and now I don't. It's March something, isn't it? Anyone?

"I'm all alone here. Everyone else is gone. I don't know…why I'm still alive. I wish someone would tell me what I'm supposed to do.

"There must be a reason why…I can't be the only one left alive…can I? Why am I still alive? Why? Please answer me."

Tears started rolling down Susan's face, tears that made little marks on the note pad she held and blurred what she was writing.

The radio continued.

"I don't know how much longer I can keep broadcasting. There's less than a half-gallon of gas left. Maybe another week. Maybe less. Maybe I should stop trying for a month. I don't know what to do. Is anybody listening?"

"Tell us where you are; tell us," Kate whispered.

The voice from the radio said, "I'm running out of food…preserves are almost gone. I should have planted, but I didn't. I should have marked the calendar. I should have…"

The voice broke down, crying. Susan cried too. Everyone else in the room was silent. After a time, the voice continued, more composed.

"This will be my only broadcast today. I'm going to make the gas for the generator last as long as possible. I'll keep going. I'm going to keep broadcasting for as long as I can, every noon. For as long as I can. Then I don't know what I'll do…"

"This is David, at the Delray Farm. Out."

There was nothing more.

Susan wiped her eyes with a tissue and tried to make her blurred notes neater.

Missy broke the silence. "He hasn't given up yet. He sounded like he was losing it, but he got it back. He regained control. He's going to take it all the way to the end."

"But he didn't tell us where he was," Kate groaned. "If he doesn't tell us soon, it's going to be all over for him."

Susan, her voice still choked with emotion, asked, "Can't we follow the radio signal? Can't we locate him that way?"

She was looking at Jim.

"I don't know how," he admitted. "I know it can be done, but I don't know how to do it."

A grim silence fell over the room. Her voice husky at first, Anitra broke the silence.

"I think I know where he is."

"Where?" Susan shouted. "Where?"

"I'm not sure exactly where," Anitra said, avoiding looking anyone in the eye. "That name, Delray Farm, it sounds familiar. I think there was a family named that somewhere around where I used to live—north of here, about seventy-five miles, north of the interstate."

"Can you show us where they lived, on a map?" Missy asked.

"I'm not really sure," Anitra answered. "That name just sounds familiar. There's a half-dozen places I can think of that might be it. But I think I can find it."

"Will you come with us, to look for him?" Jim asked.

Anitra hesitated. "Harry won't like it."

"Harry's not the boss," Bess snapped.

"A person's life may depend on you," Missy pleaded.

Anitra looked around the room at all the faces watching her. She looked out the window at the sunshine on the bridge. She looked back at Susan, whose tear-stained face issued a silent plea.

"Okay," Anitra said softly.

They talked further about their hopes of finding David. Anitra soon excused herself, saying that she had to get back.

Missy and Bess went with Jim to his place for lunch—vegetable soup and crackers. The three then spent the afternoon doing household chores, and Jim and Missy went for a walk, out to the hill in back, where they'd had their first date.

In the early evening Bess found them and told them Ernie had come over to say the car was ready. They hurried to the garage.

The car was sitting in the lot in front of the garage. Ernie and Bob had washed it, and the non-rusty parts glistened in the evening sun.

Ernie handed the keys to Jim.

"Thought you'd want the honor of startin' 'er up," Ernie said.

Jim declined. "That honor belongs to you, Ernie."

While Jim, Missy and Bess stood alongside and Bob in

front, Ernie got into the station wagon. He bounced on the seat a few times, adjusted both the rear and side-view mirrors, grinned broadly at everyone, and turned the key.

Nothing happened.

The broad grin on Ernie's face faded, slowly, slowly, gone. He cursed, leaned forward, and turned the key harder. While Ernie was banging on the dashboard and turning the key so hard it was at risk of breaking off, Bob went inside the garage, got another battery, set it on the ground in front of the car, and started connecting cables to it. When Ernie saw what Bob was doing, he gave up wrenching the key and waited, limply, for Bob to finish.

"Try it now," Bob said.

Ernie turned the key again, and the motor emitted a low whine that increased in tempo, and then a boom! A cloud of black smoke belched from the tail pipe. The smoke cleared, and the motor continued running.

Bess cheered, Missy clapped her hands, and Jim said, "Awwright!"

Bob smiled.

"Git in," Ernie shouted. "I'll take you all for a ride!"

Missy, Jim and Bess piled into the back. Bob disconnected the extra battery, closed the hood, and got in front with Ernie, who pulled out of the lot and turned left on the main street. At the intersection, Ernie drove through the red light; but not before he slowed down and, out of habit, checked for any oncoming traffic.

As he continued down the street, he laid on the horn; and at the end of the block he made a U-turn. As they drove past

Pamela's, she was standing on the curb and waving and smiling at them, holding her hair to keep it from blowing across her eyes. They waved back and then stopped. She got in the front seat next to Bob, and Ernie drove off again.

This time the light was green, and Ernie drove through without looking. They waved again as they drove past the market, where Frank and Anitra had ventured out as far as the doorway, and Frank waved back, shyly. Ernie was trying different rhythms on the horn.

Susan and Kate were already outside as they drove past, and Ernie made another U-turn to pick them up, Kate getting in the front and Susan in the back. The packed station wagon was now a jumble of humanity, one body pushed up against, and sometimes upon, another—an amalgam of diffidence, bravura, and glee. Glee won out, as the bouncing of the vehicle forced the occupants to accept the frequent personal contact of one with another.

Ernie drove the two-block length of downtown again, making one more U-turn before landing them back at the gas station, where he stopped the car; and everyone got out.

Bess, Susan, and Bob took turns driving up the street or around the block while the rest stood at the garage and talked.

"Everything's now in place," Kate said. "How soon will you leave?"

"Tomorrow afternoon, as soon as we get organized," Jim answered.

Anitra was still standing in the doorway of the market, and Jim walked across the street to talk to her. He told her they could leave the next day, and she looked at him for a moment before closing her eyes and slowly nodding her head in assent.

She said Harry was asleep, and she had Frank help them get several boxes of food and place them in the station wagon.

While helping to load the food, Missy asked if she could go with them.

Jim was concerned. "The world has changed. We don't know what it's going to be like. Maybe it's going to be easy, but maybe we're going to be facing a lot of hardship. You'd be better off staying here, where things are more settled, more comfortable."

Missy put her arms around his neck. "I'd rather suffer by your side than have to worry about you suffering alone."

Jim's eyes glistened. He acquiesced to her wishes by kissing her.

Susan gave them time to savor their kiss; and then she also asked to go. Slowly relaxing their embrace, they turned toward her.

"It's because of David," she explained, "because of the things he said. I want to be there when we find him."

Still gently in each other's arms, Missy and Jim communicated wordlessly, and Missy sensed that this was her call. She nodded yes to Susan.

The troupe continued their preparations, loading more groceries into the car, and some extra gasoline. They made plans that the four of them would leave the next day.

Before Jim left the lot, Ernie walked over to him and shook his hand.

"Thankee' for doing business with us," Ernie said. "Sure do appreciate the work."

"You and Bob did a wonderful job," Jim replied.

Ernie rubbed a less rusty part of the fender of the station wagon affectionately.

"Felt good," he said. "Bob's one fine mechanic—don't tell him I said so. We sure did need the work. Felt good."

Without looking up, Ernie continued to rub the fender.

"As soon as we get back," Jim said, "I'll bring it in for a tune up and oil change."

"Hot dang," Ernie exclaimed loudly enough for Bob to hear. "How 'bout that. Repeat customers. We're good!" Then Ernie pointed at Bob and said, "Don't you go askin' for a raise."

"More of nothing is still nothing," Bob groused.

"That's still more'n you're worth," Ernie retorted.

Jim left them to their arguing.

That evening, Pamela moved in with Bess, to keep her company while Missy was gone; and Missy spent the night with Jim at his place.

The next morning, Jim and Missy had promised to breakfast with Bess and Pamela at 8 a.m., but the time came and went.

Bess telephoned, and Missy answered.

"H'lo," Missy said.

"My, don't we sound sleepy," Bess responded cheerfully.

"Hi Bess," Missy murmured, sheepishly. "I didn't get

much sleep last night."

"Are we complaining?"

"No," Missy laughed.

Missy kissed Jim awake and dragged him out of bed. They showered together. Jim was playful, and Missy vacillated between pretending to complain, and surrendering to his ministrations.

"Hurry up," she said, without much resolve, as he was spending a luxurious amount of time lathering her breasts and her stomach. "I still want to go shopping."

"Shopping?"

"A lady going on a trip needs a new wardrobe."

They showered, dressed, and went next door, where Bess and Pamela had prepared toasted homemade English muffins, with marmalade, also fruit juice and canned sausage.

They raved about the food, most of which had come from Pamela; and Missy worried aloud about diminishing Pamela's supply.

"I'll get more, today," Pamela said.

"Yeah," Bess grumbled. "Harry's not angry at her."

"He still makes me keep his water barrel full," Pamela said. "I told him he can just turn the faucet on; but he won't listen. So when he's not looking, I just run a hose over to the barrel. It only takes a few minutes, and he thinks I'm spending hours every day serving him, carrying his water all the way from the river."

"I wish *I* could get off that easy," Missy moaned.

They finished breakfast, and Jim went back to his place to pack for the trip. Missy went across the street to shop.

The day was hot and sunny. For the trip, Missy chose to wear sandals, white shorts, and a skimpy, cut-off T-shirt that left her midriff bare. She selected a few other things and went to place them in the station wagon.

As she neared the gas station, she saw Harry in front of her, walking towards the station wagon. He was about to see all the food they had expropriated from the grocery store.

"Hi Harry, what's up?" she called out, as she hurried to catch up.

He stopped walking, and she passed him and positioned herself between him and the station wagon, in order to block his view.

He looked at her, standing before him in the morning sunshine. The thin material of her T-shirt did little to restrict his view of her chest. Hurriedly, he indulged himself in the sight of her firm legs, her taut stomach, her supple breasts.

"I need wood," he grumbled, and tried to walk past her. She moved sideways to keep her body between him and the car.

"We don't keep wood in the station wagon anymore," she said. "We don't even use that much. We've got the electric stove now."

"You'll get into trouble if you start messing with things you don't know anything about," he growled. "And I mean *big* trouble."

"We've all got our electricity back, Harry, everyone except you. And no one's gotten into trouble yet," she said. "You don't have to quit just because you're afraid. You can be afraid and still keep trying."

"You won't talk like that when someone gets fried."

"I hope that doesn't happen."

Furtively, he treated himself to another survey of her legs before returning his glance to her face.

"You coming to work today?" he asked.

"No." Her voice was firm.

"The work's got to be done."

"Counting it won't make it last any longer," she scolded. "We've got to find more. We've got to start producing some food, too."

Harry sneered, "You don't look like a farmer to me."

"I'm not afraid to try something new."

"Go ahead," he taunted. "Plant your vegetable garden. As soon as it fails, you'll come begging to me."

Missy shook her head.

"No I won't, not anymore," she said. "No matter what happens, I'm not going to come crawling to you. We don't need you. We'll find our food somewhere else."

"Good luck," he replied sarcastically and turned to start walking back to the store.

Missy breathed a sigh of relief and began to put her clothes in the car. But Harry had turned around and crept up behind her. As she moved backwards while opening the car door, she unexpectedly bumped into him, and she jumped.

"What's that stuff doing in there?" he demanded gruffly.

She was startled, but she responded quickly. She threw her clothes into the car, got part way in and reached around and locked all the other doors, pulled the keys out of the ignition, got out and locked her door, put the keys in the tiny pocket of her shorts, and leaned against the car with her arms folded over her chest.

"That's our food," she declared. "We're going away, and there's nothing you can do about it."

Harry reacted like his brain had lost control of his body. He jerked, twitched, gurgled, but failed to produce any intelligible sound or useful movement. While Missy stood her ground, Jim walked up to the back of the car and asked, "What's going on?"

Missy didn't dare break eye contact with Harry to acknowledge Jim's presence, so she continued staring at Harry with her arms folded. Once more Harry opened his mouth, but still no intelligible sound came out, so he cast his eyes to the ground, turned with his back to Jim, and began his retreat back to the store.

"What was that?" Jim asked.

"Nothing," Missy answered, beginning to calm down. "Nothing to worry about."

She took the keys out of her pocket and handed them to Jim. Then she put her arms around his neck and kissed him, while gently brushing her unfettered breasts against his chest.

Then she laughed, pushed Jim away by his shoulders, and said, "Let's go have an adventure!"

Missy's laugh occurred just as Harry was opening the

door to enter the store, and he winced as if the sound had been a jagged knife stabbing him between the shoulder blades. But he didn't turn around as he disappeared into the darkness.

Jim and Missy walked together back to the flat. While Missy threw a few last-minute things together, Jim phoned Susan, who said that she, too, was ready.

Jim then called the market, and Anitra answered on the first ring.

"Ready to go?" Jim asked.

"No," Anitra whispered. "I've changed my mind. I can't go."

"What?" Jim exclaimed. "You have to go! We aren't going to find him without you."

Missy took the phone.

"What's the matter Anitra?" Missy asked. "Why aren't you going?"

"I can't talk," Anitra whispered. "Harry's around somewhere. I'm afraid of what he might do."

"Anitra, we need you," Missy pleaded. "Without you, we aren't going to find David."

"I'm...I'm sorry," Anitra moaned. "I can't talk. I'm sorry."

She hung up.

"Someone's going to have to try to convince her to come," Jim said. "Without her, we have no chance."

Bess and Pamela went with Missy and Jim down to the

car. Susan and Allyson were already waiting for them. When Susan found out Anitra wasn't coming, she immediately went across the street to talk to her. The group around the car watched as Anitra opened the market door for Susan, and the two women talked. Susan at one point pulled imploringly on Anitra's arm. After five minutes, Susan walked back to the group, wiping tears from her eyes.

"She's coming," Susan announced. "She wants us to leave and then pick her up in back of the market. She doesn't want Harry to see her go."

"He'll find out soon enough," Jim said.

They finished their preparations, and Ernie made a last check of the car—tire pressure and fluid levels.

"How long will you be gone?" Bess asked.

"If all goes perfectly," Jim said, "We could be back in time for dinner. But if we have trouble finding him, we'll stay out for as long as our supplies last—about a week, longer if we find more food and gas."

Missy kissed Bess good-bye, and Jim kissed Bess on the cheek. As Jim was hugging her, Bess said over his shoulder to Missy, "Make sure you bring him back."

"I will," Missy promised.

They finished their good-byes and got in the car—Jim driving, Missy next to him, and Susan in the back. They drove up to the corner, turned left, and turned left again behind the market. Jim slowed down as he drove past the loading dock.

A door next to one of the bays was ajar, and as they drove by Anitra opened it and stepped out. She was wearing an aqua jump suit, bare at the neck and midriff, and many gold rings

155

and chains. She carried an oversized purse, which she threw ahead of her before awkwardly jumping down from the platform. Susan opened the car door; and Anitra got in back, behind Jim. Jim backed the car out sharply, returned to the main street, and headed north, out of town.

As they drove past the power plant, they honked and waved at Kate, who had been outside waiting for them to pass by. They then drove across the bridge and followed the road as it curved gently to the north-west.

On the roof of the market, partially concealed by the brick wall, Harry stood, watching the car as it disappeared around the bend. Even after the car was out of sight, even after the dust had settled, he stood there watching the empty road. Then, with his back against the wall, he slid down till he was sitting on his heels, and he stayed there with his head down and his eyes closed.

Like the tears running down his cheeks, his words oozed out, "…gone…gone…everyone leaves…leaves me."

The station wagon was five miles out of town, and no one had said anything. Once, Jim had squeezed Missy's hand, and she patted his arm in return.

Missy broke the silence with, "This car rides nicely."

"Yes," Jim agreed. "It may be ugly, but it's doing the job for us."

Missy turned around to the back seat.

"How are you doing, Anitra?" she asked.

With a deep breath, Anitra nodded her head several times quickly.

"I'm okay," she gasped.

"Are you worried about Harry?" Missy asked.

"I shouldn't have come," Anitra answered. "Harry's not going to like it."

"You had to do what's right," Missy insisted. "If there's someone else alive out there, we have to find him before it's too late."

"He's suffering," Susan added.

Anitra turned her head away from them and faced out the window before answering.

"I know," she sighed. "But Harry's got the <u>food</u>."

They drove on. Jim told them to watch for anything unusual, anything that might deserve a closer look.

Mile after mile went by. Nothing broke the monotony of the desert. There were no other cars, no movement, no life except for the four lives traveling inside that thin metal shell.

After they'd been driving for an hour, they passed a billboard advertising a gas station that said "Last gas for fifty miles." The gas station appeared on the left, and in the lot was a tanker truck, angled in, both doors open. Jim drove up slowly and stopped the station wagon near the truck. He got out and looked around. There was no one in the truck, no one in the station, no one anywhere.

Jim went to Missy's side of the car and leaned over at the window.

"Might as well stretch our legs," he said.

Everyone got out. Jim and Missy stood by the car

157

talking while Susan and Anitra walked around.

"It's creepy, after all this time, to find another vehicle," Jim said. "I half expected to find someone. The way it's sitting there, with the doors open, it looks like the driver just got out to take a walk."

"There's no one?" Missy asked.

"No."

Susan came up and told them there was a vending machine on the premises, "with candy bars inside."

Jim found a crow bar and was about to smash open the vending machine when Missy stopped him. She reached into her purse and took out a large handful of quarters.

Surprised, Jim asked, "What are you carrying them for?"

"Habit," Missy shrugged.

They inserted Missy's quarters, and pulled on the chromed knobs at the bottom of the machine. Faithfully, it delivered their treat every time. They loaded up on snacks; but, without electricity, they couldn't get any gasoline.

"Why does the vending machine work if the gas pumps won't?" Missy asked.

"The vending machine is old-fashioned, mechanical," Jim answered. "It belongs in an antique store."

"But what about the truck?" Susan asked. "Don't they call them mobile gas stations?"

Jim climbed up on the truck and banged on it. The tank was mostly full. He found the nozzle and spilled some of the fuel on the ground.

"Diesel," he complained.

Then he looked again at the truck.

"It won't work in the car," he said, "but it will work in the truck. With this big a gas tank, we can travel across the country a dozen times."

"Can you drive a semi?" Missy asked.

"I drove one once, for a total distance of about two miles," he admitted, "but I'll figure it out."

"I knew you were going to say that," Missy giggled.

Jim climbed into the cab. At first it wouldn't start, but he found and threw a battery switch and the motor came to life. While it was warming up, they loaded their gear into the back of the cab and parked the station wagon beside the building.

"We'll pick it up on the way back." Jim said.

With difficulty, Jim backed the rig out of the station, jack-knifing it so far that it creaked. It took him three attempts to clear the pumps.

The women got in. Though the seat was wide enough that four could sit comfortably, Susan chose to lie on her stomach on the bed in back and peer through the curtain with her head propped on her hands.

Once he was on the road, Jim moved the rig smoothly enough, keeping it in the center of the two-lane highway.

They drove more miles. Missy turned on the radio and scanned both AM and FM. There was nothing but static. She turned it off.

The truck seemed like it wasn't moving but rather that

the road was coming to them, and the white lines zipped underneath one after another.

"Another ten miles, and we'll drive past where we used to live," Anitra said. "We built the place ourselves. We were going to get married."

"You...and Frank?" Missy asked.

"What? Oh no," Anitra answered. "My boyfriend's name was Nick. Frank was just someone to hang around with, when Nick was gone. He was gone a lot, working construction. Nick said Frank was the only one he'd trust around me, because Frank was harmless."

"You mean, you and Frank aren't lovers?" Jim asked.

"Jim!" Missy scolded.

Anitra was gracious. "That's okay. But no, Frank's not my lover, or Harry either, if that's what you're thinking." There was a pause, and then Anitra added, "Maybe I can't blame you for thinking that. I suppose that's what everyone thinks. But Nick was right; Frank is harmless. And Harry, all he ever does is look."

"I've noticed," Missy groaned. "But I don't understand. If you're not involved with either one of them, why do you live with them?"

"I don't want to go hungry."

More white lines slipped away under the truck. The big windshield became a wide screen, displaying a landscape that was moving, but scarcely changing.

"So you and Frank and Harry used to spend time together?" Missy broke the silence.

"Not Harry. I didn't meet Harry till after...after the change," Anitra said. "Frank and Harry and their sister used to live a couple of miles from our place, but Harry moved out before my boyfriend and I moved in. I heard that Harry had a drinking problem, and I also heard that he'd gotten a girl in trouble, and that's why he moved out."

"What happened with the sister?" Jim asked.

"Gone, along with everyone else," Anitra whispered. "Everyone...gone."

"Where were you when it happened?" Jim asked. "Where were you at noon?"

The pause was so long Jim wondered if Anitra had heard him, but she answered softly, "I was with Frank. Nick was out of town. Frank and I were walking, along the railroad tracks. We stopped for lunch in the shade of the old water tower. I remember we had cheese sandwiches and not very cold lemonade. I fell asleep. It was nice.

"But when we got back, everything had changed. No one was around, anywhere. Frank's sister was supposed to pick him up, but she never came.

"Finally, Frank called Harry, long distance. Harry was drunk; he didn't know what was happening, either.

"Harry got a car somewhere and drove out. We were waiting outside for him but he drove right past us and went to his sister's place first.

"When he came back, Harry didn't say a word. He just stopped the car, we got in, and he drove us to town. We broke into the market, and we've been there ever since."

"You mean, the only reason Harry has the food is that he

got there first?" Missy asked.

"I guess so," Anitra answered. "Before that, Harry was a day trader. He didn't have any connection to the market."

"Wow," Missy groaned. "All this time we've been letting him walk all over us, and he didn't have any more right to the food than we did. He just took advantage of us."

In the distance, up ahead, a small bungalow with white siding appeared on the left.

"That's it," Anitra said. She sat forward and leaned her arm on the dashboard. "Slow down."

Jim slowed the truck, gradually, more and more, until they were traveling only a few miles per hour as they passed the house. Anitra watched until it disappeared from view. Tears glistened on her cheeks and made her dark eyes shine.

"Oh, Nick," she cried softly. "Where are you?"

Anitra sank back in her seat and continued crying. Jim had slowed the truck to a crawl and hadn't started it back up again.

"Okay?" he asked.

"Yes, okay," Anitra answered. "Go on. The interstate is about five miles ahead. I'll be all right."

Jim put the truck back into gear and continued down the highway.

Missy put her hand on Anitra's shoulder. After some rummaging in her purse, Susan handed Anitra a tissue, and she dried her tears.

The hypnotic effect of the white lines, sequentially

sliding underneath the truck, once more began to instill its languorous effect upon the passengers. To the right appeared a sign announcing they were approaching the interstate highway.

The two-lane-wide bridge over the expressway came into view; and Jim, not yet confident of his driving skills, stopped the truck several hundred feet before it and shifted into the lowest gear. As the big rig lumbered forward, the view through the wide windshield seemed to be changing in slow-motion. Foot by foot the semi moved closer to the bridge, and more and more they were able to see past the embankment and down into the trench below.

As the expressway came into view, Missy grabbed onto Jim's arm, and Anitra grabbed the armrest on the door. Susan gasped, once; but then silence filled the cab; and the only sound was the whoosh of the air brakes as Jim stopped the truck near the middle of the bridge.

Except for the low rumble of the engine, there was no sound, not in the cab or anywhere from the surrounding countryside.

Below them, the expressway extended straight in both directions, as far as the horizon, three lanes on each side with a steel barrier in between.

And in all the lanes, on both sides, and even on the slopes, and all heading in the same direction, heading west, were all the cars—thousands of cars, all colors, all styles, new, old, shiny, rusty, luxury, economy—packed in, bumper to bumper, and extending to infinity, beyond sight, toward both horizons.

And in all the cars, there were people.

And nothing was moving—no motion at all.

For a long time the truck remained on that bridge, standing vigil over the countless cars below that no longer moved. And the four people inside also maintained an unexpected vigil, offering their silence in appeasement for the dreadful stillness that surrounded them, remaining motionless in the face of the horrific lack of movement for as far as they could see.

A few bright, white clouds drifted by at the horizon, the earth rotated a few degrees on its axis, the sun inched along the sky.

The hearts of the four people inside the truck continued pumping blood, and their lungs continued to take in and expel air.

Trancelike, Jim wrenched the gears into low, and the big truck ponderously moved off the bridge and down the road. Jim drove a mile and then pulled the rig over to the side and turned off the motor. He put his arm around Missy and kissed her cheek. She hugged him back, hard. Missy turned to hug Anitra. Jim squeezed Susan's hand, and she squeezed his back.

They got out of the truck and walked about, randomly, burning off the adrenalin. Jim sat down on the truck's running board, and Missy stood in front of him.

"That explains a lot," he groaned, "even if we still don't know what happened."

She took his head and hugged it against her stomach; and he was comforted by her steady, rhythmic breathing. She stroked his hair while she looked off down the road, not back to where they had been, but forward, to where they were going.

Their unplanned stop became a lunch break. Susan heated up some soup on a camp stove. There was little conversation, and not much appetite, either. When lunch was over, they got back in the truck, all of them sitting on the seat this time; and they began searching for the farm.

Anitra became confused. She took them down one road that led no where, and Jim had trouble getting the truck turned around.

"All these roads look alike," Anitra complained.

On the second try, they found a place Anitra thought might be right. Jim parked the rig in the yard; and together the four approached the house, cautiously, and went inside. There was no sign that anyone had lived there recently.

"I'm sorry," Anitra said. "I'm sorry. I thought I knew where it was. I thought I knew the house. I'm not sure any more."

"Now what?" Jim asked.

"We can't give up," Susan declared. "He's still out there, and he's all alone."

"We don't have to give up," Missy responded. "We can start a farm-by-farm search. We've got enough food. And we surely have enough fuel."

"Let's do it," Jim said.

"Shall I drive?" Missy asked.

Jim's eyes widened. "Do you know how?"

"I'll figure it out," she smiled. "It's just like my old VW, except with more gears."

"And more brakes," he added.

They got back in the cab—Missy behind the wheel and Jim next to her. Very slowly, but also smoothly, Missy moved the rig through the yard and back onto the road. Tentatively at first, she shifted through the gears; but soon she had the truck moving smartly along.

Jim was impressed. "You're a better road jockey than I am!"

Missy wouldn't take her eyes off the road, but her smile was as wide as possible.

"I learned a little by watching you," she beamed, "and I learned not to be too afraid of it, either."

They criss-crossed their way around the countryside, taking any road that looked big enough for the truck to get through. Occasionally Anitra would make a suggestion of which way to go, when some place looked familiar to her. They stopped at every house or farm to look for signs that someone had been living there recently.

When it began getting dark, Missy stopped the semi right in the middle of the main road. The world was their parking place. No one felt like cooking, so they ate a cold meal and went to sleep. Anitra and Susan slept in the bed in back; and Missy slept leaning her back against Jim, who had his arms folded over her chest and stomach.

In the morning, after breakfast, Jim tried to start the truck, and couldn't. He opened the engine and began examining it.

"Are you going to be able to figure it out?" Missy asked.

"I know nothing about engines," Jim confessed.

While he was working, Anitra and Susan walked a short

distance from the truck. Susan noticed the slightest wisp of smoke wafting through the air in the distance. She looked twice to make sure that her heart wasn't playing tricks on her, and then excitedly she ran back to tell Missy and Jim.

Since Jim was making no progress with the engine, they decided to go exploring on foot.

The smoke soon disappeared, but they continued walking toward where they had seen it until they came to a neat, modest farm house and a barn. The house was closed, but the barn was open; and they walked inside and looked around. At first they didn't see anything; but then, in a separate room in the corner, they saw the figure of a young man, only about 18 years old, wearing overalls, slumped over in a chair with his head on the table in front of him. He wasn't moving.

"Just like all the others," Missy whispered.

At the sound of her voice, the young man raised his head and looked at them.

They froze where they stood and watched him. He blinked, brushed his too long hair out of his eyes, and blinked again.

And then he started crying.

"Hello," he said, through his tears.

"David?" Susan asked.

He nodded while wiping away a tear with the back of his hand.

"Today was the last day, too," he said still crying.

Susan walked up to him and put her hands on both of his

shoulders.

"I'm not crying," he denied, and the tears continued to fall. He wiped his eyes again and put on his glasses.

Susan comforted him; and after he stopped crying, she introduced every one. A little stiffly, and shyly, he greeted each one in turn.

He tried to offer them his hospitality, but he had little to offer.

"Most of my food is gone," he said. "I've got some preserves left, and some canned tomatoes. There might be something left at the house, but I don't go up there anymore."

He told them about the farm and about the crops that used to grow there. He told them about how his life had been the last several months, and how he'd been calling on the radio all that time.

He asked how they had gotten there, and they told him about the truck which now wasn't working.

"Maybe I can help," he said. "Things are always breaking around here. Sometimes I get them working again."

He got his tools, they walked back to the truck, and Jim and David worked together on it. As lunch time approached, the women picked out some food, took the camp stove, and set up for lunch at David's farm. David and Jim walked back, and everyone ate seated at a picnic table beneath a large tree halfway between the house and barn. A cool breeze comforted them, and the tension of their recent endeavors began to ease.

They made plans, figured how long the food would last, including the food David had added to their supply. They discussed how long it would take to walk back to the station wagon if they couldn't get the truck to work, and whether it would be better to send one person who could drive back, or have everyone go together.

"Leave?" David said. "I never thought about leaving here." He paused for a long while. "I guess I have to. I can't stay here anymore, can I?"

He looked at the others for confirmation.

"No David, you can't," Susan said.

There was another silence.

"I've never lived anywhere but here," he murmured.

"The unknown is always frightening," Missy comforted. "But soon it will become familiar, and then you'll have a new home."

"But my mother is here," David whispered.

"Your mother?" Jim asked. "Your mother is here? Where is she?"

David looked down at his food, and he remained motionless.

"What is it?" Missy asked.

"My mother is in the house," David replied. "She's dead."

Susan touched his hand. "Oh, David, I'm so sorry."

"Tell us about it," Jim prompted. "How did you survive? What did you do?"

David gave him a questioning glance and shrugged, "I didn't do anything."

"Tell us," Susan said gently. "Tell us what happened."

David looked at Susan, only at Susan, as he recounted his story.

"We didn't know anything different was happening," he shrugged. "A couple of neighbors came by and said we should get out, everyone was leaving, moving west before something terrible happened.

"But my mother wouldn't go. She said all we had to do was have faith, and everything would work out for the best. So we stayed here.

"It got noisier outside—people driving by, honking, shouting—people in trucks with a lot of furniture in back, people in cars with the trunks open and packed full.

"They stole our car—some people we didn't even know. They just came right up in the yard. One guy was pounding on the door, shouting at us to give him the key. My mother wouldn't let him in. But then another guy got the car started without the key, and they just drove off in it. I ran out and shouted at them, but they kept going.

"I think my mother was getting pretty scared by then. I could see her hands were shaking. But she said we should just trust in God, keep doing the job we were supposed to do, and we would be all right. I was scared too, but I didn't want her to know.

"So we sat down to lunch. It was so noisy outside. We could hear the cars on the interstate, all the honking, all the motors revving.

"I remember, my mother bowed her head to say grace, but I didn't bow my head. Everything seemed so strange. It got quiet. My dog was on the porch, looking all around, wagging his tail as fast as he could.

"Then my dog just plopped down sideways, right where he was; and he stopped moving, just like that. I looked at my mother, and her head was still bowed, and the next thing that happened was she just went limp, and fell forward, and her head landed in her plate, and she didn't move anymore either.

"I knew I was going to die too. It was so quiet. All the honking had stopped. So I closed my eyes, and I waited to die. I waited to feel something. After a while, I opened my eyes, and nothing had changed. My mother hadn't moved; my dog hadn't moved. I closed my eyes again and kept waiting to die.

"But nothing more happened. I was still alive. I couldn't wait any longer. I got up and walked around, and it felt so strange. I felt like I was taller than I really was. I was seeing things differently than I ever had before. I was moving, and nothing else was moving.

"I decided it was just going to take a little longer for me to die. I picked my mother up, I cleaned the food off her face, and I put her in her bed. I went out and picked my dog up and put him on the floor next to my mother. Then I went to my own room, and I lied down. I was so tired. I went to sleep thinking that I would never wake up again, just drift off to sleep, and everything would be over.

"But I did wake up. I think it must have been the same day, in the evening. I was hoping it had all been a terrible dream. But I opened the door to my mother's room, and she was still there where I had left her, and so was my dog. I was alive, and they were dead.

"I couldn't stand it, staying in the house. So I locked the door, and I went out to live in the barn. And I've been there ever since."

David finished his story. Susan reached across the table and took both of his hands in hers. He looked at their hands, hers so pale and slender compared to his, and then he looked at her face, her bright hair shining, her eyes glistening, as she steadily returned his gaze.

"I'm not going to cry anymore," he declared.

Susan let go of his hand, but she held his gaze.

They finished the meal, and David and Jim went back to work on the truck. Several times they thought they'd reached the limit of what they could try, and then one of them would think of something else. Several times they thought they'd found the problem, but still the truck did not start. But each false hope consumed more time, and it was the failing sunlight that made them stop their efforts.

They ate their night-time meal of canned stew and canned corn, close to the truck, illuminated by the glow from the camp stove. Then there was nothing to do but go to sleep. They began to prepare the bed in the truck, and David said good night softly and started to walk back to his farm.

"He shouldn't be alone," Missy said. "He's been alone for too many months."

"I'll go with him," Jim offered.

"No," Susan insisted. "I'll go."

She ran after David; and, side-by-side, without touching, they walked over the fields and back to the farm.

Jim and Missy slept together in the back of the truck, and Anitra slept stretched out on the seat.

In the little room in the barn, David lit an oil lamp. There were two places to sleep in the room, one a cot and the other a narrow bunk bed. David attempted to smooth out the sheet on the bunk bed for Susan, but they still looked rumpled.

"I wish I had fresh sheets," he said.

"It's all right," she answered.

She got into the bed; and he lied down on the cot, then leaned over and blew out the lamp. The cool night surrounded them. The only sounds were the rustling of their clothes as they moved or the occasional creak of a rafter.

"Good night, David," she said.

"Good night...Susan," he answered.

She fell asleep still hearing the sound of his voice speaking her name. He fell asleep listening to her steady breathing.

The gentle night cushioned them as they slept, wrapped them in protection—softened the sounds, dulled the sharp edges, and slowed the pace. Gradually the morning sun evaporated the protection; and, by the time anyone awoke, the new day was already awaiting them.

David woke up first, and got out of bed; but when he saw that Susan was still sleeping soundly, he returned to bed and waited till she began to stir. Eventually she roused herself, and then she smiled at him, and they got up together. They walked across the field to the truck, where the others were just waking up.

Jim and David went back to work on the truck. By the second hour, they had exhausted the new ideas the night had brought them, and their attempts at repair were reduced to the occasional prodding of a wire or tightening of an already-tight bolt.

By mid-morning, Jim decided that he would have to walk to the station wagon. He said so out loud, and his pronouncement was met with quiet acceptance, though Missy squirmed uneasily. They agreed it was best that one person go alone, traveling light and fast.

He stuffed some food and a container of water into a sack and started down the road. Missy walked the first quarter mile with him.

"I wish I was going with you," she murmured.

"So do I," he admitted, "but it's better if I go alone. I figure it's about 80 miles to the wagon. If I walk four miles an hour, it'll be tomorrow afternoon before I get there. That means I have to sleep alone tonight."

"I'll be thinking of you every minute," she whispered.

"Don't go to sleep tonight without looking at the moon," he whispered back. "I'll be looking at it too, and thinking of you."

"Please, my lover, fare well. Fare well for both of us."

He kissed her gently and glided his hands up and down her back. She hugged him hard and kissed him hard in return. Then he still held her arms as he looked into her eyes and filled his memory with the image of her face.

"After this is over," she pleaded, "let's promise ourselves we'll never again be more than one day's walk away from where we want to be. And I want to be with you, always."

Touched by her words, he nodded his assent, his

glistening eyes communicating to her his feelings.

"I'd better go now," he said. "The sooner I go, the sooner I'll get back. Let's both turn around and go. No looking back. Promise?"

"Promise."

With one more quick kiss, they separated and both turned and started walking. Each step he took away from her was more difficult than the last, until finally he could not resist turning to watch her depart. Having already succumbed to the same attraction, she was standing at a distance and watching him go away.

He took a deep breath at the sight of her; and then, sadly, he shook his head at their mutual deception. She gave him a tiny wave, not raising her hand higher than her waist. He waved back, once, and, with a deep breath, turned hard and continued walking away. He did not turn around again. He did not see her feeble wave good-bye continue, and only when he was at a great distance did her hand slowly fall to her side.

Jim walked straight down the middle of the road, staying atop the yellow dividing line, as fast as he could without breaking into a run. Within 20 minutes, his legs started to ache, but he maintained his pace and the pain became tolerable, just a part of the total routine. He walked without stopping, without resting, through the noonday sun, slowing his pace only when he took a sip of water or a bite of food, and then speeding up again.

The road was straight, and Missy watched him walk away till he was no more than a speck, and she even took a few more steps in his direction to prolong the moment. When she no longer could delude herself that she was still able to see him, she turned around and walked back to the truck.

Anitra met her in the road near the truck.

"He'll be fine," Anitra offered.

"Thank you," Missy answered. "Thank you for saying that."

The two women sat down under a tree, not far from the truck, and they were joined by Susan.

"Dave's packing what he wants to take with him," Susan explained. "This time I thought maybe he actually would prefer to be alone."

Some time later David joined them. He set a duffel bag on the ground, near the truck.

"Is that everything you're bringing?" Missy asked.

"It's all my clothes and the rest of my food," David answered. "I thought about bringing my telescope and my radio, but you probably won't have enough room."

"We'll fit them in," Missy assured him.

"My stamp collection, too?" he asked.

"That too," Missy said.

"I'll go get them. I want to get everything together now."

He started to walk back across the field.

"Wait a minute," Missy said. "Does your radio still work?"

"There might be enough gasoline to use it one more time," David answered.

"Leave it till last," Missy told him.

There was little for them to do. David brought the rest of his gear, except for his short-wave radio. Instead of a regular meal, they ate small amounts, sporadically. In the late afternoon, David passed the time by again tinkering with the truck. Susan stayed close to him, asking him questions, handing him tools.

David drained the fuel lines and cleaned out the fuel filters. He asked Susan to get in and push the ignition switch. She did, and with almost no hesitation, the truck roared to life.

Startled, Missy and Anitra jumped up and ran over to David. Behind the wheel, Susan was both frightened and delighted.

"What do I do now?" she squealed, waving her hands.

"Don't touch anything," Missy shouted.

Susan joined them in front of the truck; and, over the noise of the engine, they proclaimed their joy. Spontaneously, Susan gave David a hug. He turned red and awkwardly, then enthusiastically, hugged her back.

They loaded everything into the truck, and Missy drove it down the highway and over the dirt road back to the farm. She left the engine running while everyone went into the barn.

David pulled the cord on the generator, once, twice, with studied determination a third time, and it started running. An electric light came on in the corner.

"Hurry," David yelled. "It won't last long."

"What do I do?" Missy asked, excited.

David threw a switch on the radio.

"Just push the button and talk," he answered.

Missy spoke into the microphone.

"Hello, hello," she said. "Bess? Kate? This is Missy. Everything's okay. Everyone's fine. We're coming back! We've got to find Jim, and then we're coming back! We're all okay. We'll be back soon. And we've got a surprise! We'll see you soon."

Missy handed the microphone to Susan; but, before she could even start to speak, the generator sputtered, sputtered and died. The light in the corner went out.

Back in town, at the power plant, the little receiver was turned on, and the sound of Missy's voice coming from it spread out through the room.

The empty room. No one was there to hear it, to learn of their success, to be uplifted by Missy's jubilance.

At the farm, they unhooked the transmitter and packed it in the truck with the rest of David's gear, and then they started on their way back. In her enthusiasm, Missy ground the gears and made the truck shudder and bounce as they were getting going; but soon she settled down and moved the semi smoothly back onto the main road.

She re-crossed the bridge over the freeway slowly and carefully. David was the only one who had not yet seen the grim and endless line of cars, and he was the only one who looked to the sides as they passed over.

"Lord, help us," escaped from his lips at the first sight of the cars, and then he fell silent. No one else in the semi was able to invest more than the briefest glance at the horrendous sight.

Once past the bridge, Missy increased the speed, and

soon they were traveling sixty miles an hour heading back south. As the speed increased, so did her heartbeat. She sounded the horn at intersections, at billboards, at nothing at all.

Twenty minutes passed.

"How soon before you think we'll find him?" Susan asked.

"Soon," Missy answered. "Soon."

"I wonder how far he got?" Anitra wondered.

"He figured he could walk about four miles an hour," Missy responded.

"It's been almost eight hours since he left," David said. "It's nearly six p.m."

"Eight hours," Missy figured, "thirty-two miles. And we're going a mile a minute. We should catch up to him soon."

"It's amazing," Anitra observed. "We're going to do in a half hour what took him all day. What a difference!"

The miles slipped by. There was no sign of Jim. Missy had stopped sounding the horn. The sky was darkening, and a few storm clouds appeared.

"It's going to rain soon," Missy moaned. "I hope we find him before he gets wet."

"Maybe he stopped for the night," Anitra offered. "Maybe he got tired. We might have passed him already."

"No," Missy declared. "He's still on the road. He wouldn't quit until the sun abandons him. He's still walking."

More miles passed beneath them. The road ahead

remained empty.

"Maybe we should turn around," Susan ventured. "He'll feel terrible if he's off the road somewhere, and he saw us pass him."

Missy slowed down.

"I don't see how..." Missy's voice quavered. "He knew we were waiting for him. He wouldn't have quit till he had to."

"Then where is he?" Anitra demanded.

Missy slowed down further, but she kept the truck moving. No one spoke. The silence they maintained became a physical presence, a grim specter riding along with their hopes. The truck moved as if it was floating an inch above the ground, on a dense cushion of air. The wind whipped through the windows and tousled the riders' hair.

Another mile passed, and another.

Then Missy's back straightened, and she gripped the wheel harder.

"There," she exclaimed. "There he is! He's ahead of us!"

Missy pressed down hard on the accelerator, and the semi obediently surged forward.

"Where?" Anitra asked. "I don't see him."

"He's on the road," Missy shouted. "He's still walking!"

Susan and Anitra exchanged questioning glances.

"I don't see anything," Susan offered. "Are you sure?"

Missy sounded a long blast on the air horn and shifted into a higher gear. Soon the speed was approaching fifty miles an hour.

On the road ahead, a minute speck on the horizon became more and more distinct as the truck barreled forward.

"I see him now!" Susan called out. "It is him!"

Missy sounded the horn again; and, away in the distance, the figure turned in their direction. As the truck approached, Jim stepped to the driver's side of the road. Missy maintained most of the speed until they got within a few hundred feet, and then she stood on the brakes. The truck shuddered to a halt as it pulled up alongside Jim.

Missy was smiling broadly, but she refused to look at Jim. Instead, she just sat there, in the driver's seat, looking straight ahead, with both of her arms resting on the top of the wheel.

Jim stood with his hands on his hips, waiting for her to speak, but she just kept smiling and looking straight ahead.

When he couldn't take it any more, he opened with, "Well?"

She looked at him, her face aglow in her happiness.

"Hey, stranger, would you like a ride?" she teased.

"I dunno," he responded. "I was really kind of enjoying the walk."

"I'll let you drive," she purred.

He leapt to accept, saying "Okay" as he was reaching up to pull open the door.

Susan voluntarily moved into the back, and Missy slid over. Jim climbed into the driver's seat, and Missy greeted him with open arms and a kiss.

"Welcome back," she murmured, her face now buried against his neck. "I missed you."

"I'm glad to see you too," he breathed in her ear, and then he returned her kiss. "I'm glad to see all of you," he added, louder.

"Did you enjoy your walk?" Susan chirped.

"Not really." Jim's voice was somber. "It's the first time I realized how very quiet it is. Except for the wind, there was nothing making any sounds, anywhere. You realize how alone you are; and, once that takes hold, it keeps getting worse. I felt like I was standing on the top of the planet, but I didn't belong—a lump that wasn't supposed to be there. I started thinking that, any minute, a big club was going to come swinging out of the sky and knock me out into space."

No one knew how to respond.

Jim shrugged and continued, "I guess I've been thinking too much today. I don't like being alone. I'm glad you found me."

Missy put both of her hands around his arm and leaned her head on his shoulder. He put the truck in gear and started it down the roadway. Missy reached for the air horn and sounded a long blast.

"We're coming home!" she shouted.

They told Jim about what he had missed, that David had fixed the truck and that they had made one last quick broadcast to town, saying that they were on the way back.

"They'll be expecting us," Missy said. "I bet they'll even paint a 'Welcome Home' banner."

"We'll find out soon," Jim replied. "We should be back to the station wagon in twenty minutes, and an hour after that we should be back in town."

Just as they had started to settle into the monotony of the drive, a sudden flash of brown and white appeared on the road, just in front of Jim. They heard a yelp and a crunch as the cab registered a barely perceptible bump.

"What the…!" Jim cried, and he slammed on the brakes. By the time the rig came to a stop, it had traveled another tenth of a mile.

Jim got out and examined the front of the truck, but nothing looked any different. Back in the road, he saw a brown and white lump.

Missy got out and stood next to Jim. They both looked back down the road, where nothing was moving. There was no easy place to turn the truck around; so, grimly, they started to walk back. The others got out and followed them.

As they got closer, Missy allowed Jim to take the lead; and he advanced just far enough to see what had been a dog, its body now exploded and its thick blood flowing slowly across the cruel concrete. Jim backed away and sat down at the edge of the road, his head down. Missy sat next to him.

Undaunted, David ventured closer to the bloody mess, followed by both Anitra and Susan.

"It was a beagle," David said.

Susan looked over David's shoulder at it.

"Ohhhh," was all she said. And she turned her face away.

"I wonder how it got here," Anitra asked. "Where has it been all this time?"

"It doesn't matter where it's been," Jim moaned. "I killed it, and we can't bring it back." He buried his head in his hands, and his words were muffled. "I didn't see it. I didn't see it until the last second."

He shook his head slowly.

"It wasn't your fault," Susan soothed. "None of us saw it either, not until it was too late. You couldn't help it."

Jim looked up at Susan, and shook his head again. "I just don't understand. If only I'd seen it sooner. It would still be alive now. Why did it live this long? What good did it do that it outlasted all the other dogs on the planet by five months, only to die…like this. What's the point?"

His question went unanswered. Missy put her arm around his shoulder. He was numb to her touch. She stayed next to him, holding him, waiting for his grief to ebb.

Susan wandered into the field. Anitra and David walked a short way down the road, away from the dead dog.

Jim remained with his head down, staring at nothing more than the gravel between his feet. Missy stroked the hair at the base of his skull, and she rested her head on his shoulder.

Susan was pointing excitedly at something in the field, and David and Anitra ran over to her, where they all bent over to examine something concealed in the tall grass.

Jim still hadn't raised his head, and Missy had hooked

her arm in his and was just holding on to him, rocking gently. He didn't see the others walking back until Susan's tanned legs entered his blurred field of vision. Abruptly, Susan bent down and shoved something brown and soft and fuzzy close to Jim's face. He looked up, and the brown and soft and fuzzy thing licked his nose.

"Baby beagles," Susan declared. "Four of them!"

Jim took the beagle and held its little body in both of his hands. It squirmed, excitedly licked at his hands, and tried to chew on his thumb with its tiny, sharp teeth. Jim looked around. Anitra was holding another one, and David had two.

"Baby beagles," Jim repeated, dazed.

He held the little dog against his face, and it wiggled happily and scratched at his chin with its muddy paws. David handed another puppy to Missy, and she held it high up, and it tried unsuccessfully to run, its tiny feet chugging through the empty air. Missy brought it down and nuzzled its face.

"They're weaned," David said, "But just recently. They look healthy, but I bet they could use some puppy chow."

Susan crouched down in front of Jim and Missy, reached out to the puppy Jim was holding, and rubbed its little head with her finger.

"Maybe the mother knew she couldn't feed them anymore, and she wanted us to take over," Susan said. "Maybe she was desperate."

Jim stroked the puppy under its chin while Susan continued to scratch its head.

"Maybe," Jim sighed. "Maybe. But still she didn't have to die like that."

Anitra spoke softly, "When you're doing something for your loved ones, you don't always stop to think of the consequences."

No one had a response for what Anitra had said. Jim shook his head sadly, and he held the puppy back up to his face.

It was rapidly getting dark, both because of the departing sun and the arrival of black storm clouds. Everyone walked back to the truck, each carrying a puppy except Susan, who petted the one that David had. As they reached the truck, it started to rain heavily.

They clambered inside—five people with four puppies. David was the last one in: and, as soon as he closed the door, an enormous lightning bolt cracked open the sky, followed instantly by thunder that shook the truck.

Inside, it was dry and comfortable. There was a faint musty aroma from the sprinkling that fell on people and dogs before they reached shelter.

David turned on the windshield wipers, and everyone watched as wave after wave of rain washed down the road and splattered the windshield.

"I don't feel like gong on," Jim said. "In the dark, with the storm, we might miss the station wagon."

"Besides," Missy added, "It wouldn't be the triumphant return I'd hoped for."

They decided to spend the night where they were and complete their journey in the morning. When the darkness became profound, David turned off the windshield wipers and turned on the overhead lights. The storm was less violent now, but the raindrops continued to beat in a steady rhythm against the roof of the cab.

The puppies wasted no time exploring their new surroundings, and one person or another was constantly calling for the roll of paper towels, to clean up their tiny messes.

"Their mother could have trained them better," Susan pretended to scold, as she held her puppy up in the air, and it tried to lick her face from too far away.

"That's our job, now," Missy said. "Welcome to motherhood."

Everyone laughed.

The puppies became full-time entertainment, as the spotlight of attention traveled amongst them to the one putting on the best show from moment to moment. Tugging large objects, falling down, and getting into impossibly tight places were the most popular diversions.

Susan shared the truck seat with David. Jim was on the bed, between Missy and Anitra. The tattoo sound of the rain and Jim's gentle stroking of the dog on top of him soon lulled Jim to sleep; and the puppy on his chest fell asleep, too.

Missy and Anitra reduced their conversation to a whisper, which added to the feeling of somnolence that pervaded their chamber.

One by one, Missy handed the puppies down to Susan, who gave them each a bit of special attention before laying them on the floor near her, where they snuggled up with each other for warmth and went to sleep. Missy took the puppy from Jim's chest last. Jim muttered when the puppy was removed, but he didn't wake up. Then, Missy curled up near Jim, with her arm around him. Anitra mirrored Missy, except just her hand was resting on Jim's arm. Susan and David went to sleep with their backs against their respective doors, their legs intertwined.

The night-long sound of the rain patterned their dreams. It was a constant that enveloped them and defined for them that this comfortable, dry truck was the only right place for them to be for as long as the storm lasted. It was the center of their universe, the only habitable place that existed.

The night passed and morning came. The dark clouds were replaced by whiter, fluffier versions.

Left undisturbed, the people would have slept later; but, at first light, the puppies staged a surprise attack on every finger, nose, or ear that was left unprotected. Within minutes, everyone in the truck was awake with a single purpose—dealing with the squirming bundles of fur.

They ate a quick breakfast, the last of their food, some of which went to the dogs.

"Food went quicker than we thought," Jim said.

"We've got nine mouths to feed now," Missy answered. "But we'll be home soon."

David made a few make-shift leashes so they could walk the dogs without letting them get away. Quietly, he also took care to bury the puppies' mother, though Susan saw him do it and stood a respectful distance away while he finished.

"All set?" she asked, as he walked towards her.

"Yeah, all set," David answered, surprised at having been caught. Susan took his arm, and they walked back to the truck together.

Susan and David got in the back of the truck. Missy

drove, and Jim sat next to her. Anitra was by the passenger window, and the puppies went wherever they wanted, though Jim took care to keep them out from under Missy's feet and the truck's pedals.

The engine started at once; and, after less than twenty minutes traveling, they found the place where they'd left the station wagon.

This time Missy was out of quarters, so Jim smashed the vending machine; and they unloaded all the candy.

Susan agreed to drive the station wagon, and David and two puppies went with her. Missy led the way with the semi.

Within an hour, they were approaching the bridge next to the power plant, but no one came out to wave at them. She continued driving.

"Well, they didn't make a 'Welcome Home' banner," Missy complained, as they approached the town. She sounded the air horn again.

Missy drove along the curb on the left side of the road and stopped in the second block, just by the gas station. Susan pulled up alongside.

No one was in sight.

Missy shut off the truck, and dead silence greeted them. Nothing was moving except, one block ahead, the stoplight changed from green, to amber, to red.

Everyone got out. Anitra and David went into the gas station to find the dogs some water. Missy and Susan started walking up the street. Jim positioned himself in between and watched both pairs of people. Missy and Susan kept walking, and Jim took a few steps closer to them.

From behind the building next to the gas station, Bess stuck her head out and waved her arm frantically.

"Hey, c'mere, c'mere, come over here!" Bess shouted.

Missy and Susan both stopped walking and looked at her; but they were slow to react to the panic in Bess's voice.

Bess quickly looked around, ran out to the street where they were, grabbed each one's hand, screamed "Hurry!" and dragged them back behind the building.

"Run, Jim!" Bess shouted over her shoulder.

Seeing their panic, Jim hunched down and looked for danger before he too ran for shelter behind the building.

"Bess, what is it?" Missy shouted. "What's the matter?"

"It's Harry," Bess said. "He's gone crazy! He's locked himself in the store. He won't let anyone have any food. And he's got a gun."

"Where is everybody?" Missy asked. "Is everyone okay?"

"No one's hurt," Bess answered, "but we're hungry. We ran out of food yesterday. We're all inside here, inside the doctor's office. We take turns watching, because we're afraid Harry might come out after us. So far, he's stayed inside; but he won't let anybody in."

"How long has this been going on?" Jim asked.

"Since right after you left," Bess said. That first day Harry just started acting strange, told us we'd have to come back the next day for groceries. But the next day he told us we couldn't have any, that he was saving all the food for him and

Frank."

"Frank's in there too?" Jim asked.

"Yes, the two of them," Bess said. "Anyway, when Kate said she was just going to take some food, Harry pulled the rifle out from behind the counter and pointed it at her. He said if she didn't leave, he was going to shoot her right there. He pushed her out of the store. We got together across the street from the store to talk about it, and he shot at us a couple of times. We scattered, and we've been hiding and standing watch ever since."

Anitra had been watching them from inside the gas station, and she stuck her head out the door and called, "Is everything okay?"

They all shouted at her to get back inside, and Jim told her to go out the back door and come around. Anitra pulled her head back in, but as she was closing the door, one of the dogs squeezed out and stayed outside.

Anitra got down on her hands and knees and tried to coax the dog back inside; but, after a few playful leaps at her, its attention was diverted, and it wandered out into the street and began sniffing around. Anitra still tried to call it to her, but the others shouted at her to go inside, and she did.

Anitra and David took the three remaining dogs, went out the back of the gas station, and joined the others behind the doctor's office. The lone dog was cavorting in the street in front of the gas station.

"We've got to save it," Susan cried. "It might get shot."

The puppy began sniffing along an unseen trail until it reached a crack in the pavement, then it jumped at an invisible foe and scampered off in another direction.

"Someone do something," Susan pleaded.

"Wait a minute," David said.

He tied together all of his make-shift leashes and attached them to another of the dogs, which he fed a piece of chocolate and then let it wander out just to the end of the protection of the building. Before long it was playing and exploring; and, after several long moments, the first puppy joined it and sniffed at its mouth. David pulled the leash in, the first dog followed, and Susan grabbed it. It licked happily at the several hands that reached out to pet it.

Susan placed her hand on David's arm and let him see the admiration in her eyes. He returned a boyish grin.

The group moved through the back door to the inside of the doctor's office. The room contained the rest of the town's people, except for Harry and Frank. The blinds were drawn, and the room was only dimly lit by the small amount of sunlight that was able to pass through. Sleeping bags on the floor testified that they had been sleeping there when they weren't on vigil.

Kate and Pamela were standing at different corners and peering through the blinds toward the market.

The return of the search party generated excitement, and the room quickly filled with several simultaneous conversations detailing adventures one group had experienced in the absence of the other. David was introduced around and was welcomed warmly.

The puppies were allowed to scamper, and they found no shortage of hands willing to pet them or arms willing to hold them.

As the exuberant conversations began to subside, the

topic that remained regarded the problem with Harry, and the lack of food.

"We've searched through all the kitchens in town," Kate bemoaned, "but we've already eaten all the food we found. Harry has the only food left."

Missy dumped her purse out on the table. She handed out several candy bars and took an inventory of what was left.

"This won't last the day," Missy said. "We have to force Harry to give us food. Our lives depend on it."

"I tried to force him," Kate said. "I almost got shot."

"Do you think he'd actually shoot one of us?" Susan asked.

"I don't know," Kate answered, "but he scared the hell out of me. He pointed the gun right at me, and the only thing I could see was the end of that barrel. It looked huge. Then he jabbed me with it, and I was afraid the gun would go off, whether Harry meant it to or not. All I could think about was getting away."

"Harry has no more right to that food than anyone else," Allyson declared. "What makes him think he's so special?"

Ernie wiped his hand down the length of his face before saying, "We could rush 'em. Take 'em by surprise. They cain't be watching all the time. We just sneak up on 'em and take the gun away."

"What if someone gets hurt?" Jim asked.

"All we have to do is stand up to him," Allyson said. "Stay together. Tell him how we want it, and that's how it has to be. He has to listen to us, all of us."

193

"Someone has to confront him," Missy added. "I'll bet if someone just stands up to him, Harry will back down."

"It's too dangerous," Jim cautioned. "It's better if we just wait till things calm down, till Harry comes to his senses."

"Without food?" Pamela asked.

"Things are different now," Jim replied. "We can travel. "We didn't pass any supermarkets north of here, but we know the country's full of them. When we find another market, we won't need any of Harry's food. We won't need anything he has."

No one spoke till Allyson said. "I'm hungry now. There's no telling how long it will take for us to find another supermarket."

Several people chimed in that they, too, were hungry.

"Choc'lit bars just don't git it," Ernie intoned.

"Someone has to stand up to Harry," Missy decreed.

After another pause, Anitra volunteered, "I'll go. Harry knows me. I don't think he'll do anything to hurt me."

Anitra took a step toward the door. Missy stood up and took hold of her arm. For a moment they just looked at each other.

"Do you want me to go with you?" Missy asked.

Anitra cast her eyes to the ground, but then she looked up and met Missy's gaze.

"No," Anitra answered, softly. "I'd better go alone. I don't want Harry to feel like we're ganging up on him."

Anitra took another step toward the door, and this time Kate stopped her.

"Are you sure?" Kate asked. "You don't have to do this."

Anitra swallowed, and nodded yes. "I'll get us some food. We'll all feel better after we've eaten. Harry's not a bad guy. He's just a little, well, strange. He just needs to feel like he fits in. Maybe I can get him to come out."

At the market, Harry and Frank were together in the small meeting room in the corner of the building. Frank was hunched up in the corner in front of the counter. Harry was sitting on the floor under the window with his arm resting on the ledge. An empty vodka bottle lay sideways on the floor near him, and an all-but-full bottle was on the ledge near his arm. A single-shot rifle was propped up against the ledge.

"You keep watchin', Frank, keep watchin'," Harry growled. "We can't let 'em sneak up on us."

"They must be hungry, Harry," Frank whined.

"They're not," Harry shot back. "They don't need us. They don't wanna have anything to do with us. We gotta take care of ourselves. They don't care about us, and we don't care about them. They don't understand. No one understands."

"I'm tired of watching," Frank whimpered.

"Just watch, will you!"

Frank kept watching, and Harry's head slumped down onto the window ledge. His eyes were half closed.

Across the street, Anitra opened the door of the doctor's office and stepped out onto the sidewalk. Coming from the darkened room, she was temporarily blinded by the sunlight. She stood there with her hand up to her eyes, shielding them from the sun.

The many gold chains she wore around her neck glistened. Her shoulders were bare. The gold chain she wore around her waist sparkled. Her stomach was bare. As she lowered her hand from her face, the rings she wore on every finger captured the yellow light, concentrated it, and sent it shooting out in all directions.

Haltingly, Anitra started walking toward the market. She stepped one foot off the curb and hesitated, searching the building across the street for any sign of activity.

"She's out there," Frank whispered loudly to Harry, who shook himself alert, rubbed his eyes, looked out, and rubbed his eyes again. He reached for the gun.

"Harry?" Anitra called out, too softly to be heard, then louder she said, "Harry? It's all right. Let me come in. Everything's okay. I've got things to tell you. A lot has happened."

She stepped off the curb and walked carefully toward the market. When she reached the traffic island in the middle of the street, she put one foot on the curb and hesitated again.

Harry shouted at her.

"Go away!" he screamed. "Leave us alone!"

Without advancing further, Anitra kept talking.

"I'm real hungry, Harry," she pleaded. "Everyone is. I don't want to be hungry. It scares me. Please let me in, Harry. *Please*. We just need a little. Please Harry. Please."

She stepped up onto the curb and took a few more steps forward.

"Go away!" Harry shouted. "Go away!"

He pulled the trigger. The bullet struck Anitra's left shoulder, and she twisted around and back.

"Oh no, noooo," Anitra cried.

She placed her right hand on her injured shoulder and slowly sank to her knees.

Harry fumbled, hurrying to reload the gun.

Inside the doctor's office, Missy bolted to her feet and moved as if to go out the door to Anitra. Jim grabbed her around the waist and held her until she yielded, turned around, and, crying, hugged him. She buried her head against his shoulder, and he continued to look out through the blinds at the scene unfolding on the street.

"No Harry, Harry no!" Anitra screamed. Please don't. I just want…please, Harry, please! Don't hurt me."

Still holding her shoulder with her right hand, she reached out with her left hand, supplicating, and, on her knees, she moved toward the shadowy figures in the market.

"Please Harry," Anitra cried, as she crawled forward on her knees. "Please don't shoot me again. Please, not again. Please help me!"

"No!" Harry screamed, and he pulled the trigger again.

The next bullet entered her stomach. The force of it made her double over, and her hands jerked down to clutch her wounded abdomen. Her face registered surprise, that transitioned into pain, as she gently swayed and then toppled forward into the dirt.

Inside the market, Frank was crying.

"Geez, Harry," Frank sobbed. "You got her right in the belly."

"What? Who? Did I?" Harry called out, looking frantically from the window to Frank and back again.

Frank continued crying and did not answer. Harry squinted more and struggled to see.

Clutching her stomach with one hand, Anitra tried to drag herself forward with the other, but wasn't strong enough.

"Please, oh please," she whispered.

With a cry of pain, she abandoned holding her wound, and used both hands to drag her body forward, a few inches at a time, crawling through the dirt, which mixed with her blood to form lumps of black mud. She crawled until she reached the far curb of the traffic island, and the roughness of it against her cheek made her stop. She lay there with her hands dangling over the curb.

"Oh no," she moaned. "Oh please."

Anitra continued to groan softly, but the profound silence that surrounded her allowed her moans to be heard on both sides of the street.

The silent audience inside the doctor's office continued looking out the windows, as if watching a play, waiting for the next act, which was slow to begin.

With her head cushioned against Jim's chest, Missy's

voice was muffled.

"We've got to help her. We've got to…do something."

Jim shook his head. "What can we do? He's got the only gun. It's just too dangerous."

"But she's still alive," Missy pleaded. "Maybe we can save her! We can't just leave her out there and wait for her to bleed to death!"

Missy eased out of his arms and stood facing him, holding his hands in hers. He looked at her eyes, the light shining from them. He looked at their hands, hers—small, white, delicate—his—large, mottled, rough. The union of their hands became the focal point of his world, the center of all gravity. Everything that had been, everything that would be, was now being drawn in to this one place, the center of their universe. He looked back at her gleaming eyes.

"Stay here," he whispered. "Maybe I can do…something."

The silent audience watched Jim as he went to the back door and opened it. He turned to look back at the people he was leaving, especially at the woman, so beautiful, so vulnerable.

"Stay together," he cautioned. "If he tries to come in here, together you can overpower him."

Jim went out and closed the door behind him.

He was gone, and the room was silent. Missy looked around, and all eyes were on her. She looked at each of their faces without seeing any of them. She looked at the back door, through its window, trying to see what was beyond.

With his absence, she realized, "I have to go with him."

Both Kate and Bess moved to intercept her.

"You can't," Kate decreed. "It's too dangerous. He told you to stay here."

"Don't go, Missy," Bess pleaded. "You can't help him."

Missy's focus moved from the door to Bess's face.

"Maybe I can't help," she admitted, "but I still have to be with him. Whatever happens, it's got to happen to us together."

Bess was holding on to Missy's arm, but let it slip through her fingers as Missy made her way to the back door. When Missy opened the door, she turned to smile encouragement to Bess, and then slipped out.

Those who remained returned to their vigil at the windows.

By the time Missy was outside, Jim was already out of sight; and Missy had to guess which way she thought he must have taken.

Jim had made his way behind the building to the middle of the next block, where he was able to cross the street without being in the line of fire. He worked his way back to the customer entrance of the market, where he hugged the building, waiting for the pounding in his chest to abate. With shaking hand, he tried the main door, which was locked; and he quickly darted back to the relative safety of the side of the building. His breathing was rapid and hard.

He looked around him, left, right, over his shoulder, even up; then, with one more deep breath, he grabbed a portable sign cemented into an old wheel, charged the door, and smashed the window in it.

The glass scattered in all directions, and huge, jagged chunks of it clung to the door, but Jim smashed them aside and dove through the space and into the store. He scrambled past the inside door and quickly ducked down behind the closest check-out counter.

He held onto the counter. His eyes were just peering over it and his lip was pressed against the dirty black bumper along the edge, caked with the dirt and sweat of countless past customers. Breathing hard, he whispered over and over, "Oh damn, oh damn, oh damn, oh damn, oh damn."

He wondered about getting shot, how much would it hurt, how quickly would he die? Would he have time to say good-bye to…well…Missy? She was the only one he couldn't bear the thought of not being able to say good-bye to, just one last time, not for his sake but for hers, just to be able to tell her that it was okay, everything was okay, before it was all over.

He held on there until the pounding in his heart lessened. Then he zigzagged from check-out lanes to aisles back and forth, working his way closer to the corner where the meeting room was. Every time he stopped, he repeated to himself the litany, "Oh damn, oh damn, oh damn."

As he got close to the meeting room door, he planned escape routes, short runs, places he could dart to, get out of the line of fire, not be trapped, have another short run, and another, stay ahead of a man with a gun, not be a target.

At the last aisle before the door, he grabbed his only weapon, two cans of soup and, in a crouch, worked his way the final distance to the door and touched the knob with his hand. He bowed his head and took a final deep breath.

Jim burst the door open and hurled both the cans of soup into the room. He tried to pull the door closed again, but his own foot was in the way, so he wound up bouncing against the jam and falling down, on his hands and knees, inside the room.

But Jim's fears, and his heroics, were both unnecessary. Harry was passed out, harmlessly, the second vodka bottle, now half-empty, still in his hand. The gun was at his feet. Frank was curled up in the corner, crying softly to himself.

Jim kept his eyes on Harry and slowly crawled forward on his hands and knees. As Jim touched the butt of the rifle, Harry opened his eyes; and Jim froze while the two men looked at each other. But Harry did not even try to move; and, after a moment, he closed his eyes again. Jim pulled the gun away and, still on his hands and knees, began backing out of the room, sliding the gun alongside.

Just as Jim was back even with the counter, Missy burst into the room. Frank jerked, and Jim spun around on the floor and held out his hands to protect himself. When he saw that it was Missy, his hands dropped limply at his side, and he smiled weakly. Missy knelt down and bent over to hold him. By now he was shaking, and he had difficulty hugging her back. She helped him to his feet, and he held on to her with his face buried between her shoulder and neck. She kissed his ear and his chin, and she bent down and picked up the rifle.

Harry showed no signs of moving, and Missy and Jim went to the front door, opened it, and stepped out onto the street. Jim and Missy walked arm-in-arm. Missy carried the rifle. Across the street, as soon as they saw Missy and Jim emerge from the market, they came pouring out of the doctor's office. The two groups met in the middle of the street, at the traffic island where Anitra still lay, moaning.

Together, Kate and Pamela rolled Anitra over. Her

abdomen was caked with mud and blood. At the sight, Missy's legs buckled, and she almost slipped out of Jim's arms; but he caught her, took the rifle from her, and eased her down so that they could sit on the curb. Sick, she sat with one hand holding her stomach and the other pressed against her lips, and he massaged the back of her neck.

With help from Susan, Ernie picked Anitra up and carried her to the doctor's office.

"What about Harry?" Kate asked Jim. "What did you do to him?"

Jim shook his head. "Nothing. He was passed out when I got to him. He's still inside with Frank."

"We'll have to watch him," Kate cautioned. "We can't trust him. We have to guard him."

Bob offered to keep watch over Harry. The rest, except for Jim and Missy, followed Ernie and Susan into the doctor's office.

Ernie took Anitra into one of the examining rooms and put her on the table. Everyone stood around watching while, with Susan's help, Bess tried to clean Anitra's wounds. She daubed some alcohol on her, and Anitra wrenched so violently that she almost came off the table. Jim and Missy came and stood in the doorway. Bess stopped using the alcohol and stood by with the cloth in her hands, tears rolling down her face. Occasionally, weakly, she tried to clean Anitra's body but stayed well away from the places where she was wounded.

"I don't know what to do," Bess cried. "I don't know anything about this."

"You're all we have, Bess," Missy said, softly.

"It's hopeless," Bess sobbed. "I don't know what I'm doing. All I've studied so far is medicines, prescription drugs. I thought that's what I'd most likely need. I never expected a gunshot wound. I can't do it!"

"You know as much about it as any of us," Jim soothed. "You have to try."

"What if I kill her?" Bess cried. "She's still alive now, but I might be the one who kills her. The bullet is still in her. She might be bleeding internally. She'll die if the damage isn't fixed, but I can't do that. That's… that's surgery!"

"If we don't act," Pamela said, "she might die anyway. It'll just be slower."

Bess sat on a stool next to the examining table and hung her head.

"I can't do it," she moaned.

Missy whispered to Jim that she was feeling faint, and he took her back to the waiting room, and they sat down. Kate used the opportunity to move everyone else out of the examining room, except Bess and Susan.

As she was leaving, Kate put her hand on Bess's shoulder.

"You're not alone," Kate comforted. "We'll think of something. For now, just help her hold on."

Susan and Bess were alone in the room with Anitra. Susan tried to clean Anitra's shoulder wound, and Bess sat by without moving. David walked up, stood in the doorway, and watched. Susan acknowledged his presence with a nod, and Bess glanced at him once but hung her head again. David cleared his throat.

"Can I help?" he asked, meekly.

"Sure," Bess answered, bitterly, "if you've got a medical degree."

"No," David shook his head. "No." He scuffed his toe across the floor. "But I always used to help the vet when he came to our farm, though. I was with him when our calf was born. And I helped him when some hunter accidentally shot our dog."

Bess looked at him. "Then you can do it."

David was enthusiastic. "I'll help. I'll help. Maybe if we work together…"

"I don't even know how to start," Bess uttered, plaintively.

"You have to probe the wound," David offered. "And the vet used an ether drip to keep my dog from moving, while he was working. And we have to wash our hands first, as clean as we can get them."

"We have ether," Bess said, meekly.

Susan latched onto David's momentum. "You two go clean up. I can stay here with Anitra, and I can start the ether drip."

As Bess led David through the waiting room to the next examining room, where they could scrub up, she bemoaned, "I don't even know what a bullet looks like."

Bess and David disappeared into the second examining room, but Ernie took Bess's words as his cue. He asked Jim for the rifle, and Jim gave it to him. It was an old, small, single-shot .22 caliber. There was a bullet in the chamber.

Ernie took the gun outside and fired it into the ground, then dug through the dirt until he found the slug. He returned the gun to Jim and stood waiting for Bess to come back out.

There was only one sink in the second examination room, so David stood by while Bess was scrubbing her hands and arms up to the elbows.

"I can't do this," Bess bemoaned. "I don't know why I'm pretending I can."

"You shouldn't be afraid," David whispered.

Focusing on her task, Bess answered bitterly, "Tell me one reason why I shouldn't."

David crossed and uncrossed his arms, and then he put his hands in his pockets. He kept his head down as he spoke.

"My mom and I had this refrigerator," he began. "We were having hard times, sometimes we didn't have enough money to buy food. That refrigerator was so old. My ma had gotten it long before I was born. It never quit running, but it had been around so long and it had been opened and closed so many times that the hinges on the door had worn clean through, and the door started to come off, first just at the bottom, but that made the top hinge wear quicker. For a while, we were holding the door on with a rope, but the rope didn't work very well, and the refrigerator was running all the time.

"My mom had gotten some replacement hinges somewhere, I don't know where, and she thought I could put them on, but the screws were attached from the inside of the door. It looked impossible. There was no way to do it. I was afraid that if I took it apart and couldn't get it back together again, it would mean that my mother and I were going to starve.

"So we kept using the rope, and after a while the door fell off completely. My mom found the money somewhere, and she managed to buy a new refrigerator on time payments. One of the neighbors helped me haul the old one out to the barn.

"But after that old refrigerator was sitting there, unplugged, and we didn't need it anymore, I took the door apart and I fixed it in about a half hour. It was so easy! It's been working in our barn, keeping my pop cold, ever since."

Bess had finished washing up and stood drying her hands and looking at David. He stepped up to the sink and started his ablutions.

Without turning around, he concluded, "If I hadn't been afraid, I could've helped my mother a lot more than I did. I feel bad about it now. But fear is no reason to not try."

Bess waited in silence while David finished washing. She smiled a nervous smile at him.

"I guess I do have to try, don't I?"

David nodded.

As they passed through the waiting room on the way back to Anitra, Ernie was waiting for them, proudly displaying the .22 caliber slug.

"So small!" Bess declared. "I didn't think it would be so small."

In the now-designated operating room, Susan had been busy collecting anything she thought might be needed—sealed pouches, complete kits for minor surgery, swabs, a bottle of hydrogen peroxide. She had also found and opened a bottle of ether, and its distinctive aroma wafted through the room. David began dripping ether onto gauze that covered Anitra's mouth and nose.

Susan dripped peroxide onto the hole in Anitra's stomach, and Bess cleaned away the last of the blood.

"The wound looks so small," Bess exclaimed. "Even smaller than the bullet."

Bess leaned over Anitra with a probe in hand.

"Heaven help us," Bess whispered.

Bess began exploring the wound. It started bleeding again, and Susan washed more peroxide in. Bess kept probing.

"This is so…I don't know…wait…I think," Bess said. "Yes, it's here. The bullet's right here. I can get it!"

Bess used forceps, tried once, twice, pulled, and then fumbled, but the dull gray bullet dropped out of the forceps and onto Anitra's stomach.

"It's out!" Bess shouted. "It hardly went in at all! I got it out! I didn't think I…wow!"

Only the smallest amount of blood seeped out of the wound.

"It doesn't look bad," Susan observed. "It doesn't look bad at all."

Susan flooded the area with peroxide. They continued working, but Bess decided their best idea was not to probe any deeper, and added a prayer that the injury was not any more serious than it seemed. They put a dressing on Anitra's stomach wound and then cleaned up her shoulder, which proved to be no more than a gash where the bullet had grazed past.

"That's all we can do now," Bess declared. "I'll give her

some antibiotics, and then we'll just have to watch her."

When she finished, Bess leaned over Anitra and squeezed her hand. Weakly, Anitra squeezed back. Before walking out, Bess gave David a long hug, and he blushed and looked shyly at Susan, who was smiling back.

"We got the bullet out," Bess announced to everyone in the waiting room. "It wasn't in very deep at all. I think she's going to be okay. I hope so."

Smiles, cheers, and congratulations greeted Bess's announcement. She sat down next to Missy and Jim.

"I've been looking at this gun," Jim told her. "It's an antique. It's got a patent date on it of Aug. 29, 1899. If the bullets are even half as old as the gun, they wouldn't have very much force left in them."

"Then we got lucky," Bess acknowledged.

"That, and we have you," Jim answered. "Congratulations! It looks like your first operation was a success, doctor."

Bess smiled while shaking her head no.

"It can only get better," she said. "I just hope my next patient is for something simpler, like a headache, or the sniffles."

"As a matter of fact," Missy replied, "I do have a bit of a headache."

Bess jumped up.

"Doctor prescribes two aspirins," she proclaimed. "I'll get them for you." Then as she was walking through the door into the office, she looked over her shoulder and smiled, "I'm getting good at this."

"Go on," Missy laughed.

While Bess was getting the aspirin, Frank walked into the building. He stood before the doorway to the waiting room, where he also was able to see down the hall to the examining room where Susan and David were still with Anitra. Ernie was the first to notice Frank's presence and stood up to confront him.

"What do you want," Ernie growled. "Come here to gloat?"

Frightened, Frank whined, "Bob said I could come over." Then he lowered his eyes to the floor and asked, "Is she dead?"

Ernie wouldn't answer, and Frank refused to raise his head. After standing his ground for a while, Ernie gave up, backed away and sat down. When Frank realized that Ernie was no longer confronting him, he raised his eyes and searched the faces of the people in the room for an answer. Missy finally took pity on him.

"No, Frank," Missy said. "Anitra's not dead. Bess thinks she's going to be okay. At least we all hope so."

"Me too," Frank said, lowering his eyes again.

Bess returned with the aspirin for Missy.

She took one look at Frank, who was swaying mournfully, and said, "You'd better sit down, Frank." She placed her hand on his arm to guide him to a chair.

"You'd better sit down too, Bess," Jim added. "We all need to settle down a little."

Bess took his advice. For a while, no one spoke.

At length, Pamela broke the silence. "I hate to be shallow; but, now that things are under control, am I the only one who's starving?"

They looked at each other, surprised; but Pamela had opened the door to their hunger, and now it filled the room.

"Let's eat," Kate said. "Let's eat well. When we're done, we'll be better able to deal with our other problems."

"Which problems?" Missy asked.

"We're going to have to take turns helping Bess watch Anitra," Kate said. "And we're going to have to do something about Harry."

Allyson and Pamela volunteered to prepare a meal, and they drafted a reluctant but flattered Ernie to help them. They went to the market and traipsed happily from one aisle to the next, filling one shopping cart and part of another with any of the canned goods that caught their attention.

While they were making their selections, Harry staggered out of the meeting room. They remained motionless and watched Bob follow Harry as he stumbled down the aisle and made his way to the store room in back. Harry went inside, and Bob stopped at the doorway. After a moment, Bob turned to the others and said, "He's sleeping again."

More subdued, the three finished choosing their food and left the market.

Allyson and Pamela took the food to the building on the corner diagonal to the market, the Starlit Restaurant, where they began preparing a meal. Ernie returned to the doctor's office, where Jim, Missy, and Kate were still in the waiting room.

211

Frank was sitting quietly in the corner.

"We got to do somethin' 'bout that Harry," Ernie said. "He's jes' wandering around like it don't make no difference, what he did."

"We were just talking about it," Missy said, "Wondering what we can do."

"Well, fer one thing," Ernie growled, "We kin lock him up. It ain't right, what he did, shooting that purty girl like he done. We kin lock him up and keep him from shootin' someone else."

"Not that easy," Jim cautioned. "For one thing, we don't have a jail. And, we don't have a jailer. And we can't just lock him up and be done with it. We've got to watch him, and feed him, and see that he gets exercise, and make sure he doesn't escape. It's a 24-hour-a-day job. And we already have another job caring for Anitra, and another watching the power plant—three round-the-clock jobs—nine eight-hour shifts; and we only have eleven people available. That doesn't leave much time for planning our future, finding more food, producing our own food, and improving our lives."

Susan, who had been listening while tending to Anitra in the next room, appeared at the doorway.

"Maybe we don't have to jail him," she offered. "We could let him take care of himself, we could make him work even, and all we have to do is watch him."

Jim was unconvinced. "Sooner or later we'd let our guard down. We're only human. Then if Harry wanted to do more harm, he could."

"But what harm can he do?" Kate argued. "We have the

only gun, and it should be a simple matter to keep it away from him."

"But is it the only gun?" Jim asked. "A week ago we didn't know it existed. But even if there are no more guns, we can't hide every rock that could bash in a skull, every match that could burn down the town. If someone wants to do damage, they can always find a way."

The conversation had reached an impasse. No one had anything more to suggest until Kate broke the silence.

"We could kill him," she said, simply.

"No!" Frank shouted; but then, startled that he'd attracted any attention, he returned his eyes to the floor and rigorously kept from looking up again.

"We *could* kill him," Jim stretched out every word, "But then that means that we'd need an executioner, someone to pull the trigger."

Jim took a silent poll by looking around the room at the faces of the other people. Susan and Kate were both staring at the floor. Wide-eyed and frightened, Frank darted his glance back and forth; but he was looking at people's shoes, not their faces. Ernie met Jim's gaze, but only briefly, before the felt compelled to look away. Missy was the one who steadfastly returned his look when he turned her way.

With her eyes only on Jim, but spoken so everyone could hear, Missy said, "You have to hate yourself an awful lot to want to kill another human being. I don't think anyone here does."

United through each other's eyes, Jim and Missy held their gaze until their spiritual union was interrupted by Ernie's

213

voice.

"Well, what the hell are we going to do then?" he demanded. "Let him off scot-free? Let him get away with murder? Give him a chance to put a slug into another one of us?"

"We can't just let him off," Kate agreed. "He must be punished, for Anitra's sake, and also for everyone else's safety."

"Well," Missy offered, cautiously, "We could banish him."

"Banish?" Kate asked. "How?"

Missy shrugged. "Give him some food. Take him somewhere so that he doesn't know where he is and can't find his way back."

While Missy's idea settled in. Frank dared to glance up from the floor, fearfully searching the faces in front of him.

"We do seem to have no shortage of unpopulated areas, now," Kate suggested.

"S'pose it could work," Ernie agreed, "S'long as we make *real sure* he cain't find his way back."

"What we have to do now," Kate decided, "is ask the others and see if they approve.

At that moment, Allyson walked in and announced that the food was ready.

Bess didn't want to leave Anitra, but Missy insisted that Bess had been under too mush stress and needed a break. Susan agreed to stay with Anitra, and Missy promised to relieve her soon. Everyone else went across the street to eat.

Missy and Jim walked across the street arm-in-arm.

"I'm glad we're not going to kill Harry," Missy murmured, her head against Jim's shoulder. "It doesn't make sense, killing someone, if you think about how few people are left, when there used to be billions."

"Almost seven billion," David interjected. "And there'll be 80 million more next year...well...I mean, at least, there would have been."

"Seven billion. And now only a dozen," Jim sighed. "It doesn't seem possible we could be talking about the same thing."

The corner restaurant was well-lit and airy, due to window walls along both of the street fronts. Allyson and Pamela had set places at the tables closest to the corner between the window walls, and it made a close-knit, bright, convivial grouping. The women had prepared a smorgasbord of canned vegetables, and also a rice casserole.

"The instructions for the casserole said 'just add meat,' so I had Allyson stick her finger in it," Pamela joked.

The conversation was relaxed and free. They asked about how Jim had subdued Harry, and Jim told them the story, including the part about hurling cans of soup before tripping over his own feet. Bess showed him no mercy when she heard about him throwing soup cans at what he thought was an armed gunman, not knowing that all he was dealing with was a passed-out drunk. She asked him what kind of soup he had used, was "condensed" more deadly than regular? She teased him that right now they may well be eating the contents of one of his chosen weapons. Missy did not join in the banter, but she smiled all the while Jim was being put on the spot.

Gradually, the group relaxed from the tension of the day,

and the conversation slowed. The puppies, who had been banished outside for the duration of the meal, now were let inside and fed table scraps.

Kate talked about the plan for dealing with Harry.

"Isn't that cruel and unusual punishment?" Allyson asked.

"I don't know," Kate responded. "Are we still honoring the constitution?"

"Of course we are," Jim insisted, "especially the Bill of Rights. But there's nothing cruel or unusual about what the rest of us, who have committed no crime, have to face every day—long hours, harsh work, solitude, loneliness. There's nothing unusual about being alone."

"Jim's right," Bess nodded. "We're all in prison, all the time, inside our bodies, in solitary confinement. That's the *usual*. What's rare is the fleeting moment when you feel someone is actually sharing your prison with you."

Missy and Jim snuck glances at each other, while the others, with an assortment of mumbling, sighing, or nodding, provided a crowd's acceptance of what Jim and Bess had said.

"So that's it then," Kate concluded. "We remove Harry from society. How soon do we do it?"

"Tonight," Jim shrugged. "In the dark, so the sun won't give him a clue which way we're going. We'll take the truck and pack it full of food. Since we didn't find a market north of here, we'll take the back roads and head east. If we find a market, far enough away, we'll leave Harry there and bring back as much food as we can carry. Then Harry can spend his days doling out food to himself."

"Why not take the interstate?" Bess asked. "You'll be more likely to find food along a popular route."

Jim was taken aback, realizing they had not yet shared what they had learned on their journey. He looked around at their faces, fixing on Missy and David who understood his discomfort.

"The interstate's impassable," he replied, simply.

The way he said it kept the others from asking any casual questions. Jim said no more, but Missy provided the explanation.

"We found all the cars, and all the people," she began.

Missy told everyone what they had seen on the freeway. The room became deadly silent as she recounted only the sparsest details about the line of cars stretching to the horizon in both directions. When she finished talking, no one spoke. No one was eating anymore; the room was motionless. Pamela picked up a few dirty plates and took them to the kitchen to clean, but the emptiness of that room quickly drove her back to the company in the dining area where she sat, limply, with her head down.

"Thank goodness we have each other," Bess sighed.

As quietly as possible, Jim stood up and pushed his chair under the table.

"I'd better relieve Bob," he said. "He must be very hungry."

Jim gave Bess a hug as he was walking out, and he affectionately caressed the back of Missy's head.

"And I'd better relieve Susan," Missy said.

No one else was in a hurry to leave. They stayed in that sunny room, basking in the communion with their fellow living beings. Bob came in and reported that Harry was sobering up and starting to walk around. Pamela remembered seeing a pair of handcuffs at the novelty store and brought them to Jim, who cuffed a grumbling, but not yet cogent, Harry to a post in the market stockroom. Susan came from the doctor's office and reported that Anitra was awake and had asked for something to eat, and the people in the diner responded warmly to the news. Through the day, the restaurant became the center of the town's activities. People left on errands, but returned to be with the group.

The afternoon meal never ended, but blended into supper. As people got hungry again, at different times, they freely entered the kitchen and prepared more food, always finding someone else to help them consume it. One person's leftover became another's appetizer. There were plenty of requests to "taste this" or "try this" and frequent displays of culinary skill with a touch of competition.

As evening approached, Jim, Ernie, and Bob together monitored Harry as they uncuffed him and let him take care of his needs. He ate his meal sorrowfully and did not speak, except once when, unprompted, he said, "You all hate me, don't you?"

No one answered him.

When Harry finished, they cuffed him to a post next to his cot in the market storeroom, and he fell asleep. Bob and Ernie began loading the truck with food. So that he could get some sleep before the night-long drive, Jim asked David to watch Harry and get someone to help if Harry needed anything. Susan offered to keep David company.

For hours, Harry slept. Susan and David didn't want to

disturb his sleep, so they kept their watch without talking. David read a magazine, and Susan worked a book of crossword puzzles. Occasionally, she would whisper to David for help when she was stuck.

Susan got thirsty, and since there was nothing in the market that was cold to drink, she went across the street to get a can of pop for each of them.

While she was gone, Harry woke up and saw David sitting across from him, watching him. It took Harry a moment to collect his thoughts.

"I've never seen you before," he muttered. "Who are you?"

David looked around nervously, hoping to see Susan returning.

"David," he answered. "My name's David. David Delray."

Harry tried to sit up, forgetting temporarily the handcuffs, which jangled and arrested his movement. He settled for propping himself up uncomfortably on one elbow.

"You come from Lofton County?" Harry asked.

"Yes."

"Mother's name Denise?"

"Yes," David answered, surprised. "Do you know her?"

"No, no," Harry answered. "Well, I used to live around there. Everyone heard of everyone. That's all."

There was a pause. David again looked around to see if Susan was coming.

"Where's your father?" Harry asked.

"I don't have one."

Harry grunted. "How'd you get here?"

"They came and got me. I called them on the radio."

"Humph. You got your own short wave."

"Yes," David responded, still surprised. "My mother bought it for me, when I was eight."

"Your mother here too?" Harry asked.

"My mother's dead," David answered, softly.

Harry sank back on the pillow and said no more. Susan walked in and handed David a can of pop. He thanked her and opened it, but then he stopped and asked Harry if he wanted some. Harry didn't answer him.

※ ※ ※

Missy and Jim had gone to Missy's place, where Pamela was removing some of the things she brought over when she stayed there with Bess. Missy stopped Pamela from moving out. Though she teased about being kicked out of her own house, Missy took a few of her things and officially moved in with Jim.

It was the first time Missy and Jim had shared a bed in several days, and they enjoyed it, and each other, fully, until long after dark.

When Jim finally forced himself to get up and get going,

Missy was worried that, since he hadn't gotten much sleep, he would fall asleep at the wheel; and she insisted on coming along. Jim acquiesced, saying, while in exaggerated fashion nudging her and winking, that they could "sleep" when they got back. She put her arms around his neck and hung on him and kissed him softly on the mouth.

They got dressed and went to the market. David and Susan were asleep on the couch, the post next to the cot was broken, and Harry was gone.

David apologized profusely for having let them down, but they consoled him and each took a share of the blame— Susan saying she should have stayed awake, and Jim and Missy saying they should have come for Harry much sooner.

There was nothing more to do that night. Jim and Missy went back to their place, and Susan took David to her house, where he slept on the couch.

The next morning they organized and searched for Harry, but they did not find him. For several days after, they remained tense, always going places in pairs; but Harry did not show up, and as the days went by, as these things go, they allowed their guard to relax.

Anitra recovered rapidly. She complained more about the pain from the wound in her shoulder than the one in her stomach, but both injuries showed signs of healing completely. Everyone got in the habit of affectionately referring to Bess as "Doc."

David spent a lot of time with Jim. Within a day, he had immersed himself in the complexities of the power plant and the telephone switching station. David discovered that, with the restored electricity, the phones were working normally again. Bess's little switching station was put out of business, though she was happy to let it go.

On the morning of the second day after Harry's disappearance, Jim was relaxing behind his place, lounging in a chair beside a small patch of lawn and sipping artificial lemonade. Missy was upstairs, taking a shower. David came over to visit.

"Taking it easy?" David began.

"Waiting for Missy," Jim responded and poured David some lemonade. "You're doing so much of the work around here now, I find I have quite a bit of leisure time."

"I enjoy it," David beamed. "It's like having your own enormous model railroad. Except, of course," he added, "there's no train."

"This is our world," Jim replied, "and it's only what we make it. We can have anything we want, if we're willing to do the work. If we want a train, we'll add a train."

"That might be a lot of work," David said.

Jim laughed. "Well, so far, we've got our utilities—water, power, and phone. That's a lot. We'll have to go searching for another supermarket soon. Then we'll see if we want to add a train."

They heard Missy hum a few notes through the window above them.

"Do you like Missy?" David asked.

"Yes, David," Jim admitted. "I love her."

"I guess I'm kinda dating Susan."

"Congratulations," Jim said. "She's a beautiful woman."

"Yeah, she's so pretty, only, I mean, well, she's older than me."

"Not that much. Six or eight years. Besides, I'm afraid our population density doesn't allow a much closer match."

"Oh, not that. I don't mind that. It's just that, well...I mean, I don't want to change her; she's terrific. I wish $\underline{I}$ knew more. I don't know much about girls."

"None of us do," Jim sighed.

"I mean, I don't, well, I don't know anything at all about, you know, about girls."

"Ohhhh," Jim said, "I see. I guess your father never explained this to you."

"I never had a father," David answered. "My mother never really did explain much, about girls."

"She didn't, eh?" Jim said. "Well, I know it's the most important thing in your life right now—always will be, in fact. But I'm sure Susan will teach you everything you need, once she's ready for you to know. Don't be too concerned about it."

David looked unconvinced.

"Couldn't you give me a few pointers?" he pleaded. "I don't want to look, you know, clumsy."

"I understand," Jim soothed. "Something you've never done, something that important, can seem pretty intimidating. You're afraid she'll think you're a stumblebum. But sometimes not knowing something is a treasure, like a chest full of gold coins. You don't have to be in a hurry to know everything there is to know. Don't spend all your gold coins right away. Take your time learning what you don't know. You can spend your gold coins slowly, one by one, to buy your present and future happiness."

David looked disappointed.

"I don't think we'll have any gold coins there," he said.

"No, I guess not," Jim sighed. "Okay, just remember this. You're not the first one to do this for the first time. Everyone else had a first time too. And your body is a design that's been tested over countless generations and found to work, flawlessly. You and she are nearly the same height, so everything will line up, point for point. Just line up your body with hers; and, sooner or later, everything will fit together."

"And that's it?"

"Yes, except that it will feel wonderful."

David sighed and took a sip of his lemonade. Jim rested his head back and closed his eyes.

"The lawn looks nice," David said. "Did you just mow it?"

"No," Jim replied. "In fact I've never…"

He stopped talking. He opened his eyes and sat up straight. He turned his head from the lawn to David and back to the lawn, and an increasing look of horror spread over his face.

"Oh, nooo," he moaned. "Oh no!"

Jim stood up and went to the grass and knelt down. On his hands and knees, he felt the grass—handfuls of it, individual blades.

"Oh please no," he cried.

Still on his knees, he straightened his back and looked farther away, at the bushes, at the shrubs.

Missy came out, wearing slacks and a flimsy white top. She was using a towel to dry her still-damp hair. She saw Jim on his knees and looked to David for an explanation, but he only looked back at her uncertainly.

Jim was still on his knees, and Missy walked around in front of him. Quietly, he was crying. She knelt down in front of him and held him. He continued crying, softly. While holding him, she looked helplessly over his shoulder at David.

"Jim, what's wrong?" she whispered, at last.

"It's dead," he answered. "It's all dead. None of the plants are growing. The whole planet is dead. We're dead too."

Missy looked around at the plants as well as she could while still holding on to Jim.

"I don't understand," she said. "Everything looks the same to me."

"That's just it," he said. "Everything is exactly the same. I've never cut this grass, and it looks freshly mowed. *Everything stopped growing last fall.*"

"But, all this time, we would have noticed, wouldn't we?" she asked.

"We didn't," Jim moaned. "We were too busy... surviving."

He sat down sideways on the grass and continued brushing his hand through it. Missy walked over to some bushes near the building and touched the leaves.

"It's not possible," David offered. "If the plants weren't growing, then we'd be running out of oxygen right now, like a moth inside a jelly jar, with no holes punched in the lid."

Jim just looked at him.

"Oh," David whispered.

"And food," Jim added. "Our canned food is the last we're going to have. Nothing is growing any more."

Missy held her hand to her stomach.

"I...I don't feel good," she groaned.

She ran inside.

✽ ✽ ✽

Life in town didn't change much after the latest grim discovery. Once the truth became known, it was a dull ache that the residents somehow managed to ignore, like a distant war, or the knowledge of your own eventual, impending demise.

Anitra recovered enough that she could take care of herself. She was terrified of being left alone, and so she moved in with Kate, Allyson, and Susan. She avoided Frank, and she didn't speak about Harry at all.

People had gotten into the habit of taking most of their meals at the restaurant, where everyone helped out; but Pamela took the responsibility for keeping the kitchen clean and the pantry full.

The dogs had the run of the town. They resisted

forming an attachment to any particular human being; but, wherever they went, they were able to find a hand out, a friendly pat, or a comfortable place to sleep. They too took their meals at the restaurant, with Pamela providing dry dog food, along with the occasional, and very rare, table scrap.

David busied himself with the technical aspect of town life, leaving Jim with very little to do. Jim and Missy often sat on their balcony overlooking the main street, where they would read or talk, and where they could wave at anyone who passed by on the street below.

Weeks passed. Jim and Missy were on the balcony.

"David and I are going out soon," Jim said, "To look for another market. I'm sure we'll find one."

Missy nodded. She was working assiduously on a needlepoint kit.

"How are you doing?" he asked.

"Fine," she said, without looking up.

"I mean really," he persisted. "How are you handling it, knowing that it's all going to end?"

"We always knew that it was going to end," she answered. "It's just not going to be the way we expected."

"Do you ever feel like quitting?"

"If we quit, then everything stops, and what's the point in that?" she responded. "We might just as well have something, for as long as it lasts. Nothing will be here soon enough."

She continued concentrating on her needlepoint but asked, "What's your reason for going on?"

"I have to," he replied. "Someone has to keep you company."

She smiled and kept working. He picked up a book, opened it, but did not start to read.

"Did you talk to Bess, about why you're feeling sick all the time?" he asked.

"Yes."

"Well?"

"Bess is my best friend, but she needs to read a few more of her doctor books."

"What did she say?"

Missy kept her eyes focused on her needlepoint.

"Bess thinks I'm pregnant."

Jim put his book down on the table. He tried to catch Missy's eye, but she steadfastly refused to look up from her needlepoint.

"Would you like a second opinion?" he asked, at last.

"What?"

"I think you're the most beautiful woman I've ever seen."

Missy's hands fell motionless to her lap and, misty-eyed, she could only look at the man seated before her; but then she got up and went over to him. She didn't get any more of her needlepoint done that morning.

* * *

Months passed. Jim and David succeeded in finding another market to the east, not as big as the one in town, but well-stocked nonetheless. They had the unpleasant task of removing the canned goods from a building filled with the stench of putrefied meat and produce, but they collected enough food to last through the coming winter, with a considerable variety as well. They even found gourmet dog food for the beagles.

Nothing was seen of Harry. Kate suspected he was hiding in the valley; and Frank was sneaking him food; but despite several attempts to monitor Frank's movements, no one was able to catch him at anything.

David and Susan kept steady company. He set up a system to receive a wide band of radio frequencies, in case someone else was trying to contact them; and she helped him monitor it.

Ernie and Bob had fine-tuned the station wagon and the truck until they hadn't left a single bolt untouched, and Jim was working with them to get one of the other junkers operational, a big, old, red Plymouth.

Anitra recovered fully, except for a little stiffness in her shoulder, and joined Kate and Allyson in managing the power station.

Missy was no longer able to ignore the new roundness in her previously-flat abdomen. Jim had gotten into the habit of kissing her good night twice, first on the lips and then on her stomach.

Missy professed that marriage, per se, wasn't that

important in their new, little, twelve-person world; but when Jim knelt down before her and proposed, she couldn't stop smiling all day.

Kate was proclaimed mayor by voice vote, and she presided over Jim and Missy's wedding. Bess was the maid of honor; Ernie was the best man; and both of them cried during the vows, though Ernie strongly denied it later.

Missy and Jim honeymooned by walking upriver toward the mountains and pitching a tent, where they stayed for several days—eating, bathing in the cold stream, exploring each other's bodies and minds, and making love.

The flavor of their excursion returned with them to their flat. In place of the mountain stream, they took bracing showers together. Instead of in a tent, they explored and loved each other in a large, comfortable, cool bed. The honeymoon continued.

Change occurred slowly in the new world. Life got easier; Missy got rounder.

A couple of evenings a week the group would meet at the restaurant, where Kate and Pamela collaborated to show taped movies. Pamela made a marquee which even had a spot for coming attractions, and she served popcorn and fruit drinks. Kate only had about fifty movies, so she was careful to husband them so her audience would not tire of them too quickly.

Susan revealed that she could play the piano, and she was occasionally cajoled into performing for an always attentive audience.

Sometimes, Jim simply took out a book and read to the group. His deep, mellow voice would roll through the night air and caress them as they listened; and, no matter how long he read, they'd always ask for "just a little more," like children listening to a bedtime story.

David's contribution to entertainment was to announce the approach of a lunar eclipse, which they decided was an excellent excuse for an all-night party.

The site they chose for their moon watch was the rise in front of the power plant, where they could lie close to the river, and where they had an unobstructed view of the valley.

When the night of the eclipse came, they brought chairs and blankets, also wine, crackers, and a canned cheese spread; and they clustered together on the rise to await the celestial event. David set up his telescope. The dogs had followed the crowd and frolicked on the hillside above them.

The moon shone brightly and revealed most of the details of the valley below.

"How beautiful it is," Missy sighed. "Everything looks so fresh, so perfectly in place, like a little scale-model world. Everything looks so wonderful, so new."

"We have met the enemy, and they are us," Jim observed.

"What?" Missy asked.

"Nothing," Jim answered. "Just something I read in the funny papers once."

At precisely the minute David had indicated, a sliver of darkness began its encroachment on one side of the full moon.

"There it goes," David announced.

As they watched, the moon became redder and began to disappear. They ate, and drank, and talked in subdued tones as around them it got darker.

"If you stare at it long enough," Susan said, "It's like it's hung on a string in the air, not moving at all."

"Actually," David responded, "It's moving quite fast, over 2000 miles per hour. But then that's relative, because we're moving, too."

"How fast are *we* moving?" Susan asked.

"That depends on how you mean," David answered, warming to the topic. "Our rotation is only about a thousand miles an hour at the equator, less this far north. But our speed around the sun is much more, about 67,000 miles an hour."

"Wow," escaped Frank's lips.

The dark part of the moon continued to grow and grow.

"It's not going to disappear altogether," David explained. "Even though the earth right now is moving into position to completely block the straight line of light coming from the sun, enough light will be bent by our atmosphere to give the moon that reddish glow. At this moment, we have our backs turned to the sun."

"I don't understand," Frank ventured, plaintively. "It looks just like the same moon we see every night."

"Not at all, not at all," David responded, getting more excited. "The crescent moon we see most nights has nothing to do with Earth at all. It's just our view of a side of the moon that's partly sunlit and partly unlit.

"But tonight we're looking at ourselves. That's our own shadow up there, proof that the world is round. Tonight, if we were big enough, and we stood in the right place, we could make shadow puppets on the moon the same way we used to on a projection screen in our living rooms."

From their place on the blanket where Jim was holding her, Missy whimsically reached up and tried to cast her own shadow puppet on the moon.

"Maybe if you stood on my shoulders," Jim offered.

She punched him.

When the moon reached its darkest and reddest, Missy sought out Bess.

"You're not afraid?" Missy asked.

"It's too beautiful for me to be afraid," Bess answered.

The group vied with each other to be the first to detect the return of the white light, but no one could agree on when it was present. Gradually, the brightness returned.

"Another half hour or so, and the moon will be full again," David instructed.

"It makes you feel so small," Allyson said, "So insignificant."

"We are small," David agreed.

"But we're not insignificant," Bess added, "At least not to each other."

The amount of blue-white light increased, on the moon, and, by reflection, on the landscape around them.

"I remember when I was a little girl," Susan reminisced. "I used to lie on the grass in the backyard, and look at the moon, and wonder if there were any people living there." Her voice broke. "Now I'm wondering if there's anyone else alive anywhere."

"It's been so hard," Kate moaned. "Such a change, living in a world without all the people."

"What the hell happened?" Ernie broke in. "That's what I want to know. What the hell went on last year?"

"Seven billion people" Jim observed. "What could it have been?"

"And why didn't it happen to us?" Bess asked.

"We didn't panic," Kate offered. "Except for David, none of us even knew that anything unusual was happening, until it was all over. Maybe that had something to do with it."

"Well," Jim offered, "At least it kept us from being out on that highway, trying to head west with everyone else. That sure was the wrong place to be. But it doesn't explain what happened, or why it didn't happen to us."

"Or what our purpose is—here, now, still alive—witnessing, for the first time, an unpopulated planet," David said.

"Do you believe everything has a purpose?" Jim asked.

"Yes," David answered, firmly.

The moon had recovered all of its light, and the brightness around them made it almost as easy to see as in the daytime. Frank was nodding off to sleep, as were Allyson and Anitra. Bess was spritzing the last of the cheese spread on crackers and passing them around, and Pamela was pouring more wine. Missy was hugging Jim's arm and cuddling up closer to him.

Without thinking, Jim swatted at a mosquito that landed on his neck, then held out his hand and looked at the spot which was its crumpled body. It wasn't until Missy had grabbed Jim's wrist and looked too that he realized the importance of what had just happened.

"Life," Missy whispered.

They were staring at his hand with the twisted form of the mosquito still unfolding when, just beyond their focus, a fish jumped out of the river and splashed back in.

"What was that?" Bess asked.

Missy and Jim both shouted.

"A fish!"

"A fish jumped out of the water!"

There was much confusion. Sleeping people awoke; wine got spilled; everyone spoke at once.

"A fish? Are you sure?"

"Who saw it?"

"Did someone throw a stone in?"

"Where was it?"

"No one threw anything."

"It was a fish."

"Was it big?"

"Where'd you see it?"

Missy begged them to be quiet.

"Maybe we'll see it again," she said, "If you don't scare it away."

They waited, quietly. Once in a while, someone would fidget, or talk; and someone else would silence them.

The light from the moon, which was now behind them, twinkled on the water, and the shimmering blurred the clear demarcation between reality and fantasy.

"Maybe not," Jim whispered, at last. "Maybe it was just a wave."

"No," Missy said, firmly. "Wait. It was alive."

At her bidding, they waited. And they waited. Bess passed around a few crackers, devoid of cheese. Pamela poured the last of the wine. Sometimes their attention wandered away from the river for a while.

But, as they sat there, like children waiting for the show to start, the fish broke cleanly from the surface, glistened green and red and orange and silver, stayed suspended in the air like time itself had stopped, and then disappeared again back under the water.

The fading sounds of the fish's return to the water were lost in Jim's joyous shout. He jumped up and started to dance, and Missy jumped up with him.

"Yahooo! It's alive; the sea is alive!" he shouted.

He took both of Missy's hands in his, and they danced a jig.

"We can breathe! We can eat!" he hollered.

He stopped dancing and put both his hands on Missy's

stomach.

"We have a future," he cried. "Little whosits is going to grow up to be a fisherman!"

"Fisherperson," Missy corrected.

The others joined in their glee. But the night had been long, and the celebration tapered off quickly.

Jim, however, would not be dissuaded.

"Fishing! We've got to go fishing," he declared. "Today, before dawn, we'll go. We'll drive to the ocean. We'll catch fish!"

"But honey," Missy cautioned, "You don't even like fish."

"I know," Jim answered, "But I'll learn. That's not important right now. We don't even have to keep the fish. All we have to do is catch just one, to prove that we can, to prove that it's possible to sustain life on this earth. Then we can relax. Then we know we'll have time to plan our future. Then we know that we *have* a future."

There was much good-natured grumbling, but Jim's enthusiasm was irresistible. They agreed to pack picnic lunches, scrounge up fishing equipment, get a few hours sleep, and assemble at dawn for a fishing excursion to the ocean. They picked up their blankets and chairs, trooped back in to town, and said their good nights.

Missy fell asleep at once, but Jim was too keyed up to sleep. He lay there, with his chest against her back, with his arms around her; and he gently kissed her neck and lovingly caressed her distended belly while she slept.

237

By the time the sun was just starting to rise, Jim was already dressed and in the street, sounding the air horn on the truck, which reverberated mercilessly through the otherwise quiet town.

Missy was the first to appear, carrying a bag of food. Her eyes were half-closed, her hair uncombed and her blouse improperly buttoned and showing more than the usual amount of her firm breasts. Uncaring, she climbed into the truck, stuffed the food in the rear, laid her head back and said "Wake me when we get there."

Ernie and Bob arrived, and they prepared the vehicles. They unhooked the semi from its trailer, and they brought the big Plymouth up for its first use since they repaired it.

The others began to straggle in. Pamela and Bess were late, and Jim went up to their place. He found Pamela almost ready, but Bess was still in bed.

"Fish are biting!" Jim shouted, and he grabbed Bess's legs and pulled her out of bed with a thump.

"Fish maniac," Bess groused, as Jim left her rubbing her bottom where she'd landed.

Everyone except Pamela and Bess had by now assembled in the street. In addition to the lunches, Jim felt they should have some extra food in case they had any trouble on the road or at sea; and Frank volunteered to drive the Plymouth to the market loading dock and put a few cases of canned goods in the trunk.

"Let me, please," Frank begged. "We used to have a car like this when I was a teen-ager."

While Frank was getting the extra food, Bess and

Pamela came downstairs, Bess still grumbling and rubbing her bottom; but Jim gave her a kiss on the forehead, and she forgave him.

Frank brought the car back and stayed behind the wheel with the motor running.

"I take it you want to drive?" Jim said to Frank.

"Huh? What? Oh, yeah. I like driving," Frank replied, without looking at Jim or taking either hand off the steering wheel.

"Okay, okay, we'll let you drive," Jim agreed, and he patted Frank's shoulder.

Susan and David got in the truck with Missy and Jim. Bob drove the station wagon with Anitra in the passenger seat and Ernie in back between Bess and Pamela, who had even rounded up the dogs and apportioned them to the different vehicles. Kate and Allyson got in with Frank.

Jim stuck his head out the truck window, made a circling motion with his hand like he was heading up a wagon train, and grinned broadly. Then he sounded the air horn, put the truck in gear, and it lurched forward.

"Gee, it never bounces like that when Missy drives," Susan observed.

Jim grunted. Though Missy's eyes were closed, just the very ends of her mouth curved, almost imperceptibly, upward.

With the others following, Jim moved the truck south down the main street, over the straight stretch, past the fork where he and Bess had found the station wagon that spring, and on towards the ocean. He accelerated to about 60 miles per hour and kept it there, so that the two cars wouldn't have any trouble keeping up.

The jostling of the truck gently brought Missy to full wakefulness, and she joined in the conversation. As they drew near to their destination, the road they were on ended in a T as it joined the coastal highway. Jim stopped the truck at the intersection and studied the signs advertising the diverse facilities, including a marina in either direction.

"Well, which way?" Jim asked. "East or west?"

"West," Missy answered, without hesitation.

Jim looked at her. She answered his unspoken question.

The other way is the marina Bess and I were at last year," she explained. "I don't think it would be good for Bess to go back there. Me either."

Jim understood.

"West it is," he said, as he wheeled the truck into a right turn, and their three-vehicle caravan continued down the road.

"Last year," Missy mused. "It doesn't seem like it's been a year."

"Does it seem longer or shorter?" Susan asked.

"Both," Missy answered. "Sometimes it seems like it was just a few weeks ago. And sometimes it seems like that other life was a dream, that it never really happened."

"Does Bess ever talk about her boyfriend?" Jim asked.

"Not any more," Missy replied. "That's…the past."

"Were they close?" Jim asked. "Were they engaged?"

"No," Missy said. "Well, not engaged, at least. I don't think they were that serious. Who knows? But the way things happened, they didn't have time to grow apart. When things end that quickly, through no one's fault, you always wonder what might have been. Poor Bess's feelings are frozen, not fading, but not growing either."

They came to the marina, where about a hundred boats of all sizes and types were nestled into a little harbor; and on shore there was an office, a repair shop, a restaurant/clubhouse, and a storage shed.

Jim stopped in front of the office, and the other two vehicles pulled up behind. Everyone got out; and they stretched their legs, basked in the early morning sunshine, or did some short-range exploring.

"The first thing we have to do," Jim said, "is choose a boat. I choose…" He pursed his lips and squinted his eyes as he scanned the docks. "…that one."

He pointed to a fifty-foot sedan-bridge cruiser, by far the biggest vessel in the marina.

"Might as well go first class," he declared.

He fired up the crowd and set them to work—searching the office and repair shop for boat keys, collecting more fishing gear, looking for extra food. He had Ernie and Bob look for a way they could get more gas, either by siphoning it from other boats or pumping it from the underground storage tanks. Frank was holding onto the car keys the way a child clutches his favorite teddy bear, so Jim had him back the car up to the cruiser and place the spare food from the trunk on board.

Susan found a rack in the repair shop that held spare keys to every vessel in the marina; and, with a few attempts, they found the ones that fit the cruiser.

The boat's gas tanks were nearly full, so it didn't take long, with everyone participating in a gas-can brigade, to top them off.

Jim tried the engines, and neither one would start at first; but Ernie found an ether spray, and a squirt of it in each carburetor brought the engines to life.

There was only a slight breeze. They cast off the dock lines, and Jim gracefully backed the boat away from the dock and then turned it to go out of the marina. Missy stood next to him on the bridge.

"Ever do <u>this</u> before?" she asked.

"Nothing as big as this," he answered, "But the principle is the same."

They cleared the harbor entrance and headed for the open sea.

Excited by the task at hand, David joined them on the bridge, and Jim began showing him the controls with an eye to letting him take the helm.

"Hey, Popeye," Bess teased Jim. "You're getting us out okay, but are you going to be able to find the way back?"

"Nothing to it," Jim boasted. "We just keep an eye on the compass, and reverse course for the return trip. Easy as pie."

Eager to be of assistance, David uncovered the compass and took a first reading, but then he frowned.

"Compass is broken," he complained.

"What? What's wrong?" Jim asked.

"We're headed away from the coast," David explained. "We must be heading more or less south. But the compass says we're headed due north. That's impossible."

Jim tapped the compass, then wheeled the helm one way, and then the other, and watched the compass respond obediently.

"It seems to be working," Jim mused. "It's just giving us a 180 degree wrong reading, pointing south instead of north. But it'll still get us out and back."

"You'd better stand back," Bess teased. "Maybe it's your magnetic personality!"

Jim let go of the helm long enough to grab Bess and tickle her, and David immediately took the opportunity to grab the wheel. Jim let him take command.

"You have the con, first officer. Keep her steady and true."

"Aye, aye, sir!" David responded, happily.

As the harbor was fading in the distance behind them, Jim inhaled deeply, proclaimed "What a beautiful day!" and started singing boating songs. He jostled Missy and Bess and goaded them into singing with him. A few more voices joined them from the deck.

They motored for a half hour, until all around them was nothing more than a hazy gray seam between the sea and sky. Since the water was calm, Jim had David simply shut down the motors and let the boat drift.

Fishing commenced. Ernie rigged a fancy line with colorful lures, multiple hooks, bobbers and sinkers, a sight to behold. By contrast, Allyson had a pole, a line, a hook and a piece of bread for bait. Bob spent most of his time setting up lines for other people. Fishing poles protruded from every side of the vessel.

No sooner had they settled in at their positions, the first round of sandwiches and drinks been distributed, the first claims of fishing prowess been made, than everyone started catching fish.

Allyson caught the first one and needed help taking it off her hook. Ernie started hauling them in, two and three at a time. Bob was constantly on the move, unhooking fish, throwing them back, trying to fix a line but being called away to start the process again.

Jim set his pole down and laughed nonstop at the antics around him. Then he grabbed Missy and kissed her as hard as he could.

With their foreheads touching and his eyes so close to hers he couldn't focus, he said, "The land may be dead, but the sea is alive. We're going to make a comeback!"

Then he kissed her again.

The criterion for "keepers" kept increasing and still the fish locker filled up. Soon most of the poles were stowed away, and people began enjoying the gentle sea and the warm sun.

Allyson had caught the biggest fish, and Ernie refused to give up. Allyson accepted the challenge, and they kept their lines in the water.

Ernie was fishing off the port quarter, and Allyson complained he was taking away all the best fish, so she moved to the starboard bow. There she kicked a pile of gear covered by a tarp; then she pulled on the tarp, and Harry appeared.

Allyson screamed, dropped her pole, and ran toward the back of the boat.

Harry was dazed, blinded by his sudden exposure to the sunlight. He made a move to return to his hiding place under the tarp, thought better of it, then nervously looked around for some other place to go. There was no place.

Alerted by Allyson's cry, the others began moving to the front of the boat to see what was happening. Kate was the first there; and, when she saw Harry, she retreated several steps; but soon she was joined by the rest of the party. They assembled on the foredeck, and Harry retreated, inching his way toward the bow.

"Don't touch me," he shouted, holding his hands up to ward them off. "Don't touch me!"

His backing up induced the group to advance. When Harry bumped against the bow pulpit and could go no further, they also stopped.

Anitra hung back, keeping the rest of the group between her and Harry, and Kate stayed with her.

"Don't touch me," Harry shouted again.

"No one's going to touch you," Pamela snapped back. "No one wants to touch you."

"How the hell did you get here? Jim demanded.

Harry didn't talk, but Frank did.

"I didn't want to do it, but he made me do it," Frank whined. "He said I had to do it, 'cuz we're brothers."

"Do what?" Missy asked.

"Bring him," Frank answered. "He was in the trunk."

"I'd think the last place you'd want to be is with us," Jim said, "when you could have had the whole town to yourself. Why did you come?"

Harry showed no sign of answering.

"He was afraid we weren't coming back," Frank whimpered. "He was afraid we'd find a new town, and stay there, and then he would be all alone."

"You mean you haven't been alone?" Bess demanded. "Where have you been living all these months?"

"Wouldn't you like to know," Harry sneered.

"Yes, we would," Jim answered.

"I saw you two," Harry said, pointing at Jim and Missy. "I was in the mountains. I saw you, when you were camping out."

Missy shuddered and pulled her beach towel closer around her shoulders, now needlessly covering her body that wasn't covered when she and Jim were honeymooning at the campsite.

"You never saw me," Harry bragged. "None of you did. I've been right under your noses for weeks."

"Where?" Jim asked.

Harry was silent.

"In the freezer," Frank admitted, "At the market. No one ever looks there."

Jim shook his head.

"Damn," Ernie said. "In the freezer. Shoulda looked."

"Now that he's here," Jim asked, "What are we going to do with him?"

"Fish bait," Ernie answered.

"No!" Frank cried.

Harry looked frightened.

"We can't do that," Frank whimpered. "He's my brother. Can't we just make him go away, like we said before?"

"What do you say, Anitra?" Jim asked. "You weren't in on it, the last time we talked about this."

Anitra seemed to grow smaller, as she shrank away from the attention to the shelter she found next to Kate. But as she grew smaller, she grew harder, too.

"Throw him overboard!" she declared.

"You can't!" Harry shouted. "It's not fair."

"You shot me!" Anitra screamed back. "I could've died!" And then, softer, she added, "Part of me *did* die."

"I had to," Harry pleaded. "You were going to take it all away from me. I had to protect myself. I had to protect my goods!"

Anitra broke down crying, and Kate hugged her and tried to console her.

The half-circle of people closed in tighter on Harry, who had his back pressed against the bow pulpit and one leg up on the rail. He had retreated as far as he could without going into the sea.

Harry continued talking, "You don't understand. None of you understand. Food is the most important thing. Food is all we have left. I didn't have to give it to you. It was _mine_! I could have kept it all for myself. I let you have some because I wanted to. And none of you appreciated it. Not one of you!"

"Throw him overboard," Anitra cried again, though her voice was muffled because she was crying with her head against Kate's shoulder.

Missy grabbed Jim's arm and pleaded, "We have to stop this! She wants him to drown!"

"I would too, if he'd shot me," Jim answered. "But we can wait until we get to shore to decide what to do. Right now we just have to get him under control."

Jim took a step toward Harry.

"Don't touch me!" Harry shouted. "You have no right! None of you are any better than me! You've always been against me, because you were jealous. You wanted what I had."

Harry kept talking, but the others had stopped paying attention.

Behind him, the water had started churning, and a metal object appeared above the surface, followed by more metal—the conning tower of a submarine.

Harry continued talking until he could no longer ignore the rush of water or the fact that the eyes of the others were no longer on him. He looked once, quickly, to the side, and saw nothing; but no one in the group had advanced on him, so he turned around farther and saw the large gray mass of metal in the water in front of the boat. Startled, he stumbled away and fell into the arms of the others.

No one tried to hold Harry, and he didn't try to escape as they all watched the submarine.

A hatch on the submarine opened, and uniformed men appeared on deck. Through an amplifier, one of them called out, "Heave to and stand by to be boarded."

This stunning turn of events cowed them all; and, sheep-like, they did as they were told. A raft launched from the submarine came alongside and took half of them to the ship, then returned for the other half. Even the dogs were included. Once on board, dogs were handed down and everyone else climbed down a ladder past two levels to the crews mess—a chamber of stainless steel, fluorescent lights, and space-efficient tables and chairs. The dogs were sequestered in another part of the vessel.

They had no time to become accustomed to their new surroundings before they were joined by the captain—a tall, lean man with a trace of gray hair at his temples.

His demeanor was stiff, formal.

"Are there others?" was the first thing he asked. "Other survivors?"

No one spoke at first, until Kate took it upon herself.

"No," she said. "This is all we know about."

"Good, that's good," the captain responded. "We don't have time for others."

"What's going on?" David asked.

"I'm sure you have many questions," the captain said, "And we have some for you. We'll give you a briefing as soon as we can. Right now we have to get under way."

"How far are you taking us?" Susan asked.

"Far? Not far. A few hundred feet is all," the captain answered, and he left the room.

Other seamen came in to ask after their needs and bring them food and drink. When they found out Anitra had been shot, they took her away for a medical exam. Missy's pregnancy also earned her a trip to the infirmary.

When they returned, both women were smiling.

"I'm fine," Anitra announced. "The doctor sent you his compliments, Bess."

Bess beamed.

Missy walked up to Jim and tapped her stomach.

"Twins," she said.

Jim's eyes grew wide.

"Are you sure?" he asked.

"The doctor didn't guarantee it, but he's pretty sure he heard two heartbeats."

"Wow," Jim said, and he kissed her.

Shortly after Missy and Anitra returned from the infirmary, the captain came back into the room, accompanied by another officer.

"My name is Captain Wright, and this is Lieutenant Commander Mitchell. I'm glad to hear you all seem to be in fine health."

He looked at Missy, who was holding hands with Jim.

"Congratulations, on your condition," he said.

"Thank you," Missy answered softly.

The captain continued his remarks to the group in general.

"I suppose you have some questions…" he began.

"Are we going to submerge?" David asked.

"We are submerged," the captain answered. "It's necessary for us to be submerged at this time."

This piece of information hit them dully, and they looked uncertainly around the room at each other.

"We'd like to know more about you," the captain continued. "What life is like on land now, how you survived, whether you were all together when it happened."

"What? No. We weren't all together," Kate said. "We were all in different places. But what was it? What did we survive from? Was it a chemical war?"

"Was it nuclear radiation?" David asked.

"No, no," the captain responded, more solicitously. "I'm sorry. I'm not addressing your concerns. Of course you have questions. I'll let Mitchell explain it, at least as much as we understand."

"Was it space invaders?" Frank asked, breathlessly.

The lieutenant commander, a shorter, rounder man than the captain, cleared his throat and moved closer to the center of the room.

"No, nothing like that at all," he said. "There was

nothing man-made, nothing artificial about what happened. There was nothing 'alien' either. It was a totally natural phenomenon. It came from the sun, something we've never seen before—*a different light.*"

Jim was incredulous. "Sunlight? You're telling us ordinary sunlight killed almost every living thing on the whole planet? All our friends? All our families?"

"Far from ordinary," the lieutenant commander said. "This was a most extraordinary force. Light waves, part of the electromagnetic spectrum, come in a variety of sizes, frequencies and energies. But this light was beyond gamma rays, with a shorter wavelength, higher frequency, higher energy than we've ever known before. It went to each and every living cell in its path and turned them off, individually. And," he added, "If it helps you to know it, the process was absolutely painless."

"How horrible!" Missy gasped.

"How did it happen?" Bess asked.

The lieutenant commander continued, "The first clue we had that something untoward was happening was that the earth's magnetic poles reversed—something that has never before occurred within human history."

"The compass wasn't broken!" David whispered to Jim, but the captain heard him, and the military rigor of his face betrayed the slightest smile. He nodded at the young man.

"That opened Pandora's box," the lieutenant commander proclaimed. "The process originated at one point on the sun and emanated out in a shape like a wedge of pie, only a few feet thick but thousands of miles wide. At first it didn't touch the Earth at all.

"But, as the Earth moved closer to the area in space where this force was beaming, it reacted to our presence. It varied from its natural course, curved through space, and locked on to our magnetic poles. It stayed locked on; and, as the earth moved through, it followed us back to a straight position and then curved in the other direction, staying locked on to our magnetic field until finally the earth moved far enough through space that the force snapped back to its normal position."

"That explains why it always struck at noon, local time; and why it seemed to be moving from east to west," David said.

"Bright boy," the lieutenant commander answered. "Exactly. The light only fell upon a wafer-thin slice of the planet at any one time, but the rotation of the earth slowly and inexorable caused almost the entire planet to be bathed in its rays. It first turned on over the Pacific Ocean; and, since it stayed on for over thirty, nearly forty hours, the eastern hemisphere got a double dose."

The captain interrupted, "That ought to satisfy your initial burst of curiosity. We need to know more about you." He turned to Missy first. "We need to know what you did to survive, how you shielded yourself from the light."

"We didn't do anything special," Missy said. "Bess and I were together. We didn't know anything different was happening. We were just scuba diving."

"Under water, exactly," the captain said, as he made a note on a clipboard he carried.

"Our friends on the boat were killed," Missy added.

"I'm sorry," the captain said. "Very sorry." He turned to Jim. "And you, where were you at noon?"

"I was underground," Jim answered, "Exploring a cave. I guess that's what saved me."

"Not sufficient," the captain responded. "The President and several of the Joint Chiefs were deep inside a mountain when the light came, and they all died instantly. There must have been something else."

Jim scratched his head. "Part of the cave was under a lake. I guess I might have been there at noon."

The captain nodded. "Water. Water so far is the only protection we've found. And the rest of you? Were you all in some way shielded by water?"

"We were in a hot tub," Allyson volunteered. "Susan and Kate and I."

"That would not be enough to protect you, the lieutenant commander said. "The layer of water has to be between you and the sun."

Allyson looked confused.

"But we're alive," she said.

The captain smiled at her.

"There was a water storage tank right overhead," Kate said. "I designed the house myself, and I did it that way so the water could flow straight from the roof into the hot tub."

"Well, <u>we</u> wasn't in no dang hot tub," Ernie proclaimed loudly. "Bob'n me was working, working hard, fixing the boiler at the old school house."

"And was there water in the boiler?" the captain asked.

"Mebbe," Ernie said, subdued.

"And was it between you and the sun at any time?"

"Prob'bly," Ernie answered, more quietly.

The captain nodded and scribbled down a few more notes.

"How about you?" the captain said, looking at Anitra.

"Frank and I were out walking, out in the open," Anitra said. "We were eating lunch in a field, surrounded by sunshine. We weren't anywhere near water."

"Yes, we were," Frank said softly.

"No, we weren't Frank," Anitra insisted.

"Yes we were," Frank blustered, and his face got red and his cheeks puffed out as he spoke. "We were in the shade of the old railroad water tower; and there's water in that tower, too. I know, because I go swimming in there sometimes; I do."

"That's right," Anitra admitted, "You're right."

Frank settled back.

"I told you," he muttered.

"Looks like water is the only protection we're going to find," the captain said. "Whom haven't we asked?"

Pamela raised her hand but said nothing.

The captain spoke to her, gently. "How about you? Was there water in your story?"

She shook her head.

"I was home, in bed," she responded, almost in a

255

whisper. "My husband was upstairs. He died that day. I didn't."

"I'm very sorry about your husband," the captain replied. "But, are you sure; was there anything, any water, protecting you?"

"No, nothing," Pamela said. "Just the..." She stopped talking and lowered her eyes. "...the water bed. My husband was on it. I was one floor down. I must've been under it."

"Thank you," the captain said. "I know this is difficult for you. Have I left anyone out?" He looked at Harry. "What about you, sir?"

Harry had kept his eyes to the floor; but, as the silence grew heavier, he looked up and saw that they were all watching him.

"I don't know," he offered, reluctantly.

"You don't know?" the captain asked. "You don't know how you survived?"

"I don't know," Harry repeated. "It was my day off. I was enjoying it. Maybe I had a drink or two. Everyone was running around, talking crazy, shouting, saying we had to get out of town, had to hurry. I...fell asleep.

"When I woke up, everyone was gone—all the cars and all the people. I shouted, but no one answered. I ran down the street; I pounded on doors; but they were all gone. I was alone."

Harry stopped talking. He avoided looking at anyone.

"And where were you, when you...fell asleep?" the captain asked.

This time Harry did not raise his eyes. "On the traffic island, in the middle of the street. I tried to get someone to give me a ride out of town. No one would stop for me. No one would help me. They all left me. All alone."

Someone cleared her throat. Someone shifted his position. No one could fill the silence left after Harry finished speaking.

The Navy men conferred quietly with each other. Phrases of their conversation were heard in the room.

"…was drunk…"

"…can't be sure…"

The captain again addressed the group.

"Is that it then? Is that everyone?"

"Jim answered, "Except for David."

David looked toward the captain, sheepishly, now that the spotlight was on him.

"It's like I already told you guys," he said. "I was eating lunch with my mother. My dog died. My mother died." His voice quivered. "I waited to die, too; but it didn't happen."

"Where was your water shield?" the captain asked.

David had no answer.

"Was there a supply of water near you, at least a couple of feet thick?" the captain asked.

"The only water we had was well water, and I was far away from it," David said.

"You saw your mother die?"

"Yes."

"How far were you from her?"

"Across the table."

"Did you feel anything strange?'

"No."

The captain exchanged glances with the lieutenant commander.

"And there was no water anywhere?" he asked.

"No," David said.

The Navy men left the room for several minutes. When they returned, they told David and Harry they needed to submit to medical exams, and then led them out of the room.

A while later, David, with a bandage on his arm, was escorted back to the room by the captain.

"Are you okay?" Susan asked.

"Sure," David responded. "They didn't do much, took some blood and tissue samples—asked a bunch of questions, mostly. Harry's still in there."

"Why are you doing this?" Susan demanded of the captain. "What's wrong with David?"

"Just good procedure, miss," the captain soothed. "Nothing to be alarmed about. We had a report from our sister ship, working the eastern seaboard, that they found people who survived without water protection, who simply seem to be immune to the light. Perhaps your friend is, also. If an immunity does exist, learning about it is of tremendous importance to the survival of mankind. We need to get a complete medical history of him and give him a thorough exam, right down to blood chemistry and genetics, to see if we can pinpoint something that makes him different from the rest of us, some medical occurrence or natural condition that affords him immunity. I promise he won't be harmed, nothing worse than giving those tissue samples.

Susan nodded her understanding.

Kate spoke up. "You mentioned survivors. There are others?"

"Yes," the captain answered. "There are submarines, of course, a few dozen from several different countries, all those that happened to be submerged when the light occurred. On land, we know there are a few survivors. Very few, I'm afraid. Almost no one in the eastern hemisphere at all, because of the double hit. The odds are astronomical that anyone who, by sheer chance, was shielded by water the first time would still be under protection 24 hours later. And either there were few cases of immunity in the east, or the immunity isn't strong enough to stand up to the second dose."

"All those poor people," Missy moaned. "Not knowing what hit them, not safe anywhere, on land or sea."

"Only under the sea, and no one knew," Bess said.

"And all the planes that crashed," Jim added.

"We have no indication that any planes crashed," the captain said.

"How can that be?" Susan asked.

"The light hit Australia, Japan, and eastern Russia first," the captain explained. "Once the panic started, many governments banned all non-military flights. In hindsight, that was a mistake; but, as a practical matter, it didn't make much difference. With the panic, no one could get off the ground, because the planes and the runways were packed with terrified people. But planes already in the air were able to fly through the wedge of light unscathed, perhaps because of their speed, or Mitchell thinks it may be because they were away from the magnifying effect of the planet itself.

"So planes in flight before the panic began were able to land. Intercontinental flights to the western hemisphere flew through the light and reached the ground, only to have the ray catch them later. But the poor devils flying to the eastern hemisphere were the unluckiest of all. They landed their planes, unassisted, at airports where everyone was already dead. They must've had a hell of a time, trying to deal with the enormity of what was happening, until, still on the ground, they perished the following day at noon."

"What about your airborne command center?" David asked.

"What?" Allyson asked.

"He's right," the captain answered. "The military does keep a plane in the air at all times, to serve as a command post in the event of an emergency. It stayed up until long after the light was gone and was only forced down when it ran out of fuel and had no way to refuel in flight. We were in contact with that crew for a while, but I'm afraid they couldn't handle the emotional aspects of it. They're listed as AWOL, now."

"And you?" Kate asked. "How are you handling it?"

The captain straightened.

"This crew is just fine," he declared firmly. "But then, except for when we loaded provision at the navy yard, no one aboard has been on land for over a year. We haven't seen...what you've seen. I need to hear about that now."

They told him what they could about the freeway filled with cars. They also told him what life was like now, what they had done to take care of their needs without a society to support them.

The captain was impressed. "Under the circumstances, you seem to have done very well for yourselves. You are 'survivors' in more than one sense of the word."

A seaman came into the room and told the captain, "The time is getting close, sir."

"That's fine, thank you," the captain responded. "I might just as well stay here as anywhere."

"Time for what?" Kate asked.

The captain cleared his throat. "I want you to know, first, that we're sitting on the bottom with several hundred feet of water above us. You also have to know that...today is the one year anniversary of the day the light hit, and the time is approaching noon."

"You mean," Allyson cried, "It's going to happen again?"

"We're just being cautious, miss," the captain replied. "Everything we've told you about this force is based on scientific conjecture, along with a computer simulation incorporating all known data. But this phenomenon exceeds all human knowledge. We don't actually have any way of detecting the light, or knowing whether it's still effective. So, for the sake of safety, we're recreating the actions we took a year ago today, actions which were sufficient to protect us at that time."

Susan was clutching David's arm. "You think we'll be safe here?"

"I'm quite sure of it, miss," the captain assured her, "so you can just relax. This vessel will protect you."

They looked around at the shiny metal of their surroundings with a combination of fear and nascent reverence.

"This means," Kate said, "If you hadn't found us today, we'd be up there right now, exposed to it again. It's incredible that you found us at the last minute like this."

"We have suspected for some time that there were survivors in this general area," the captain said.

"How?" Kate asked.

The captain smiled at her. "Satellites, ma'am. They're still working. And you folks were heating your homes last winter."

Kate thought for a moment. "If you knew about us, you must know about others—other survivors. Are there any close by?"

"I can't say with any precision," the captain answered. "It's probable that you in this room represent all the survivors anywhere close by."

"But you have the bigger picture," Jim said. "Do you know how many survived? What is the country's population today?

The captain thought for a moment. "A few thousand,

perhaps. The world's population is in the tens of thousands. No more."

"It's frightening," Bess murmured at last, "to think how few of us are left."

Haltingly, Frank added, "It makes me feel...more important."

Everyone looked at Frank, and Pamela patted his arm.

"Wait a minute," Ernie said to the captain. "If you knew we was around, you cut it mighty damn close, coming to rescue us."

The captain addressed him directly. "We're very glad we were able to take you aboard this morning, but I'm sorry to confess it was not our plan. Our orders are not to venture inland, not until the Navy has a clearer picture of what it's like there. It was only this morning, at the navy yard, when we finished restocking, that we detected your vessel on radar and decided to investigate. Otherwise, we'd be started on a six-month voyage by now."

"You were just going to leave us, unprotected?" Bess asked.

"As I say," the captain answered. "It's our belief the light is no longer operational. This is merely a precautionary measure, and we're glad fortune found it that we could include you."

"What time is it?" Pamela asked.

The captain looked at his watch.

"Just a few minutes, till noon," he said.

Standing behind Missy, Jim put both of his arms around her waist. Susan and David held hands. Nervously, instinctively, Bess moved closer to Jim and Missy. Missy took her hand, and Jim opened his hug and put one of his arms around her.

The seconds ticked away. When one person made eye contact with another, they would smile or nod encouragement, but the smiles quickly faded.

Jim held on to both women with his head between each of theirs. Susan squeezed David's hand tighter and held it in both of hers.

Pamela sighed, quietly; but it was the only sound in the room; and the others looked at her; so she mumbled a barely audible apology. Sound triggered sound, as several people took the opportunity to adjust their position or clear their throats, but then silence again won out over the sounds of humanity.

More seconds ticked by.

Finally, Bess asked, "Is it time, yet?"

The captain looked at his watch.

"Yes," he said, "It's just past noon."

Conversation returned to the room, slowly at first. The captain excused himself; and shortly after, the noises around the outside of the submarine increased. Harry, also with a bandage on his arm, returned to the room but spoke to no one.

Several minutes later, the lieutenant commander came and announced the submarine had surfaced, and he invited them all onto the deck.

Single file, they climbed back up the two levels, out of

the submarine, and into the sunlight. The captain was already on deck, as well as several crewmen, who were working to retrieve a small raft.

"We left some sensing equipment on the surface," the captain explained. "We thought we might learn something; but, apparently, none of it recorded anything unusual."

The sun shone brightly, and just a few white and fluffy clouds drifted lazily by. The fifty-foot cruiser they'd used that morning was bobbing about a half-mile away.

"It's just another beautiful, sunny day," Bess remarked.

They watched while the crew finished securing their equipment.

"As soon as we get stowed away here," the captain said, "We'll be getting underway for the east coast. Members of your group are welcome to join us. Life aboard a submarine can be Spartan, but I can promise you an existence that's familiar, akin to the civilization you've known in the past. Or, we can return you to your vessel and wish you good fortune."

"What are you going to be doing?" Kate asked. "Where will you be?"

"We've already placed on board several pieces of sophisticated medical equipment, as much as we could fit," the captain explained. "We'll be heading to New England to rendezvous with our sister ship and there to collaborate on learning more about what happened to us last year, why did it happen, what can protect us from it happening again and, especially, why some people survived without any protection."

"You'll be back in six months?" Kate asked.

"I can't promise that," the captain replied. "This

mission will last six months, but where we go from there is anyone's guess. I can't promise when, or even if, we'll come back this way."

The group talked among themselves. The discussion was brief, the words soft-spoken. Kate spoke for them all.

"No," she said, "We want you to take us back to our boat. We're going to stay here, and continue on the way we have. Ours may be a new world, but we're going to make the best of it we can. It's going to be okay."

"Actually," the captain said, "I was hoping one of you would be excited by the idea of a ride on a submarine. We want David to come with us."

"What? Me? Why?" David asked.

"It's important," the captain answered. "You're the one we think most likely was not protected by water when the light was on. We need to perform tests more elaborate than a simple blood test, and we need to be able to compare the results with those of people on the east coast who seem to have immunity."

"I don't want to go," David cried.

"You'd be performing an invaluable service for your country, son," the captain answered.

"I don't want to leave here. These people are my friends," David whimpered. "My only friends."

The captain took his hat off, adjusted the sweat band, and put it back on.

"I was hoping it wouldn't come to this," he said. "But the matter is too important to leave up to the wishes of one young man. I have to insist that you come with us."

"No!" David shouted, and he sought the shelter of Susan's arms.

Jim stepped in. "You have no right to force him."

"These are extreme times," the captain answered. "And we're justified in utilizing extraordinary measures. You can think of it as the imposition of martial law; or, if you prefer, he can consider himself drafted. He's of the appropriate age."

"But you still work for us," Jim responded angrily. "As the only known organized electorate in the country, we can take a vote right now, and I can bet you that we'll rescind martial law and ban the draft."

"Your saying it doesn't make it law," the captain answered. "You're just one man."

"And you're just one man," Jim retorted.

"But I am an appointed leader, and I am the commander of a nuclear submarine."

The two men squared off and stared at each other. They stood, eye-to-eye, neither one budging. Not only the civilians, but also the crew had stopped what they were doing to watch the confrontation.

The tension mounted as neither man blinked. Then Harry spoke up.

"I'll go," he whispered.

Reluctantly, the captain broke his gaze from Jim to look at Harry.

"You're not our first choice," the captain said. "We need to be sure that you were away from any water protection during the event."

"I was," Harry answered, and then he hesitated and looked out toward the horizon. "I was drunk. I passed out. I was in the middle of the street. I was there for hours. There was no water protection. I just passed out and when I came to, everyone was gone. Everyone had left me. I was alone."

The captain delayed speaking.

"Okay," he allowed, at last. "David can stay with his friends. We'll take you to the east coast."

David relaxed his grip on Susan's body, and Susan gave him a squeeze and kissed his cheek.

The captain gave the order to move the submarine closer to the cruiser, and then it was time to dispatch the first raft-load of people and dogs.

While the civilians were clustered on the deck, waiting to board the raft, the lieutenant commander spoke up. "One thing I'd like to mention, you have to start thinking about re-populating the planet." He looked at Missy. "I see some of you have already started."

Missy smiled and looked down at her protruding stomach.

The lieutenant commander continued, "We don't know yet how great a population this changed planet can comfortably support, but it's certainly more than we have today. The important thing, and I hope you'll excuse me if this sounds blunt, but the important thing is to use as large a gene pool as is possible."

There was an awkward pause, accompanied by a few furtive glances among the group.

Bess took the captain's arm and asked coquettishly, "I don't suppose you'd like to lend us a few sailors?"

Resistant to her charm, the captain's answer was rigid. "Sorry, miss, but I'm afraid *our* duty is here."

Bess pouted and shrugged.

The raft made the first trip to the cruiser and returned. Harry, his hands at his sides, stood on the deck, between the captain and the lieutenant commander, and watched as they left.

As the raft was loading for the second trip—the last two beagles, Jim and Missy, Pamela, Bess, David and Susan aboard—the captain asked Harry, "Aren't you going to say good-bye to your friends?"

"They all hate me," Harry answered.

The people on the raft avoided looking at Harry as he stood there, forlornly, the only civilian on the deck, surrounded by men in uniform.

At the last moment, just as the raft was being shoved away from the ship, David looked back at Harry and, after hesitating, raised his hand in a single gesture of farewell.

"There," the captain said. "There's one young man who doesn't hate you."

In the instant just before the raft lurched forward and turned away from the submarine, leaving Harry behind, he quickly raised his hand and waved back, and he continued waving at the diminishing figures as the raft sped away toward the cruiser.

Finally, Harry let his hand sink down to his side.

"It's a nice thing you did for that young man," the captain said, "coming with us for an indefinite time to an indefinite place so that he could stay with his friends."

"Yeah," Harry grumbled.

"He certainly is a fine young man," the captain responded.

"I think he's my son," Harry whispered.

"We suspected as much. Natural immunity seems to be exceedingly rare, and the chances are highly unlikely of there being two such, living so close together, without a concomitant genetic link."

The raft unloaded its final passengers and returned to the submarine. The people on the cruiser watched as the tiny figures on the submarine, one by one, disappeared from view. Then the sub began moving and, gradually, disappeared beneath the waves.

Only when the submarine was gone from sight did Jim start the engines on the cruiser. David, beside him, was enthusiastic about plotting the course back to their port, but his calculations were letting him down.

"To reverse our course out," he complained, "we should be heading 180 degrees, but now the compass says we're going almost 0 degrees. It's the opposite of what it should be. It doesn't make sense."

Jim assured him that they were heading the right way; and, in short order, familiar landmarks appeared. They retraced their course; and, once inside the harbor, although he bounced a bit hard off of a few of the pilings, Jim managed to return the cruiser to its original well. They began unloading their gear.

"No one's saying very much," Jim remarked.

"It's been a long, exhausting morning," Missy answered.

They loaded the vehicles and started back. Jim and Missy, Susan and David, in the semi, again took the lead; and the other two vehicles followed.

Shortly after they turned off the coastal highway onto the road back to town, in the distance a black convertible with a lone male driver churned up the dust from a side road, wheeled onto the main highway, and sped away in front of them. Taken by surprise, Jim let the truck idle until the other two vehicles caught up.

"Did you see that?" Jim asked.

"Another survivor!" Missy shouted.

The convertible was rapidly becoming no more than a dot on the horizon in front of them.

Susan said, "I don't think he saw us. He hardly even looked this way."

Missy grabbed Jim's arm.

"We've got to catch him," she cried. "We've got to find him."

"We'll never catch him in this," Jim answered.

"We've got to try," Missy answered.

Jim shouted out the window to the other two vehicles that they'd meet them back in town. Then he revved the engine on the truck and started it in motion. He shifted his way through five gears, then pulled a lever and did five more. The speedometer pegged at over one hundred miles an hour.

"Wheeee," David cried. "We're going to catch him."

"I don't know," Jim muttered. "I can't even see him anymore."

"He must be ahead," Missy said. "This is the only road."

Watch for dust," Jim said, "or any sign than he turned off."

Within a half hour, they reached the town; and Jim slowed down a little; but still he ran the red light in the center of town at fifty miles an hour. There was no sign that the convertible had turned west toward the mountains, so they continued north, past the power plant, over the river, and toward the freeway. Jim wound it back up to top speed and held it there for another half hour.

"It's hopeless," Jim shouted over the roar of the engine. "We haven't seen him in over an hour. We should turn back."

"Just a little farther," Missy pleaded. "Maybe he'll slow down."

They kept going. Still there was no sign of the convertible.

"We're almost to the freeway," Jim said. "Let's stop. I don't want to look at that again, not today."

"Wait!" Missy shouted. "Was that him? Did I just see a car turn down the entrance ramp to the freeway?"

"Where?" David asked.

"I don't see him," Susan said.

"Keep going," Missy shouted.

Jim kept going, but he slowed the truck down as they neared the freeway. The roar of the engine had set their ears ringing; but, as the engine quieted down, the ringing was being replaced by a different sound. Missy heard it first, and she looked at Jim to see if he heard it also, but he was too busy controlling the truck to return her glance.

But then Susan heard it, and she grabbed both Missy's and David's hands. The closer they got to the freeway, the more Jim slowed the truck down. The quieter the engine got, the more the other sound became undeniable.

Car horns. Car horns honking. Hundreds of them. Thousands of them. From both directions. Honking together in an outrageous cacophony that on any other day would have numbed the senses. Honking together in a cry to the heavens.

Jim eased the truck onto the overpass and brought into view the biggest traffic jam any of them had ever seen.

The cars were inching along, trying to fit into spaces too small for them. The drivers were frantically shouting and gesticulating. Children were crying. Dogs were barking. And the horns, the blessed horns, were being sounded on every note of the scale and to every rhythm.

The four got out of the truck and stood on the bridge along the rail. Jim laughed, and he cried. Missy cried, and she laughed. They kissed each other's tear-stained faces. Jim pounded David on the back, and David responded in kind. Jim kissed Susan, and Missy kissed David.

They leaned over the rail and waved happily at the motorists beneath them, who angrily tried to ignore the lunatics on the bridge above.

Jim pulled a sheet out of the back of the truck; and with

lipsticks from both women's purses, they made a sign which said "ALL OVER—GO HOME," and Missy drew a flower in one corner. They hung the sign over the rail and continued waving at the motorists, who, after a long while, did mellow their efforts slightly in response to the unharried example of the four people on the bridge above them.

The four waved until their arms were tired, then they just stood and smiled, then they waved some more.

Then, at David's suggestion, they drove to his house, where his dog ran out to greet them, and his mother was nervously pacing along the porch.

"I couldn't imagine where you had gotten off to," David's mother complained. "I must've fallen asleep. Everything seems so...odd."

David introduced everyone, and his mother greeted them warmly, though she was surprised by the pretty, young woman whose waist her son's arm so readily encircled.

"I'd like to offer you some hospitality," David's mother said, "but all the food in the refrigerator seems to have gone bad. Now isn't that the strangest thing?"

Missy and Jim soon excused themselves, saying they were anxious to meet their friends back in town and also that the other three had much to talk about. They made plans to get together soon, and David's mother offered to cook dinner for her son's "new friends."

On the drive back to town, Jim and Missy occasionally encountered a car or two returning home, now that the panic was subsiding; and Missy would sound the air horn, and both would wave enthusiastically. The people in the other vehicles usually responded, though often first registering surprise at the inordinate friendliness of the couple in the truck.

Missy and Jim drove into town and parked the truck at the gas station, where Ernie came out to greet them.

"Everyone's back!" Missy gushed. "The light must've brought them back, just like it took them away!"

"Already figured that out," Ernie drawled. "People just started showing up, acting like nothing happened, like it was just another day. Sure is good to have them back though."

"Where is everybody?" Jim asked. "I mean, the people _we_ know?"

"Took off," Ernie said, "Onc't they realized what was going on. Said they all had to get someplace, find their husbands and girlfriends and such. Bess said she had to get back to the marina, something about her boyfriend. Even that dang fool Bob is out looking for his brother. They said to tell you though, that they're all coming back, for a big party, tonight or mebee tomorrow, as soon as they could make it. Everybody's bringing everybody."

"What about you, Ernie?" Jim asked. "What are you going to do?"

"I reckon I'll jist wait here," Ernie said. "Sooner or later I figure they'll all come to me. Everybody's always going to need a good mechanic."

Missy hugged Ernie; and he shrugged, and blushed, and drew his hand down over his face.

"Shucks, ma'am," he mumbled. "Your husband's watching."

Missy hugged him again, then took Jim's arm. After

promising they would get back with Ernie as soon as the party started, Jim and Missy returned to their flat and settled in while the flow of normal life began to wash around them. Cars drove down the street, and people walked by. Snatches of conversations drifted up to them from the different quarters.

When the woman who owned the hardware store downstairs came knocking at their door to ask them what they were doing there, Missy quickly wrote her a check for the first month's rent.

"Are we going to stay here a month?" Jim asked.

"The check's no good," Missy answered. "I put last year's date on it. I didn't know what else to do."

On a whim, Missy turned on the television, and the stentorian voice of the newscaster intoned, "It's being called 'The great Hoax of the Decade,' the practical joke we played on ourselves, a mass hallucination of global proportions.

"No one knows where it started, but fear that the world was coming to an end spread rapidly world wide, surmounting all other concerns and touching the lives of every living being.

"Countless millions of people frantically tried to avoid the apocalypse which didn't come. The entire nation, the entire world, convinced that the end was at hand, either panicked and tried to flee, most in a westerly direction, or surrendered to the inevitability of it all and joined others in prayer meetings at houses of worship or at impromptu gatherings at community halls and even basements.

"Beside the widespread hysteria, the only other news of the day is that there is no news. No fighting was reported at any of the world's hot spots. Traffic deaths, perhaps due to a global gridlock, were at an all-time low. The stock market in New

York did not open; and the market in Japan, in response to the confusion and a total breakdown in communications, took the extraordinary step of closing shortly after noon, Tokyo time. With some exceptions, crime, too, took a vacation today, but even the exceptions are remarkable—major stores looted completely, picked clean, in the few hours store personnel were away."

The newscaster continued talking. Missy turned the volume down. Jim gave her a squeeze and walked out to the balcony, where he sat down to savor the approaching sunset. She stood to the side behind him and lovingly stroked his hair. He turned his head toward her, picked up her blouse and kissed her naked stomach. She responded by bending over and kissing the top of his head.

"Do you think the Navy will ever tell them the truth?" she asked, "that they've all been asleep for the past year?"

"They'll have to," Jim answered. "Not everything is the same. The planets are in a different place. And a lot of people will be expecting a lunar eclipse which has already happened. And, of course, we're going to have to use the information at our trial."

"Our trial? What trial?"

"We have a year's supply of groceries we haven't paid for," he teased. "Then there's the matter of the stolen truck, not to mention your bad check."

Missy stopped tousling Jim's hair and slapped him on the shoulder. Then she kissed his cheek.

"I married a lunatic," she murmured.

"That's why you love me," he answered.

She returned to stroking his head.

"What are we going to tell people?" she asked.

"Nothing. Not for a few days. Not till they're ready to hear the truth. Not till they start wondering about the thousand little changes that have occurred."

"Why do you think it happened?" she asked. "Why do you think everyone, everything but us, got put to sleep?"

"I don't know," he answered. "We'll probably never know. Maybe it's part of nature's plan, every million years or so to let the planet take a year off. Now that it's over, I realize that I did find a certain charm in having the entire place to ourselves, our own private planet to do with as we willed."

"Me too," she agreed. "There were some wonderful moments. But I'm glad it didn't last. I'm glad everyone's back now."

"So am I."

She bent over and rested her chin on his head.

"And what are we going to do next year at this time?" she asked, "just in case the light is still on?"

"I know this lovely, underwater cave," he offered.

Missy frowned. "No, my darling, the twins and I are not going down into some icky, wet cave." Her face brightened. "I know. I'll get Kate to invite us into her hot tub next year. We'll make an annual reunion out of it."

"It might be a little crowded."

"You'll love it," she answered.

Missy moved from behind Jim and, carefully navigating her rotund abdomen, sat in the lounge chair next to him.

"You know," she said, "we're going to have to visit my mother soon."

"I have to deal with in-laws already?" he pretended to complain.

"You might think it's funny," Missy answered, "but as far as mom is concerned, she saw me only two weeks ago; and my belly was nice and flat then. This..." She put both hands on her stomach. "...is going to be hard to explain."

Jim groaned. "We are going to be hitting your mother with an awful lot at once. I don't suppose I could arrange to be busy, say painting our new living room, the first time you go to see her?"

"Sorry, lover," Missy answered, "but we're in this together, you and me, side by side, come what may."

"Okay," he sighed. "But then you're going to have to come with me to see my older brother, to help me explain how it is that he's not older than me anymore."

"It's a deal," Missy agreed. "We'll just have to plan it out in advance, rehearse what we're going to say."

Jim straightened up in his chair and looked over the railing to the street below.

"You're going to get a chance to rehearse sooner than you think," he said. "Bess just pulled up, and she's got two guys with her in the car. Technically, I think you're still in the middle of an unfinished double date."

"Oh no!" Missy moaned.

On the street below, Bess got out of the car, looked up, saw Missy, and waved happily at her; and Missy waved back. Both of the men with Bess also looked up at Missy and waved and smiled; but, as Missy stood up, and her very large, round stomach became visible over the railing, their hands froze in mid-wave, and their mouths dropped open.

"Help me," Missy pleaded to Jim through clenched teeth. "What am I supposed to do now?"

Jim stood up next to her, put his arm around her, and started to wave too.

"Just smile, beauty," Jim said. "They get the picture."

Missy smiled.

THE END

CPSIA information can be obtained at www.ICGtesting.com
Printed in the USA
BVOW041309101011
273228BV00001B/3/P